"Take one ~~step~~
your clothes ~~on the fire.~~"

"What's gotten into you, woman?" A grimace of pain twisted Thorn's features as he lurched to his feet. "You're not my mother, for pity's sake. You don't even want to be my mistress anymore. So leave off trying to coddle me."

He tried to take the threatened step, but the strength of his legs clearly failed to match the strength of his will. He staggered toward Felicity, who mustered all her strength to push him back onto his bed. At the last instant, his hand closed around her wrist and pulled her down on top of him.

The indignation she tried to summon melted like summer hail.

A bewildering sense of completeness stole over her as the fleet skip of her heart tangled with the strong, swift beat of Thorn's until it became one thrilling, intricate rhythm...!

Praise for bestselling author
DEBORAH HALE's latest titles

Whitefeather's Woman
"This book is yet another success for Deborah Hale.
It aims for the heart and doesn't miss."
—*The Old Book Barn Gazette*

The Wedding Wager
"...this delightful, well-paced historical
will leave readers smiling and satisfied."
—*Library Journal*

A Gentleman of Substance
"This exceptional Regency-era romance
includes all the best aspects of that genre....
Deborah Hale has outdone herself..."
—*Romantic Times*

LADY LYTE'S LITTLE SECRET

DEBORAH HALE

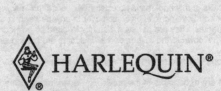

HARLEQUIN®

TORONTO • NEW YORK • LONDON
AMSTERDAM • PARIS • SYDNEY • HAMBURG
STOCKHOLM • ATHENS • TOKYO • MILAN • MADRID
PRAGUE • WARSAW • BUDAPEST • AUCKLAND

ISBN 0-373-29239-2

LADY LYTE'S LITTLE SECRET

Available from Harlequin Historicals and
DEBORAH HALE

Please address questions and book requests to:
Harlequin Reader Service
U.S.: 3010 Walden Ave., P.O. Box 1325, Buffalo, NY 14269
Canadian: P.O. Box 609, Fort Erie, Ont. L2A 5X3

To Graham McDonald,
nuclear engineer, rock climber
and all-around answer to a maiden's prayer,
as well loved by his sisters as Thorn Greenwood.
Nobody deserves a "happily ever after" more than you,
Big Red!

Chapter One

Bath, England
May 1815

"Felicity!"

The sound of her name, bellowed in a resonant masculine voice from the entry hall of her Bath town house, roused Lady Felicity Lyte from a restless doze.

It must be after midnight. What could Thorn be doing here at this unholy hour?

Not that Mr. Hawthorn Greenwood was a stranger to Number 18 Royal Crescent after dark. Quite the contrary. A mere two nights ago, at this very hour, he had been warming the bed beside her, serenely unaware that his days as her lover were numbered.

Until this moment, she'd had no communication with him concerning the polite note in which she'd terminated their discreet love affair.

Off in the distance, Thorn roared her name again. Felicity heard his footsteps thunder up the stairs. Her pulse fluttered in her throat, as she threw off the bedclothes and groped for her dressing gown.

She'd never heard Thorn Greenwood raise his voice. Nor move with anything but quiet, temperate steps. The racket of his current approach frightened Felicity just a little—and stirred her a great deal.

The man must be well-foxed, she decided as she thrust her arms into the sleeves of her dressing gown and fumbled in the dark to tie the sash. Had he fortified himself at some fashionable drinking establishment, then come here intent on begging her to take him back? Perhaps to demand some better account of why she'd decided to cast him off so abruptly?

The notion that he cared enough to demand or beg anything gave Felicity a queasy sensation that was not altogether unpleasant. Rather like looking out at a breathtaking vista from an alarming altitude.

Much as she longed to, she could not afford to continue her enjoyable love affair with Thorn Greenwood. Neither did she dare tell him the true reason why.

Darting the length of her bedchamber, she threw the door open just as Thorn came skidding to a halt before it. Expecting to encounter the reek of spirits, so familiar from her experience with her late husband, Felicity was surprised when she smelled nothing of the kind.

In the faint glow cast by a night lamp in the upstairs hall, Thorn looked perturbed to a degree Felicity associated with immoderate drinking. His greatcoat was unbuttoned, his hat absent altogether, and his dark hair ruffled either by the wind or his own haste. His eyes, usually the calm, steadfast brown of freshly turned earth, now flashed with the sparks of flint struck against flint.

Gazing up at Thorn as he towered over her, his broad shoulders and muscular torso filling out his greatcoat, Felicity had to anchor herself against the intense attraction that threatened to propel her into his arms.

If only he'd come to confront her any time but now—anywhere but here. Late at night, on the threshold of the room where they'd made love so often. Yet, not often enough. If they held their breaths and listened, they might hear her bed calling them with its sensual siren song.

Her skin warmed with the physical memory of his strong but gentle touch. The sensitive tips of her bosoms thrust out against her nightgown and dressing gown to lure his lips. The sweet fissure between her thighs took fire in readiness for another delicious coupling.

If Thorn Greenwood dropped to his knees and begged for one more night, his face pressed to her bosom and his large deft hands cradling her backside, no power on earth, least of all her own badly divided will, could force Felicity's lips to frame a refusal.

"Is Ivy here?" he demanded.

The words were so contrary to anything she'd expected that Felicity struggled to understand them.

"Ivy? Your…sister?"

"Of course, my sister." Thorn's brusque tone rasped against her kindled passion like a man's unshaven cheek grazing the sensitive flesh of her bare neck. "Do you think I've come here at this hour because I've developed a sudden passion for horticulture?"

Felicity's fragile sense of anticipation shattered into sharp splinters of ice.

"What on earth would your silly sister be doing in *my* house in the middle of the night? If this is some

spurious pretext for you to barge in here and wake me
from a sound sleep, you will regret it, Mr. Greenwood,
I assure you.''

"Depend upon it, Lady Lyte, nothing less dire than
the defence of my sister's virtue and reputation could
induce me to cross a threshold over which I'm no
longer welcome." Even in the dim light Felicity could
see the muscles of Thorn's firm jaw tighten further.
"As to why Ivy might be under your roof, I suggest
you put *that* question to your nephew, the young
scoundrel."

Every word out of his mouth splashed cold water
over Felicity's fevered flesh. Bad enough Thorn
Greenwood should come here at this hour of the night,
exciting all manner of absurd expectations in her only
to smash them to pieces again. But to insult her late
husband's nephew, a young man Felicity loved like
the son she'd never expected to have, that was an outrage she would not bear.

"Pray, watch your tongue, Thorn Greenwood! I
know of few young men who less deserve to be called
a scoundrel than Oliver Armitage. What is my nephew
supposed to have done to have compromised your sister's reputation that she couldn't do quite as readily
on her own? I vow, I never met a more heedless little
romp."

That wasn't true, Felicity's conscience reproached
her. On those few occasions when she'd encountered
Thorn's younger sister on the town, Felicity had been
captivated by the child's sweet high spirits, so at odds
with her brother's gentle gravity. Despite the difference in their ages, the two women had gotten on fa-
mously and Lady Lyte had been known to make quite
a fuss over young Miss Greenwood.

Felicity turned a deaf ear to her own reason. Thorn's unwarranted slight against Oliver demanded tit for tat. He wouldn't mind any insult to himself half so much as one to his beloved sister.

Thorn's powerful hands clenched and unclenched, as though barely restrained from grasping her upper arms and shaking her until her teeth rattled. Or perhaps pulling her close to kiss her until her knees gave way. Just contemplating those possibilities left Felicity a trifle dizzy.

"B-besides," she added, "I doubt Oliver even knows your sister. There cannot be a young man in all of Bath less anxious to venture out on the town."

Not that his doting aunt hadn't cajoled him often enough. A fortnight ago, Ivy Greenwood would have been just the sort of winsome creature Felicity might have urged on her nephew to lure him away from his books and his laboratory.

Thank goodness she hadn't. A shiver snaked through Felicity. Any match between Oliver and Ivy would have bound her inextricably to the Greenwood family, just when she needed to get as far away from Thorn as possible.

The words he hurled at her next echoed Felicity's deepest fears. "I have reason to believe your nephew and my sister have eloped to Gretna Green."

Felicity Lyte had no patience whatsoever with women who swooned. She considered it a vapid affectation. The last thing in the world she wanted was for the shock of Thorn's news to make her wilt into his arms. But as everything around her began to twirl like a child's spinning top, she found herself with no choice in the matter.

"Felicity!"

* * *

Breaking his vow never to budge a step across the threshold of her private chamber again, Thorn hoisted his erstwhile mistress into his arms and carried her to the bed.

As he laid Felicity on the rumpled sheets, the familiar fragrance of rosewater wrapped around him strand by delicate strand, pulling him toward her. It took every crumb of Thorn's considerable self-control to curb the urge to indulge in one final kiss. The last time he'd pressed his lips to hers, he hadn't realized it would be *the last time*.

For a moment, his passion for Felicity blotted every rational thought from Thorn's mind, including the concern for his sister which had brought him here in the first place. The wild brown tangle of her hair against the pillow tempted his hands to touch. If he inhaled until his head spun and he pitched on top of her supine body, Thorn doubted he could breathe in enough of her subtle fragrance to satisfy him.

He should have known from the moment this beautiful, sought-after creature first invited him to become her lover that she'd made a foolish mistake. What could such a diamond of the first water want with a tiresomely respectable fellow like him? A man of sound but scarcely brilliant intellect, and no pretensions of wit or charm. Not ill-looking, but hardly a beau of fashion. A man with family responsibilities and financial obligations, unable to shower her with presents or even tender an honorable bid for her hand.

Yet, she had chosen him. And for the first time in his steady, dutiful life Hawthorn Greenwood had done something less than respectable. Something furtive.

Something scandalous. Something so exhilarating, he could scarcely believe it was happening to *him*.

Felicity Lyte had offered him a banquet of forbidden fruit. Even as he'd gorged himself upon it, Thorn had found his appetite piqued rather than sated. By mutual agreement the span of their time together had been limited to this one Season at Bath. Then, with several blissful weeks still ahead of them, Thorn had received a tersely-worded letter from Felicity ending their relationship.

As he should have expected, she'd grown tired of him. Found a superior replacement, perhaps.

Now Thorn glanced around her shadow-shrouded bedchamber, satisfying himself that Felicity had been sleeping alone—for tonight, at least.

He shook his head hard to banish his selfish desires and motives. Certainly he'd been angered by the casual manner in which Felicity had cast him off. Hurt, too—might as well admit it. Still, that didn't give him the right to burst in on the woman at such an uncivilized hour and shock her into a swoon with his distressing suspicions.

"Felicity?" He'd bellowed her name in the entry hall, then gasped it when she'd collapsed into his arms. Now he spoke it in a coaxing murmur as he chafed her hand. "Wake up, please. I'm sorry I broke the news to you so baldly. I should have known it would come as a terrible shock."

A wave of alarm swelled within him when she did not rouse right away. He pressed his fingers to the tender flesh at the base of her throat, searching for a pulse.

"Thorn?" Felicity's eyelids fluttered. She spoke his name with the peculiar softness of affection as her lips half curved in a drowsy, quizzical, trusting smile. "What happened? Where am I, darling?"

Thorn's heart lurched in his chest. Could he have misunderstood her letter? Might she still want him, for a few more weeks at least? The possibility elated him and that precarious sense of elation unsettled him.

What terrifying power over his happiness had he yielded to this woman?

As if to demonstrate that very capacity, Lady Lyte opened her glittering green eyes wide as a tremor of aversion quivered through her. She flinched from his touch.

"What are *you* doing here?"

If she'd raised her hand and slapped him hard across the cheek, it could not have stung like the steely chill of her tone. Thorn winced from it, pulling upright from his solicitous crouch beside her bed.

A sharp intake of her breath told Thorn she recalled why he'd come.

Her next words confirmed it. "Oliver and your sister? Run off together to Gretna? Are you certain?"

Slowly, she rose to perch on the edge of the bed. Thorn bit his tongue to keep from warning her to be careful. If the woman wanted to risk another fainting spell, it was no business of his, after all.

"If I'd been *certain,* I would hardly be wasting my time here, Lady Lyte. I'd be on the road to Bristol this very moment trying to catch them before they got any further with such folly."

"You must be mistaken." Felicity's doubtful tone belied the certainty of her words. "I breakfasted with Oliver just this morning. I never saw a young man who looked less like he meant to elope."

Her balance appeared equally dubious as she surged

to her feet. Though Thorn willed his arms to remain
straight at his sides, one reached out of its own accord
to steady Felicity.

Thorn Greenwood had always taken modest pride
in knowing his own mind and acting in a deliberate
manner upon carefully reasoned decisions. Unused to
being pulled in contrary directions, he did not enjoy
the sensation.

He *wished* he did not enjoy the sensation of Felicity
Lyte clinging to his arm.

"I hope you're right about your nephew."

Thorn wasn't certain he meant it. If they discovered
Oliver Armitage tucked up sound and alone in his own
bed or burning the midnight oil in his study, then Ivy's
disappearance would take on a far more sinister
complexion.

"Will you at least humor me by confirming his
presence in your house?"

"Very well." Felicity wrenched her hand back from
Thorn's arm as though she regretted the necessity of
accepting his support. "Anything to speed you on
your way."

As she stalked past him toward the door, Thorn followed, ready to catch her again if she so much as
swayed.

She did not.

Indeed, her steps seemed to gain assurance as she
marched down the hallway.

"I'll try his study first." Felicity tossed the words
over her shoulder as she halted before a door at the
end of the wide corridor. "He often forgets the time
when he's absorbed in his work."

Tapping gently on the door, she called her nephew's
name, but received no response.

"Oliver?" She turned the knob and pushed the door open a crack. "Are you there?"

A musty odor of old books wafted from the room, mingled with the faint reek of chemical solutions. But all was dark and still within. Oliver Armitage did not answer his aunt's call.

"He must have retired to bed at a decent hour for a change." A note of uncertainty crept into Felicity's voice.

Pushing past Thorn to the door opposite her nephew's study, she knocked harder and hailed him in a more urgent tone. "Oliver, wake up! It's urgent I speak with you at once."

No acknowledgement.

"He's a sound sleeper."

Thorn wondered whether she meant the remark to reassure herself or to confound his mounting conviction that he'd been right all along.

Forsaking subtlety, Lady Lyte thrust open the bedroom door. "Oliver, pardon us for waking you, dear boy. But Mr. Greenwood has come with the most preposterous…"

The rest of her sentence evaporated into the dormant shadows of the empty bedchamber. The hall lamp's dim glimmer revealed crisp outlines of furniture, including an undisturbed bed.

"Perhaps he has gone out, after all," Felicity suggested, clearly forgetting her earlier claim that there was not a young man in Bath less anxious to venture out on the town.

"Perhaps."

A splash of white against the bed's dark coverlet caught Thorn's eye. He brushed past Felicity. His hand closed over a sheet of paper, neatly folded and sealed with wax. Pulling it into the faint ribbon of light that spilled through the open doorway, he squinted to decipher two words written on the outside.

He shoved the paper toward Felicity. "It's addressed to you."

still wet. Felicity drew the final stroke of a light, apostrophizing t, then blotted her . . . signature with a rocker blotter. Two words, written in an elegant script. No . . . She slipped the paper beneath . . . . locked in.

Chapter Two

Felicity willed her hand not to tremble as she held it out to receive the communication Oliver had left for her.

"Can you fetch me a light, please?" she asked Thorn.

Whatever message this paper held, she had no intention of returning to her own bedroom to read it. Certainly not in Thorn Greenwood's company.

Why, the place was crammed to the ceiling with vivid, bedeviling memories of the nights they'd spent together. The last thing Felicity wanted to contemplate just now was any reminder of Thorn's deliberate, attentive lovemaking and her own ardent response to it.

Ever obliging, Thorn headed out into the hall and returned bearing a lamp.

The thickness and texture of the paper in her hand put Felicity in mind of the letter she'd written to him just the other day. Reluctance had tugged at her elbow. Regret at having to end their affair prematurely had sharpened her words. She hadn't wanted to hurt him, but neither had she wanted him to hold any false hope that she might change her mind.

If Thorn had entreated her with those steadfast brown eyes and the earnest set of his handsome features, Felicity had feared she might capitulate.

With disastrous consequences.

"Well?" Thorn prompted her, his gaze fixed on the paper. "Do you intend to open it or not?"

"Of course." Felicity stirred from her musings. Her fingers fumbled as she broke the seal. "Don't badger me!"

Events had so far confirmed Thorn's preposterous suggestion. Still, Felicity persisted in the vain hope that this note from Oliver would not say what she feared it might.

To the best of her knowledge, her nephew had only the barest acquaintance with Ivy Greenwood. And even if he knew the young lady well and cared for her deeply, a man of science like Oliver hadn't the rash temperament to bolt for Gretna Green on the spur of the moment.

Then again, Ivy Greenwood had an impulsive streak quite wide enough for both of them, not to mention a winsome beauty that might make a fool of the cleverest man.

Felicity's insides churned as she forced herself to read what Oliver had written. Thorn held the lamp high, peering over her shoulder. The warm tickle of his breath on her ear made it nearly impossible to concentrate on deciphering the young scientist's spiky scrawl.

"Dear Aunt Felicity," Thorn read aloud. "By the time you find this, I will be well on my way to Scotland, where I plan to wed Miss Ivy Greenwood. As Miss Greenwood is below the age of consent and she feared her brother might not approve the match..."

Under his breath Thorn muttered, "Too right, lad," then picked up where he had left off. "...We have decided to elope. Knowing how fond you are of my wife-to-be, I trust you will wish us every happiness. We look forward to making our home with you when we return. Ever your affectionate nephew, Oliver Armitage."

By slow degrees, Thorn let the hand in which he held the lamp drop. Likewise, the hand in which Felicity held the letter fell slack.

Neither of them spoke for a moment, as the indisputable truth did battle with Felicity's adamant denial and beat it senseless.

"W-why, this is madness," she insisted when she found her voice at last. "I cannot imagine a more ill-matched pair than my nephew and your sister. What can have gotten into those foolish children?"

As she spoke, Felicity turned to face Thorn. When she saw how close he hovered behind her, she swallowed a little gasp and stepped back. Not that she was frightened of the man—only of the intense, bewildering effect he had upon her. Her fingers itched to reach up and nuzzle his soft side whiskers in the familiar gesture that was their signal to retire to bed.

Had been their signal, she reminded herself, clenching both hands by her sides to restrain them.

Perhaps some restless hunger in her eyes betrayed her barely checked desire, for Thorn lowered his voice to the mellow, intimate cadence of lovemaking.

"I'll tell you what's gotten into those foolish children, Lady Lyte." His gaze ranged over her face like a fond caress. "The same madness that sometimes afflicts older and wiser hearts."

"Surely, you can't mean us?" Felicity forced a

laugh. It tinkled like the cut-glass crystals on a chandelier striking against one another. ''I, for one, am well past years of discretion and quite cured of girlish romantic illusions. And you're the last man in Bath, perhaps in all of Britain, inclined to madness or any other excess.''

Sensible, steady, forthright, respectable Hawthorn Greenwood. Felicity knew, for she had weighed all those somewhat tiresome virtues in his favor before selecting him to become her convenient paramour. She hadn't wanted a more romantic or fanciful fellow, apt to imagine himself *in love* with her. Whatever that meant.

Thorn did not look as pleased with her tribute to his equanimity as a sensible man ought. His full dark brows drew together and the line of his wide, generous mouth stretched taut. Felicity shrank from the shadow of distress in his too-candid eyes.

''I bore you.''

''Don't be silly!'' Her denial rang a trifle hollow even in Felicity's own ears.

He didn't *bore* her, she insisted to herself. He'd only failed to surprise her.

Until tonight.

Now she couldn't make up her mind whether or not she liked such surprises.

''I'm incapable of being silly.'' He made the remark in such dire earnest, it might have been amusing.

But Felicity was not inclined to laugh.

''You make it sound like a crime,'' she chided him. ''It isn't. There are far too many silly people in this world, and they cause no end of trouble for us sensible folk. These two youngsters of ours, for instance. The way you barged in here tonight leads me to believe you're no more in favor of this ridiculous elopement than I am.''

"Of course I'm not.'' Thorn looked offended that she might believe otherwise. "My sister is much too young to know her own mind when it comes to an important matter like marriage.''

Ivy Greenwood could be no more than eighteen, Felicity reckoned. The same age at which she'd embarked on her own misadventure in matrimony.

Thorn shook his head. "And, as you've said, they are a vastly ill-suited couple.'' He glanced heavenward. "My sister—the wife of a scientist. Ivy is sweet-tempered and goodhearted,'' he amended, "but rather…''

"Impulsive?'' suggested Felicity. "Fickle?''

Thorn looked ready to contradict her, then he shrugged. "You're probably right. I imagine Ivy has got it in her head that an elopement is terribly romantic. But she's seen so little of the world. How can she know young Armitage is the man she'll want to spend the next fortnight with, let alone the rest of her life?''

"How, indeed?'' Felicity expelled a sigh of relief. She and Thorn were in agreement about this situation, at least. They had all the same reasons for wanting to stop her nephew from marrying his sister.

Almost all.

She had an additional one that Thorn must not know about on any account. The same reason she had ended their affair prematurely when she would much rather have lingered to the very last second of the Season then perhaps made plans to take up where they had left off again next year.

Now, that could never be, just as her nephew marrying into the Greenwood family *must* never be.

"We're in agreement, then?" Thorn cursed himself for having let that remark about boring her slip out. What could be more tiresome than a cast-off lover who refused to take his leave quietly? "They must be intercepted, made to see sense and brought home."

A look of dismay clouded Felicity's luminous tawny eyes. Then she gulped a deep breath and squared her slender shoulders. "Very well. I'll toss a few clothes into a portmanteau and leave tonight. They can't have more than twelve hours' head start. I'll probably catch up to them before they reach Gloucester."

She started for the door. In her virginal white dressing gown with her rich dark hair falling over her shoulders, she looked little older than Ivy.

"Don't be ridiculous." Thorn reached out and caught her wrist. It felt so fragile beneath his fingers. "You can't go tearing off the length of England—a woman alone."

Shaking her hand free of his, Felicity glared at him. "I'll hardly be *alone*. I plan to take my traveling carriage, of course, with a good experienced driver and at least one footman."

As if that settled the matter, she slipped out of her nephew's bedroom and headed down the hall toward her own. Thorn trailed after her.

"Besides." She glanced back at him. "I won't have to chase Oliver and your sister every mile of the way to Scotland. Heaven only knows what they're using for transport. A hired vehicle, most likely. With luck, I'll overtake them tomorrow. Then I can deliver Ivy safely back to you the following day."

She paused in her bedroom doorway and held out her hand. For a moment, Thorn wondered if she

wanted him to bow over it in parting. Then he understood that she was asking for the lamp.

Stubbornly, he hung onto it. "Do you honestly believe you'll just pull up behind them on the road, flag
them down and cart Ivy back to Bath? What if they've
stopped at an inn to change horses and you drive clean
past them?"

The look that flitted across her face told Thorn she
hadn't taken that, or a great many other possibilities,
into account. To be fair, he'd had more time to consider and plan since he'd discovered Ivy missing from
their modest rented premises in a less fashionable part
of town.

"I'll inquire after them whenever I stop for refreshment or a change of horses." Felicity took up the
gauntlet of his challenge. "It shouldn't be that difficult
to pick up their trail. And if I must follow them all
the way to Gretna, I'm quite prepared to do it. Now
kindly give me the light so I can see to dress and
pack."

Almost as an afterthought, she added, "You could
oblige me by waking my driver and footman and informing them of the urgency of my errand."

"No, Felicity. I won't let you do this." Thorn held
the lamp away from her when she lunged for it. "It
will be a difficult journey, perhaps even dangerous."

Her eyes flashed like a pair of finely cut topaz.
"You are not my keeper, Mr. Greenwood. And though
you have shared my bed, you are not my husband. If
I elect to do this, you have no power whatsoever to
prevent me."

Impossibly mulish woman! Did she have to fling
both her rejection and her superior station in his teeth?

Thorn fought to quell his slow-burning temper. It would serve her right if he let her indulge in this folly.

To his surprise, she caught his free hand in both of hers and softened her voice. "I thought we agreed Ivy and Oliver must be stopped. Why are we arguing, then? What other choice do we have?"

Wasn't it obvious? Thorn battled the intoxicating effect of her touch to frame the only reasonable alternative. "I shall go, naturally. I can make better speed on horseback. Ride cross country, if need be, to intercept them."

She appeared to give his offer at least passing consideration. Though his pride bristled at the notion that *his* taking action in the matter had never crossed her mind, Thorn tried to marshall his arguments in good order.

"I can seek information from hostlers, toll collectors or other folk a lady might hesitate to question."

He was winning her over—Thorn sensed it. He battled an inclination to spout any nonsense that might keep Felicity holding on to his hand a second longer.

"Once I manage to overtake them…" Thorn brought forth his most convincing argument. "…I do have the power, as my sister's guardian, to compel her to return home with me. You would have no such influence over her or your nephew. For this and for all the other reasons I've mentioned, I am the logical choice to pursue them. Only…"

"Yes?"

Thorn would rather have cut out his tongue than admit this, especially to her. As the hot blood rose to burn in his cheeks, he let the hand in which he held the lamp sink so Felicity might not witness it.

"I do not have the resources at my disposal that I

once had.'' Though he mustered every scrap of dignity at his command, Thorn could not look one of England's wealthiest women in the face as he tried to keep from gagging on those words.

They had never spoken of the enormous disparity in their fortunes. Indeed, they had never talked at length on any but the most superficial of subjects. Still, she must know his family had fallen from prosperity.

His humble address down the hill should have been a clue, in a town where the price of housing rose in direct proportion to the elevation of the neighbourhood. His clothes—well tailored, but several years out of fashion, could easily have given him away. The fact that he didn't keep a carriage should have confirmed any suspicions.

In all likelihood she had known his situation before she'd ever approached him with her intriguing, potentially scandalous invitation to become her lover. A wealthier fellow might have taken offense.

Oh, just spit it out, man!

''My father left rather considerable debts behind him when he died, several years ago. I have been making good headway in settling them and have every hope of seeing my family prosperous again, one day.''

Thorn addressed himself to the doorjamb, several inches above Felicity's head. ''At the moment, however, I find myself short of ready money. Since we both have an interest in seeing your nephew and my sister prevented from marrying, I suggest we join forces. If you will finance the journey, I will spare you the bother of undertaking it by going in your stead.''

At some point during his little speech, Felicity had let go of his hand. Thorn held himself tall and tense as he waited for her answer. He still could not bring himself to glance down into her eyes, lest he see some gentle mist of pity in them to complete his humiliation.

The seconds stretched taut as a fiddle string, until Thorn feared something must snap with a harsh jangle.

It did.

In a single swift motion that left him agape and unable to stop her, Felicity pounced for the lamp, plucking it from his hand. Then she darted back over the threshold of her bedchamber and slammed the door.

Before Thorn could break from his paralysis to push it open again, a solid-sounding bolt snapped into place.

"Felicity!" He hammered on the locked door. "What's the meaning of this?"

Her voice drifted out to him, cool and composed. "I think that should be obvious, sir. I regret I must decline your generous offer."

Thorn heard scurrying footsteps and whispers from the first floor. Some burly young footman might arrive at any moment to evict him from the premises. He wondered that Lady Lyte's servants had shown him so much forbearance until now.

He ceased knocking and lowered his voice. "Did you not listen to a word I said?"

"Listened, considered and made my decision," came Felicity's somewhat muffled reply. "I appreciate your offer to go in my stead, but I have elected to undertake the journey myself. I'm sure you overestimate the difficulties involved."

"I've done nothing of the sort, in fact—"

"Mr. Greenwood, please!" Her voice sounded exhausted of patience. "I have made up my mind, and I will not be swayed, least of all by your bluster. Time is of the essence, and I have any number of preparations to undertake.''

And I need you to get out from underfoot. She didn't say it, but the implication hung in the air, as palpable as the stench of glue rising from a hatter's workshop.

''I pray you will spare your dignity and mine by letting yourself out quietly. Otherwise I shall be obliged to ring for one of my servants to escort you from my house.''

Inside her bedchamber, Felicity strained to catch Thorn's answer as she tossed clothes into a case.

His arguments for being the one to go after Oliver and Ivy had been most compelling. She'd very nearly yielded to his logic. One final consideration had induced her to refuse.

Thorn Greenwood possessed too soft a heart, and his reasons for wanting to prevent this foolish marriage were far less urgent than her own.

What if, having intercepted the young lovers, Thorn allowed the pair to convince him that they were truly in love and fully understood the consequences of their actions? As if they could understand.

He'd probably relent, sanction their union with his blessing—even give the bride away. Then they'd all three return to Bath and present her with a *fait accompli.* What could she do about it then?

Felicity pushed down the little mound of clothing and snapped her case shut.

Thorn might have legal influence over his sister, but she had financial influence over Oliver, and she would not scruple to exercise it if necessary. This whole elopement put Felicity in mind of a high stakes card game. One in which she had by far the most to lose. She did not dare let her hand be played by proxy.

Still no sound came from beyond her door.

"Thorn, are you there?"

A moment's hesitation. "Yes."

He had such a pleasant voice. Not too high in pitch, not too low. A fine rich resonance. She would miss it.

"Did you hear what I said?"

"Yes."

She needed to get dressed but somehow she could not bring herself to remove her clothes with Thorn so near at hand. Not even with a good stout door locked between them.

"Goodbye, then. I promise I'll fetch Ivy back to you safe and sound as soon as I can."

"If you're so intent on going, Felicity, will you at least take me with you?"

Thankfully, there was a locked door between them. If she'd been obliged to look into his eyes, her traitorous lips might have given him a different answer. "No, Thorn."

"I realize it could be awkward under the circumstances, but you and I are civilized adults. Surely we could travel together for a day or two without..."

Felicity grasped the bell pull and jerked it vigorously.

"What you propose is out of the question, Mr. Greenwood. Now, please, please *go*."

She heard rapidly approaching footsteps out in the corridor, then Thorn's voice. "Very well. I'll leave."

Whether those words were addressed to the servants or to her, Felicity could not be sure.

While she waited for the commotion in the corridor to subside, she took a seat at her dressing table and began to do her hair. Beneath her hairbrush, folded in a neat, prim rectangle lay a length of starched white lawn.

Thorn's neck linen.

Felicity's fingers trembled as she fondled the cloth. One of her maids must have come across it while tidying the bedroom.

This was the first time Thorn had left so much as a collar button or a watch fob behind to betray his presence. In the early days of their liaison, he'd been fastidious about undressing. With far fewer garments to shed herself, Felicity had taken pleasure in watching and admiring him as he removed his clothes.

As time had passed, they'd become increasingly eager. Helping one another out of their clothes had become a tantalizing prelude to lovemaking.

Stroking her cheek with Thorn's cravat, Felicity detected no cloying whiff of sweetwater, only the bracing scent of plain soap and the subtle musk of a man. As vexing moisture rose in her eyes, she dropped Thorn's cravat and swiped the sleeve of her dressing gown across her face. All the while, she chided herself for turning into a sentimental fool.

This was no time to mope and moon over Thorn Greenwood. If she must surrender to such nonsense she would wait until later, when it would not be so bothersome. At the moment necessity demanded she act decisively and keep her wits about her.

A tentative tap sounded on the door.

Felicity started, her heart hammering.

"Mr. Greenwood," she cried, "must I have my butler summon the constables and swear out a complaint against you?"

"The gentleman's gone, ma'am," came an apologetic squeak from Hetty, her lady's maid. "He left real peaceable like. I saw the light under your door and wondered if you might be needing me, ma'am?"

Shaking her head over her mistake, Felicity rose from the dressing table and unlatched the door.

"Thank you, Hetty, I could use your help. I expect this disturbance has already roused the entire household. Will you kindly advise Ned and Mr. Hixon to ready the big carriage and make their personal preparations for a journey north? I mean to leave within the hour."

The girl regarded her mistress with bulging eyes. "Will you be gone long, ma'am? Do you need me to pack your bags? Should I make ready to come with you?"

Felicity considered the idea. "I...think not."

If it had been Alice, her former lady's maid of over eight years service, she would have accepted the offer of company in a trice. Since Alice had left her employ to marry a prosperous young butcher, Felicity had made do with Hetty, a willing little creature, though inclined to prattle.

In brief spells it was rather diverting, but to be shut up in a carriage for hours at a time with such a one held little appeal for Lady Lyte just then. She would much prefer to be alone with her thoughts and her plans for the future.

Besides... "I should not be gone long. A day or two at most, I expect. Surely I can manage without a maid for that interval."

A look of relief eased the girl's features as she smothered a yawn. "If you're certain, ma'am, I'll just go deliver your message to Ned and Mr. Hixon."

She bobbed a curtsy and set off down the hall. Before Felicity could close her door, Hetty spun around again.

"Should I tell Cook to brew you a cup of tea before you set out, ma'am? Or make you up a basket of sandwiches and such for the road?"

At the mere mention of food, Felicity's stomach revolted.

"For the men," she ordered. "Nothing for me."

Slamming the door shut, she dove for her washstand and retched into the basin until nothing more would come.

Spent from the effort, she wetted the edge of a towel in the tepid water from her ewer and hoisted herself into the chair before her dressing table. As she dabbed her cheeks with the damp towel, Felicity contemplated her pale face in the looking glass with dismay and wonder.

After twelve barren years of marriage and widowhood, Providence had played a fine joke on her. Her meticulously regular courses had suddenly ceased far too early for her age, and she woke every morning bilious. Before the summer waned, her belly would begin to swell.

Infinitely generous man that he was, Thorn Greenwood had granted her the dearest desire of her heart, and one of which she had long despaired.

A child.

But in doing so, he had made it necessary for Felicity to cut him out of her life.

Chapter Three

If she thought she could get rid of him that easily, Lady Lyte had better think again!

As Thorn Greenwood rounded The Circus, he cast a glowering glance at the darkened windows of the New Assembly Rooms, long since deserted of ball-goers. After the mauling his pride had taken over the past two days, he was tempted to curse the place where he'd first set eyes on his troublesome mistress.

Where would he and his sister be now, Thorn wondered, if he hadn't let Ivy coax him out to that first ball of the Season?

If some magical being from a nursery tale had suddenly materialized and offered him the chance to go back and relive the past two months differently, Thorn wasn't certain whether he would accept or refuse.

True, it had vastly complicated his life and it had all ended on a sour note. While his affair with Felicity Lyte lasted, though, it had been very sweet indeed.

"Quit your mooning, man," Thorn muttered to himself. He must think about raising the blunt he'd

require for a journey—all the way to Scotland if
need be.

His steps slowed from the indignant stride that had
carried him away from Royal Crescent. A mild night
breeze wafted up the gracious hills of Bath from the
River Avon. It carried the aromas of fine cooking from
the kitchen windows of many a fashionable town
house, as well as the music and laughter from a number of private parties winding to a close. The air of
conviviality and careless wealth mocked Thorn's
predicament.

Refusing to entertain regrets, he studied the problem
with the same resolve he'd brought to bear on the calamity of his family's fallen fortunes. If one thought
hard enough and ruled out no potential solution as too
difficult or distasteful, almost any dilemma admitted
of a solution. Thorn had more experience than most
men of his age and class in learning how to salvage
something satisfactory from the bleakest of prospects.

As he wandered down Gay Street and turned onto
George, Thorn mulled over the problem in his deliberate, methodical way. Raising one possible solution
after another, he weighed each in turn, discarding the
unworkable, then proceeding to the next.

He still had a few items of value he could part with
to finance his journey, though most would be worth
far more to him in sentiment than to a prospective
buyer in gold. As his footsteps echoed on the cobbles
of Milsome Street, Thorn cast that idea aside. The
pawnshops on this busiest of commercial thorough-
fares would be locked up as tight as all the other places
of business. If he did manage to rouse some broker at

this hour, the man would hardly be disposed to cooperate.

Reason counseled Thorn to go home, assemble his valuables, get what sleep he could wrest from the night then set out in the morning. The thought of Ivy and young Armitage gaining a greater lead spurred him to action *now,* as did the notion of Felicity trundling along dark and deserted highways in a fine carriage with only an ancient driver and a juvenile footman for protection.

Thorn cast his mind upon another prospect.

"Of course." He chuckled to himself when it finally occurred to him.

He might be short of cash, but he was still comparatively wealthy in a man's most precious asset—friends. If only he could get word to his brother-in-law. Merritt Temple had horses, carriages and funds he would have put at Thorn's disposal in the blink of an eye. Unfortunately Merritt's country estate lay many miles to the east. A detour in that direction would result in an even worse delay than waiting for the pawnbrokers to open in the morning.

Surely there must be a friend *in Bath* to whom he could appeal.

Weston St. Just! If any man owed Thorn assistance in his present entanglement, surely it was the fellow who had introduced him to Lady Lyte in the first place. Thorn's stride picked up speed and purpose.

Finding himself near his own doorstep, he ducked inside long enough to scribble a note to their housekeeper saying he and Ivy had been called out of town and might not return for several days. When he emerged once again onto the dark stillness of the street, he turned south toward Sydney Gardens. St. Just kept elegant premises nearby.

Thorn had no worry of waking his old schoolmate at such a time. On the contrary, his concern was whether such a notorious night owl as Weston St. Just might not return home for several more hours. Fortunately, a light burned in the sitting room window and a young footman wasted no time answering Thorn's knock.

When the boy ushered Thorn into his friend's presence, St. Just looked mildly surprised to see him. Perhaps mildly amused, as well. "What ho, Greenwood? Has the beauteous Lady Lyte put the boots to you so soon?"

"I'm surprised she hasn't told you." Thorn knew all too well of St. Just's insatiable appetite for gossip. "I received my marching orders from her two days ago."

"The little minx!" His host gestured for Thorn to take a seat. "I must say, though, I envy you even a few weeks of her company."

St. Just lifted his snifter of tawny liquid and nodded toward a side table arrayed with a decanter and more glasses. "Care to drown your sorrows?"

After his unsettling confrontation with Felicity, the offer tempted Thorn sorely. Perching himself on the settee opposite his host, Thorn shook his head. "I daren't."

St. Just cast him an indulgent look. "Of course, you never drown your troubles, or run away from them, or any other such cowardice, do you? Always look 'em squarely in the face and soldier on."

"Tiresome, isn't it?" Thorn wondered how the pair

of them had remained civil, let alone friendly, all these years with such contrary temperaments.

Felicity might have done better to take St. Just as her lover, instead of merely using him as a go-between to approach his less suitable chum. Besides the classical masculine beauty of a Greek statue come to life, Weston St. Just had an easy agreeable way with women that made them flock to him like bees to a tall fragrant flower.

"Tiresome? On the contrary, dear fellow." St. Just lounged back in his upholstered armchair and sipped his drink. "I tire of most people in no time, for the majority of them are like me—duplicitous, idle, selfish. Salt of the earth folk like you baffle me at every turn. I live in constant anticipation that you may slip from the straight and narrow into some diverting orgy of wickedness."

"I thought I had."

"With Lady Lyte, you mean?" St. Just shrugged. "A tantalizing little stumble to keep me on my toes, but far too discreet to tarnish your honor. Now, do tell me what brings you here at this hour? In the case of ninety-nine men out of a hundred, I could guess at once, but you persist in confounding me."

"It's my sister, Ivy. She's taken it into her head to elope with young Armitage—Lady Lyte's nephew."

"Has she, by George?" St. Just sat up a little straighter, his dark languid eyes glittering with something like interest. "I wish I had a scapegrace little sister to get up to all kinds of mischief and keep me productively occupied rescuing her bacon from the fire."

"I'd offer to lend you mine," growled Thorn, "but I wouldn't trust you within a mile of Ivy."

He related the rest of his predicament. How Felicity had insisted on pursuing the young lovers without him. His desperate need to get ahold of a good horse and some money to finance his journey.

Whenever he was tempted to resent St. Just's ironic amusement over the whole situation, Thorn did his best to conceal it. If he wanted to be on his way tonight, this man was his most promising source of assistance.

"I suppose you'll expect me to keep all this lovely gossip to myself, now that you've confided in me." St. Just drained his glass and rose from his chair none too steadily.

Thorn leaped to his feet. "It wouldn't do me much good to fetch Ivy back from Gretna only to have her reputation ruined by word of all this leaking out. Then I'd be obliged to wed her off to Armitage in order to satisfy honor. For all you prattle on, Wes, you've always been a good friend in the pinch. What do you say? Can I count on your discretion and your assistance?"

"As to the first," St. Just raised his hand, "I swear on my rather dubious honor."

"As to the second," he turned out his pockets, "I've just come from a monstrous night at the tables. I won't tell you how much I lost or you'd be scandalized. Enough, I fear, that I couldn't lend you a brass farthing until I have an opportunity to meet with my banker upon the morrow."

"Damn!" The word was hardly out of his mouth

before Thorn started to cudgel his brains for someone else who could help him.

Weston St. Just pressed the tips of his fingers together. "Unless…"

"Unless?" prompted Thorn. The word had a hopeful sound, but the tone in which his friend had said it made him uneasy somehow.

"Got anything on you of value?" St. Just cast a glance at Thorn's signet ring as if appraising how much it might fetch.

"This." Thorn twisted the ring back and forth on his finger, a sensation he'd always found curiously comforting. "And my grandfather's gold watch and fob. It's no good, though. I thought of that already. The pawnshops are all locked up tight as drums until morning."

"I don't mean you to hock them, old fellow." St. Just stretched his long graceful limbs as though he'd recently woken from a refreshing night's sleep. "But how would you feel about wagering them?"

Thorn opened his mouth to protest, but his host cut him off. "One good hand at the game I left behind and you'd have blunt aplenty to see you to Gretna and back. Three good hands and you could probably finance a Grand Tour." He ushered Thorn toward the sitting room door.

"I've never been a gambler." Thorn protested. "You know that as well as anybody."

In a sense, he'd taken a flutter on his liaison with Felicity Lyte—hoping to win a jackpot of pleasure. He'd dealt himself a hand believing he had everything to gain and nothing to lose. Too late he had come to realize that he'd bet on his ability to bed a woman without falling in love with her.

The stakes had been nothing less than his heart. And he had lost it.

Weston St. John paused at the doorway and regarded his friend. "You may try as hard as you like to play it safe, old fellow, but life *is* a gamble any way you look at it. You're welcome to stay here the night, then roust me out at some uncivilized hour of the morning to see my banker. Or, if you're determined to be on your way before sunrise, you can come along with me and risk your *invaluables* on the turn of a few cards. Which will it be?"

Rubbing the face of his signet ring, Thorn struggled with his decision. The watch was so old it showed only the hour, which limited its use in all but the most leisurely time keeping. The signet ring was older still. Both had passed down, father to son, through the Greenwood line to him.

He had slight reservations about leaving his watch and ring as security against a loan, to be redeemed at the earliest opportunity. To run the risk of losing them altogether…

Of course he would still be head of the family without these ancestral badges of authority. Yet somehow, deep in his heart, it felt otherwise.

Reason assured Felicity Lyte she was following the only sensible course of action open to her. Her heart warned her otherwise, but she had learned long ago to place no trust in that capricious organ. Not even when her coachman agreed with it.

"Are you sure this journey of yours can't wait until

morning, ma'am?'' Even Mr. Hixon's massive hand could not stifle the great yawn that threatened to tear his face in two.

"I regret having to drag you out of bed at this time of night.'' Keeping her tone polite yet insistent, Felicity resisted the urge to yawn in reply as Hetty helped her on with her cloak.

Even in May, the nights could be chilly, particularly when one would be sitting in an unheated carriage for many hours.

"I'm afraid this cannot wait. Is the carriage ready to go?''

"Aye, ma'am.'' The coachman turned his old-fashioned tricorn hat around in his hands as he nodded toward the front door. "Where are we bound, if I may ask?''

"I hope to be in Tewkesbury by tomorrow evening.'' Felicity made a few quick calculations, guessing when Oliver and Miss Greenwood might have left Bath.

She prayed her nephew had hired a post chaise, rather than relying on the faster stage coaches or, worse yet, The Royal Mail. "I hope we shan't have to venture much farther than that before we can return.''

The coachman nodded, as evident eagerness to be out on the open road battled his fatigue. "At least we've clear weather and a good moon.''

He opened the door and held it for his mistress as she emerged onto the moonlit street. "What with leaving now, we'll be through Bristol before even the market traffic. If we make good time, we should be able to stop at The King's Arms in Newport for breakfast.''

"A capital suggestion, Mr. Hixon." Felicity descended the front steps of her town house and climbed into her carriage.

They nearly always stayed at that clean, well-run inn on their way to or from Bath. If Oliver had hired a coach and spirited Miss Greenwood away some time after noon, they would almost certainly have spent their first night at The King's Arms. Felicity could catch news of them there, perhaps even intercept them if they did not get back on the road at too early an hour.

The coachman scrambled up to his perch, and, a moment later, Lady Lyte's elegant traveling carriage rolled off toward Bristol Road. Inside, Felicity smiled to herself in the darkness. She could picture the astonished look on Thorn's face when she arrived back in Bath tomorrow evening with his chastened little sister in tow.

When she tried to *stop* picturing Thorn's face, however, she encountered considerable difficulty.

Unbidden images of him plagued her. Thorn appearing at her bedroom door in search of his sister, his dishevelled state rather endearing. Thorn hovering over her when she'd stirred from her foolish swoon, a warm air of concern radiating from him. Thorn, angrier than she had ever seen him, full dark brows brooding like thunderheads on the horizon. No sooner did Felicity banish one memory of Thorn Greenwood than another rose to take its place.

Perhaps it was just as well she'd been forced to make this break with him now, before the unsettling influence he exerted upon her grew stronger.

As the horses settled into a steady, mile-eating trot,

Felicity pulled her cloak tighter and wedged herself into one corner of the carriage. Resting her head against the smooth fabric of the upholstered seat, she tried to elude all thoughts of Thorn Greenwood by fleeing into dreams.

When that didn't work, she decided to concentrate her mind on one subject sure to divert her from anything else.

Her baby.

Under her cloak, Felicity passed a hand over her flat belly in a gesture at once tender and fiercely protective. Despite all evidence, she still had trouble believing there could be a baby growing inside her.

How many times, during the early years of her marriage, had she prayed for this very thing, only to be cruelly disappointed again and again? Meanwhile, Percy's tribe of merry-begotten offspring had grown apace. Each one an added insult, proof of his virility, to be cared for and educated by the bounty of *her* fortune.

How many odious *cures* had she endured for her barrenness? Sometimes downright painful, always humiliating.

Year after year, she had watched the lack of an heir eat away at her husband and at her marriage. Until she could no longer bear to look him in the face because she knew what he must be thinking. Why had he married this tradesman's daughter, to refill the empty coffers of his noble family with her fortune, when she could not produce a child to inherit what he'd sacrificed so much to restore?

As Lady Lyte's carriage drove through the tranquil shadowy countryside of Sommerset, a queer sound like the bastard spawn of a sigh and a bitter chuckle echoed within, too quiet for either the driver or the footman to hear from their outside perches.

Who had been the more gullible goose, Felicity asked herself—she or Percy? How could neither of them have suspected his mistresses might've had other lovers to sire their children? Foisting their maintenance off upon him because he had the wealth to provide for them and because he was so pitifully eager to prove his virility by claiming them as his own.

Now here she was, with child at last. By a man she had no intention of marrying.

Would Thorn Greenwood ever have consented to become her lover if he'd thought there was any danger of her conceiving? Felicity knew the answer to that, for Thorn had raised the question himself when she first approached him with her scandalous proposition.

He'd blushed and stammered with an awkwardness she'd found endearing in such a consummate gentleman. It had taken two or three tries before he could frame his query in blunt enough terms for her to understand what he was asking.

She had almost abandoned the whole undertaking then and there, rather than expose her painful past. Then some baffling compulsion, deeper than her embarrassment and self-pity, had made her confess the truth.

"Don't trouble yourself on that account, sir. While we were married, my husband sired several children— none of them by me."

To forestall any word or look of pity, she had forced herself to laugh. "So you see I am as free as a man to take my pleasure."

Perhaps those words had tempted fate to play her for a fool. She would have the last and best laugh, though. Her fortune and her widowhood would make it possible for her to enjoy the pleasures of motherhood without the bothersome encumbrance of a husband.

Her conscience protested her thinking of Thorn Greenwood as an encumbrance, but Felicity turned a deaf ear. Even if she had been willing to risk marriage again for the sake of propriety, she'd gauge a husband's suitability on a different scale than the one she'd used to pick a lover. Thorn would have been far down on her list of candidates.

"Perhaps I should have brought Hetty along, after all," Felicity grumbled to herself. "At least her tiresome prattle might have distracted me from thinking about *that man.*"

Mustering more of the desperate resolution she'd employed to lock Thorn out of her bedchamber and order him out of her house, Felicity tried once again to evict him from her thoughts. She concentrated on making plans for herself and her baby once this troublesome business with her nephew and Ivy Greenwood was settled.

First, she would retire to the country for her confinement. Somewhere quiet, with a healthy climate. Far away from Bath and equally far away from the Lyte family seat in Staffordshire. Somewhere in Kent might do quite nicely. Except...

Did Thorn have a country estate in Kent? Felicity rummaged her memory, but could not recall. Had they ever talked about it?

No. They'd seldom spoken of anything beyond immediate trivialities, perhaps out of fear that it might lead to a deeper attachment on one side or the other.

"You're thinking about him again," she scolded herself.

If she wanted to know his home county, she should save her questions and put them to Miss Ivy on the drive back to Bath.

That sensible idea hit upon, Felicity settled herself to imagine the quiet, cosy household she would fashion for her family of two. She scarcely noticed her breath slowing to keep time with the gentle bounce and sway of the carriage.

Some while later, she roused slightly as the sound and tempo of the ride altered. Awake only enough to tell herself they must be traveling over the cobbled city streets of Bristol, she sank back into slumber.

She woke next in a sudden, disorienting manner as the carriage slowed abruptly, sending her hurtling forward onto the opposite seat. Darkness still wrapped the landscape outside. How long had she been asleep? Where were they?

High skittish whinnies from the horses penetrated the interior of the carriage as it came to a full stop. Felicity regained her seat, then reached up to rap her knuckles on the ceiling and demand an accounting from Mr. Hixon. The next sound from outside made her hand freeze in midair and her stomach churn in a way that had nothing to do with her pregnancy.

"Stand and deliver!"

Could someone be playing a tasteless prank? Felicity wondered as she scooped her reticule from the floor to hide in the folds of her cloak. Surely highwaymen were a fixture of the last century, not this one.

Or had travelers become more cautious about venturing over deserted stretches of road after dark? Thorn's prudent warning echoed in her thoughts. *It will be a difficult journey—perhaps even dangerous.*

She'd been so anxious to distance herself from him and so impatient with his attempts to take control of the situation. What had she expected? Thorn Greenwood was a man, after all, not a lapdog.

"Give us leave to pass," shouted the coachman. "What do ye want, anyway?"

"Wha' d'yer think?" came the reply, followed by harsh laughter that made Felicity break out in gooseflesh. "Nice lookin' rig like this, bound to have good pickin's, eh? Let's take a look."

Felicity wedged herself into the corner farthest from the carriage door as she heard a rider dismount and footsteps approach.

"I've got a pistol cocked and I ain't afraid to use it," called the highwayman for the benefit of anyone inside the carriage.

Felicity fumbled in her reticule, extracting several pound notes from the large number inside. This *knight of the road* would never miss them. Though her pulse throbbed in her ears, she lunged for the carriage door and threw it open.

"Here." She thrust her reticule toward a man-shaped shadow. "Take it and let us be on our way. I must get to Gloucester by morning—my mother is very ill."

If such nefarious creatures had hearts, that story together with her ready cooperation might save her from being molested further.

Or perhaps not.

"I'm right sorry to 'ear that, ma'am," the high-wayman replied.

He shook the reticule. Several golden guineas at the bottom jingled. "Thanks for this little gift. But don't be in too big a hurry to get on your way again. Those prads of yours sound a bit winded to me." He referred to the horses.

When he took a step nearer, Felicity retreated into the depths of the carriage.

"Are ye as pretty as ye sound, I wonder?" A gloved hand reached in and groped toward her.

"I'm not at all pretty, and..." Felicity floundered for anything she could say that might deter this criminal from doing what he appeared intent on. "...and...I have the pox!"

Felicity heard a dull thud, then the highwayman pitched into the carriage. The scream she'd been choking back for some minutes ripped from her throat.

Chapter Four

Thorn Greenwood shifted in his saddle. He'd been riding hard for several hours on a succession of narrow county roads which skirted around Bristol to reach the highway that ran between that bustling port and the city of Gloucester, over thirty miles to the north. A bilious sense of urgency gripped his belly as he spurred the spirited mount St. Just had loaned him.

A brisk west wind from off the mouth of the Severn whipped the horse's mane and threatened to snatch away Thorn's hat. He jammed it down tighter and kept riding.

"I should never have let her leave Bath without me," Thorn muttered aloud the words that had drummed in his head over and over while he'd been riding.

The full moon hung low in the sky, casting a pale ghostly light over the heath and on the black ribbon of road that wound through it. Thorn squinted into the shadowy darkness, straining to catch the faintest sign of Felicity's carriage.

Might he have reached the highway before her? Or

was she several long miles ahead of him on this lonely,
perilous stretch of road?

Thorn did not have long to ponder the question, for
just then his horse reached the crest of a slight rise.
From that vantage he could make out a small bobbing
light not far ahead—one that he prayed was being cast
by a driving lamp on Felicity's carriage.

A sigh of relief rose to his lips, only to be sucked
back in a gasp. The light had abruptly stopped moving.

That might mean any number of things, but at the
moment Thorn could think of only one. Crouching low
in the saddle, he urged his flagging horse to one last
desperate dash, fearing he might be too late. The
pounding of his heart outstripped even the fast-rolling
thunder of hooves against the road.

In the instant he drew close enough to see, Thorn
recognized Felicity's equipage. The flame of satisfaction that flared within him rapidly quenched at the
sight of a man preparing to enter the carriage box.

A man with a white handkerchief shrouding the
lower portion of his face.

As Thorn drew near the carriage, he reined in his
mount, then hurled himself from the saddle onto the
intruder. The two of them pitched into the carriage as
a woman's scream pierced the darkness.

The boneless sprawl of the man beneath him told
Thorn the fellow had been knocked senseless. Just to
be safe, he groped around the carriage floor until his
hand closed over the highwayman's pistol.

"Keep away from me!" cried Felicity. "Keep
away, do you hear?"

Thorn struggled to speak so he could reassure her
that all was well—at least better than it had been a
few moments ago. But his flying tackle of the high-

wayman had both winded and stunned him. Unable to coax out any words louder than a whisper, he scrambled up from the floor, intent on comforting Felicity in his embrace, instead.

As he reached for her, she screamed again, loud enough to make his ears ring. At the same time, her heeled slipper came into violent contact with his midriff. Thorn doubled over with a grunt of pain.

He lurched backward, only to trip over the unconscious highwayman and crumple onto the seat opposite Felicity. Before he could catch his breath or collect his wits, she fell on him, scratching, slapping, pummelling like a wild creature. Thorn fell back before the onslaught, his hands raised to fend off the worst of it.

"Felicity!" he gasped.

Her attack did not abate. If anything, it gathered speed and force, each blow punctuated by a squeal or high-pitched grunt.

"Felicity, it's Thorn." He caught her deceptively fragile wrists in his hands to stay her assault and gave her a good hard shake to bring her to her senses. "You're safe, now."

She froze for a moment. "Thorn? Is it really you?"

Some overwound spring inside him fell blissfully slack. "Do you know anyone else daft enough to chase you halfway across the county at this hour of the night?"

"Thorn." She choked out his name again. Then, with all the power and passion she had thrown into fighting him, Felicity hurled herself into his arms, weeping in great gusty sobs.

"Hush, now, hush." Thorn gathered her close, stroking his side whiskers against her hair and fighting a fast-rising tide of desire that threatened to drown his self-control.

First, the headlong race to overtake her, spurred by his fears for her safety. Then, confronting the worst of those fears, only to have Felicity launch her furious assault upon him. It had fired his blood as hot as any love play—the physical contact, the heightened passions, the pounding hearts and panting breath.

And now, cradling Felicity in his arms as she unleashed a torrent of tears on his topcoat, her backside warm against his thighs, with only a flimsy barrier of muslin and broadcloth between his flesh and hers.

At that moment, Thorn would have bartered everything he owned for them to be back in Felicity's bedchamber, rather than on the open road in a cold carriage with a dazed highwayman beginning to stir at their feet.

"M-Mister Greenwood?" a tremulous young voice inquired from beyond the open carriage door. "Is that you, sir? What happened?"

"Has Lady Lyte come to any harm, sir?" asked a second, deeper voice.

"Apart from a nasty shock, I believe she's well enough." Chilling thoughts of what might have befallen Felicity sharpened Thorn's tone. "No thanks to the pair of you."

"He did have a gun, sir," the young footman protested.

The driver offered no excuse, but his voice sounded thoroughly chastened. "Is there aught we can do, now, Mr. Greenwood?"

The highwayman groaned and tried to sit up. Thorn applied some weight to his right foot, which rested between the fellow's shoulder blades, forcing him back down.

To the driver and footmen who hovered outside, Thorn ordered, "Find a bit of rope to truss this blackguard up."

"Very good, Mr. Greenwood, sir."

"Tie him to his horse if you can find it, or to mine if you can't," Thorn added. "Then tether it to the carriage. We can turn this fellow over to the proper authorities at the first town we reach. For now, I believe we'd better continue on our way as quickly as possible, in case others of his ilk might be lurking about."

Perhaps goaded by that warning, Lady Lyte's driver and footman wasted no time finding some material with which to bind the highwayman, who sounded too befuddled to put up much resistance.

By the time the carriage had recommenced its journey northward, Felicity's weeping had quieted to a volley of sniffles. Still, she made no effort to distance herself from Thorn. Greedily, he drank in the touch and scent of her, all too conscious of how much he had missed her in the short time they'd been apart.

Might the trouble he'd taken to ride to her rescue have changed her mind about terminating their liaison prematurely? he wondered as he cradled Felicity in his arms.

Hard as Thorn tried not to be enticed by that willo'-the-wisp of false hope, he failed.

She ought to push Thorn away, order him out of the carriage or, at the very least, rail at him for frightening her half to death. But as her carriage sped on toward Newport, Felicity found herself unable to take any of the actions she ought.

There would be many long years ahead for her to manage without the warm, steadfast comfort of Thorn Greenwood's embrace. For the present, she needed it more desperately than she had needed anything in a great while. And Lady Felicity Lyte was not accustomed to denying herself anything she needed.

She could not remember ever being so badly frightened. Her heart kept up its rapid flutter in her bosom, and despite a good warm wrap, she began to tremble.

"There, there." Thorn stroked her arm.

Was it her imagination, or did he press a fleeting kiss on the top of her head?

"Are you all right, Felicity? Or did I speak too soon when I told your servants you were unharmed?" The tender concern that radiated from Thorn's tone and touch soaked into her heart like warm ointment.

Pride would not allow her to accept comfort for the most grievous wounds life had inflicted upon her. No matter how she might crave it.

"You spoke aright, I suffered nothing worse than a nasty shock." She sniffled. "Have you a handkerchief I can ruin?"

She would have hated anyone else who'd witnessed her break down into hysterical tears. Perhaps she would hate Thorn for it in the cool light of day when she could see how the betrayal of weakness had diminished her in his eyes. But for this sweet, dark moment she would allow herself the dangerous luxury of relying on a man.

"A handkerchief?" Thorn shifted her a little so he could pry his coat open and rummage in the pocket of his waistcoat. "I believe I have."

He pressed the folded square of linen into her hand. "There. Do your worst. That's what laundry's for."

"Thank you," Felicity managed to squeak. The gentle fumbling brush of Thorn's hands had set her flesh atingle.

She wiped the last residue of moisture from her eyes, thankful that by the time Thorn could see her clearly, the worst ravages of her silly tears would have faded.

If that was vanity, well, so be it. She could not abide having an attractive man see her at less than her best.

As she blew her nose, masked by the forgiving darkness, a thought struck her. "Are *you* all right, Thorn? After bringing down that awful man…then the way I went at you. I am so sorry. I can't imagine what got into me."

"You were only doing your best to defend yourself." Thorn chuckled. "And making an admirable job of it, too. I don't believe I took any lasting damage, though."

A few blows from her wouldn't have done him any harm, of course. But if that odious highwayman had managed to get off a shot with his pistol… Felicity would never have forgiven herself if Thorn had been injured on her account.

"Well?" she prompted him, bracing herself for the reprimand she probably deserved. Thorn Greenwood seemed like a man who could deliver a stern scolding when one was called for.

"Well…what?" He sounded genuinely puzzled.

"The dressing-down you've been rehearsing in your mind ever since you left Bath." Felicity blew her nose again. "Where is it?"

"Oh…that." Thorn gave a wry chuckle which succumbed to a deep, weary yawn. ''It'll keep until morning. For now, I believe we'd both be better served by an hour's sleep if we can get it.''

The poor fellow, he must be perfectly exhausted after spending the evening in search of his sister, then the last several hours in pursuit of her.

''You talk sound sense, as always, Mr. Greenwood.'' Felicity made a halfhearted attempt to rise from Thorn's lap. ''No doubt you would rest more comfortably without the burden of a blubbering woman to squash you.''

She would likely benefit from putting some distance between them, too. It was difficult enough to keep regrets at bay without the sensation of his arms around her to remind Felicity what she would soon be missing.

''You're no burden.'' With gentle insistence, Thorn drew her back into the protective circle of his arms. ''Besides, I'm apt to sleep more soundly for the reminder that you are out of danger.''

''In that case...'' Felicity settled back into Thorn's embrace. ''I'm content to remain where I am.''

More than content, in fact. Though she did not dare tell him so.

''Thorn?''

''Yes?'' He sounded halfway to sleep already.

She shouldn't pester him with questions, Felicity chided herself, but she so liked the sound of his voice. ''Wherever did you get a horse to come after me?''

''From St. Just.'' Thorn patted his pocket. ''I've got blunt, too. Won it in a card game.''

If Thorn had confessed to stealing the money, Felicity could not have been more surprised. ''I thought you never gambled.''

"Never did till tonight." His words had the slurred, dreamy quality Felicity had heard so often in the past weeks when he'd held her close after their lovemaking. "Don't know the devil about cards. It may have helped that I was the only sober fellow at the table."

"Perhaps a little beginner's luck?" Knowing full well she shouldn't do it, Felicity could not stop herself reaching up to brush her knuckles against Thorn's side whiskers.

"Perhaps." He whispered the word as if it was the sweetest of endearments.

Then, before Felicity could withdraw her hand, he tilted his head to catch her fingers between his shoulder and his cheek, nuzzling them in a chaste gesture of affection that brought a lump to her throat.

She forced her question out past the obstruction. "How could you possibly stake yourself in the sort of bankrupting card game Weston St. Just favors?"

Thorn's head snapped up again, flinching from her touch in a way he had not flinched from her earlier attack. "I'm not a complete pauper, you know."

His fortune—or rather his lack of it. Even as she regretted her question, Felicity could not stifle a twinge of annoyance. How many years had she tread with bated breath around the subject of her late husband's want of prosperity?

At least Thorn Greenwood was making an effort to repair his family's fortune. And by a more principled means than simply marrying the first available heiress.

"I didn't say you were a pauper. Most men don't carry a great deal of ready money around in the middle of the night, that's all."

Thorn did not answer at once. Had he fallen asleep, Felicity wondered, or was he too offended to reply?

"I have an old watch and a signet ring," he said at last, as if confessing to a crime. "St. Just managed to convince the other players they were worth something."

His admission stung Felicity in a vulnerable spot, just as her question about his gambling stakes must have done to Thorn. She knew very well the watch and ring to which he'd alluded. What price they might fetch from a jeweller, she could not guess. Yet they were priceless to Thorn—a reminder that he belonged to an old family of good breeding.

Despite her fortune and the title for which she'd paid so dear a price, Felicity knew many people still scorned her as an upstart tradesman's daughter. Suitable only as a mistress for a respectable gentleman like Thorn Greenwood, but never a wife.

Such a union would cause no end of talk. And respectable gentlemen abhorred being a topic of gossip among tattles like Weston St. Just.

Thorn's arms relaxed their grip on Felicity, and his breath warmed her hair in slow, rhythmic gusts. As she steeled herself to put a great deal more distance between them on the morrow, a further significance of his gambling stakes struck her.

He had gone to a great deal of trouble on her account. First, gambling his most valued possessions, then riding through the night to overtake her carriage. Finally, risking his life to rescue her from danger. Thorn Greenwood was not a man given to pretty speeches, but his actions spoke eloquently of his feelings for her.

Percy Lyte had never valued her as anything more than a source of hard cash and heirs. And when she'd proven deficient in the latter capacity, her husband's thinly veiled contempt had eroded something vital within her. Something that Thorn's honest, unconditional affection promised to nourish.

He had put aside his natural prudence to take a gamble for her sake, Felicity mused as the first feeble glimmer of daybreak gilded his strong, agreeable features. She, on the other hand, would need to curb her own daring impulses, lest they induce her to take a reckless gamble on Thorn Greenwood.

And risk losing far more than she could afford.

Thorn woke with such a violent start he might have dumped Felicity onto the floor of the carriage, if her arms had not been clasped so firmly around his neck.

The jolt did succeed in rousing her from her own sleep, though.

"What's the matter, my dear?" she asked. "Did you dream about that awful highwayman?"

"Ah…something like that." Thorn struggled to curb the sensation of panic that galloped within his chest.

He could scarcely recall his dream, now, though it had seemed so real and urgent only a moment ago.

He'd been playing some curious game of cards for stakes that had grown larger and larger. Until he could no longer fold his hand without being ruined. Fear and reckless confidence had warred within him when he'd finally lain down his promising handful of hearts, only to be soundly trumped by strange cards that looked like miniature banknotes.

As the winner raked in the pot, Thorn had realized that he'd risked both his honor and his heart. And lost.

"Where do you reckon we are now?" He concentrated on slowing his breath as he disengaged himself from Felicity.

Something about the unsparing light of day made it impossible for him to continue holding her in his arms, even within the privacy of her carriage. No matter how much he wanted to.

Felicity made an unsuccessful effort to smother a yawn as she peered out the window. She seemed no more anxious than Thorn to continue their awkward embrace. Perhaps he had only imagined the wistful warmth in her voice last night and that delicious brush of her fingers against his side whiskers.

"We're coming to a small bridge," she said. "I believe Newport lies just the other side of it, and I have good reason to hope we may catch up with our runaways there."

As she told Thorn about her custom of stopping in that village when coming and going from Bath, Felicity shifted onto the seat opposite him. "Do you know the hour?"

He fished the venerable timepiece from his watch pocket and consulted it.

"After seven." Thorn shook his head. "Your poor driver and footmen will be done in, to say nothing of the horses."

"I hope we catch Oliver and your sister before they've had a chance to stir." Felicity stared out the window, ignoring Thorn's gaze. Or, perhaps, avoiding it. "Then we can all take a day's rest before returning to Bath at our leisure."

Thorn nodded and made vague noises of agreement, though with scant conviction.

Of course, he wanted to recover his scapegrace little sister before she mangled her reputation beyond repair.

But that would mean parting from Felicity again. This time, with no chance of reprieve.

In spite of his disquieting dream, Thorn had trouble working up the least enthusiasm for that.

Chapter Five

Six hours after it had left Bath, Lady Lyte's carriage rolled to a halt in front of a prosperous-looking inn. It stopped beneath a sign emblazoned with some royal coat of arms from years long past.

Felicity made herself look Thorn Greenwood in the face as she strove to keep her tone casual. "Surely Oliver and your sister won't have gotten on the road yet."

She was thoroughly ashamed of the way she'd lost her nerve last night. Screaming like a lunatic when Thorn and the highwayman had landed in the carriage, then pummeling her poor rescuer within an inch of his life. As if those weren't bad enough, she'd further humiliated herself by bursting into tears, and clinging to Thorn like a frightened child.

That he had borne it all with such generous sympathy should have made her feel better...but it did not.

If the past thirty-odd years had taught Felicity Lyte one thing, it was that a woman must be prepared to look after herself and take her own part against the world. No one else could be trusted to do it for her—least of all anyone who wore breeches.

She could not afford to let Thorn Greenwood convince her otherwise.

On the seat opposite Felicity, Thorn stretched his long limbs as a wry chuckle rippled out of him. "If young Armitage can roust my sister out of bed at a reasonable hour of the morning, he's a better man than I."

The significance of his words must have struck him, for Thorn's brow furrowed. "Your nephew would hire separate rooms for them, I hope?"

For some reason, that question rasped against Felicity's tightly wound nerves.

"Of course Oliver will make certain they have separate lodgings," she snapped. "My nephew is an honorable young man. Just because he was foolish enough to run away to Scotland with your sister doesn't mean he'll compromise her virtue. It's not as though *she* were an heiress and *he* a fortune hunter."

For over half a century, Lord Hardwick's Marriage Act had made it more difficult for unscrupulous men to prey on naive young ladies of fortune. A truly determined number now chanced the long journey to Scotland where underage women could still wed without the consent of their families. Many an unprincipled scoundrel took the added precaution of relieving the young lady of her virginity during the journey.

Thorn glared at Felicity. "Are you accusing my sister of pursuing your nephew for his fortune?"

"She would not be the first."

The words had barely left her lips before Felicity wished she'd bitten her own tart tongue. Whimsical and imprudent Ivy Greenwood might be. For all that, she seemed a warmhearted, unaffected little thing—

unlike some of the avaricious creatures who'd stalked
Oliver during their past several Seasons at Bath.

If she and Thorn found the young lovers at the
King's Arms, as Felicity was certain they would, she
might never see him again after today. Perhaps if she
picked a quarrel with him and they parted on bad
terms, it might trouble them both less.

Felicity wished she could believe it.

Instead she feared the look of injured dignity in
Thorn's expressive eyes would plague her sleepless
nights for years to come.

"It might surprise you how many men and woman
form romantic attachments with no thought of fortune,
madam." He could have hurled the words at her like
an accusation. Instead, Thorn spoke them in a tone of
quiet forbearance that vexed Felicity even worse.

The acid retort flew out of her before she could
contain it. "When there is no fortune involved,
perhaps."

Thorn did not flinch or strike back, yet something
in his steady gaze told Felicity she had just diminished
herself in his eyes.

At that moment, her young footman pulled open the
carriage door.

Plucking his hat off the seat beside him, Thorn
Greenwood prepared to debark. "Let us go collect our
strays and be done with it, shall we?"

"By all means." Felicity let him help her down
from the high carriage box, acutely conscious that the
chaste touch of his hand would probably be her last.

Once she had firm ground under her feet, she forced
herself to pull her hand away. Then she swept into the
King's Arms, leaving Thorn to follow in her wake or
not, as he chose.

She found the large entry hall abustle with a party of travelers anxious to make an early departure. Felicity peered around for any sign of Oliver or Ivy among the crowd, but saw none.

She did recognize the innkeeper's wife, threading her way through the departing guests bearing a breakfast tray for others who would not stir from their lodgings until a more civilized hour.

Might a dish of buttered eggs and kippered herring nestle on that tray beneath the crisp white napkin? Felicity wondered. Oliver insisted a morning diet of fish and eggs stimulated his mental processes.

Once again, his aunt asked herself how an aloof scholar like Oliver Armitage had become entangled with such a flighty little chit as Ivy Greenwood. However it had come about, Felicity vowed to disentangle her nephew. Even if it meant threatening to disinherit him.

The innkeeper appeared just then to present the departing patrons with their bill.

The moment he spied Felicity, he left his other guests to tally their charges while he marched over to greet her with an exaggerated bow.

"Lady Lyte! A great pleasure as always, ma'am. We weren't expecting to see you back from Bath for a few weeks yet. I fear your usual rooms have been let until the day after tomorrow, but of course we will endeavor to accommodate you as best we can. I remarked to Mr. Armitage just last night that his arrival was all the more welcome for being something of a surprise."

"So he is here!" Dizzy with relief, Felicity barely refrained from clasping the fastidious retired soldier in an embrace that would have flustered him to death.

"If you would be so good as to show us to Mr. Armitage's room, I have an urgent need to speak with him."

The innkeeper's smile faded as he shook his head. "There must be some mistake, ma'am. Mr. Armitage and his lovely bride dined here last evening. But after that they left for Gloucester to spend the night."

Behind her, Felicity sensed Thorn give a start at the word *bride,* though he said nothing.

"Gloucester?" she repeated. "Are you certain?"

"Indeed, ma'am. Mr. Armitage was most particular about it. I recollect thinking it a late hour for them to be on the road and hoping they'd be able to find vacant lodgings once they arrived there."

The innkeeper glanced at his other guests, who looked impatient to be off. "If you'll excuse me a moment, ma'am...?"

Felicity tried not to let her dismay show. "By all means."

Once the innkeeper and his guests were occupied, she turned to Thorn. "Gloucester? What could have made Oliver press on so far? We always stop at The King's Arms on our way to Trentwell."

"I'd say the *why* is rather obvious, wouldn't you?" replied Thorn. "They're eager to reach Gretna as soon as they can. Besides, Armitage is a clever young fellow. No doubt it occurred to him that if you gave chase, this would be the first place you'd come looking."

How dare Thorn Greenwood sound so calm and rational when her whole world had turned on its head? She had so counted on finding Oliver here and putting a quick stop to this whole troublesome business.

Felicity felt her gorge rise on a bilious tide. "If we

keep driving, might we reach Gloucester before they move on?''

"It's well over fifteen miles." Thorn shook his head. "With market traffic, we'd do well to get there by noon. Even Ivy isn't that excessive a slugabed."

If Felicity could have got her hands on her nephew and Miss Greenwood, she would have throttled them both. The last thing she needed just then was to be chasing the length of the country after them.

"Besides." Thorn gestured toward the window, through which Felicity could see her carriage. "We can't simply pile back in and keep on driving. We need fresh horses, and your poor coachman and footman must get a little rest. Then there's the small matter of that highwayman. We have to deliver him to someone in authority and swear out a complaint."

Was the whole world conspiring against her? Felicity asked herself as her palms went clammy and her stomach grew more sour by the minute. If she hadn't emptied it so thoroughly the night before, she might have been violently ill in front of a room full of strangers.

And, worse still, in front of Thorn Greenwood.

It would serve the woman right if he left her there, Thorn fumed. With his winnings from last night's card game, perhaps he should pursue young Armitage and his sister on his own, leaving Felicity Lyte to fend for herself.

Except for those few sweet hours after he'd rescued her from the highwayman, Lady Lyte had made it abundantly clear she wanted neither his advice, his assistance nor his company. Why could he not wash his hands of her, as any rational man would?

Until recently, Thorn had prided himself on being a rational fellow. Then he'd stared into Felicity Lyte's incomparable green eyes and lost himself.

At the moment, that vibrant green looked rather washed-out, while the rosy springtime hue of her complexion had blanched and chilled.

"What's the matter, my dear?" He caught her icy hand in his. "You look dreadful."

"And you have a great deal to learn about being a lady's man, Mr. Greenwood." Wrenching her fingers from his grip, Felicity looked as though she longed to slap his face with them.

"Of course I look dreadful. Why shouldn't I? Woken out of a sound sleep to trundle over the countryside in the middle of the night. Accosted by a highwayman. And now with the prospect of chasing the length of England after my ungrateful nephew. I'd probably shatter a mirror if I looked in one."

The other inn guests were casting inquisitive glances their way. Thorn detested few things worse than being an object of curiosity. He drew Felicity off to a little alcove by the main staircase.

"That's not what I meant, and you know it. You're as lovely as ever. Only, you look wrought up…or ill."

Before she could fire off a retort, he held up his palms in mock surrender. "Both of which you have good cause to be, I admit. For once, hold your tongue and listen to me. You need proper rest and food, as do your servants and the horses. I'll arrange that with the innkeeper. Then, while you're recovering from last night's journey, I'll hunt up someone to take that outlaw off our hands."

For a wonder, Felicity did not interrupt him. She

waited until he'd finished before asking, "What do you propose we do after that?"

Thorn tried to hide his surprise. He'd expected more of a battle from her. "After that we must talk. To decide on our next move."

"Very well."

"Do you mean it?"

The old verdant sparks leapt in her eyes once again, igniting an answering flame in Thorn's formerly rational heart. "What manner of question is that? Do you think I oppose you for amusement?"

"Of course not," Thorn lied. "I only meant—" What could he say that wouldn't dig him deeper into trouble? "Never mind."

The other guests, having settled their bill at last, departed with a maximum of noise and commotion. Thorn found himself glad of the distraction.

Once they had gone, he approached the innkeeper. "We will have to be on our way before nightfall, but in the meantime, Lady Lyte, her driver and her footman all need rooms in which to rest."

The innkeeper's eyes lit up. No doubt he relished the prospect of hiring out the same rooms twice in one day. "Always delighted to oblige her ladyship, sir."

"The horses will need tending, as well."

"I'll make certain the hostlers know to take special trouble with them, Mister…"

"Greenwood. Hawthorn Greenwood." Thorn steeled himself against the fellow's meddlesome scrutiny. "I'm an old friend of Lady Lyte's. Her nephew's…er…bride is my sister."

"Indeed, sir?" The innkeeper beamed, as people tended to do when speaking of Ivy. "A lively little creature. Not one I'd have picked for a serious young scholar like Mr. Armitage if I'd had the ordering of it. But love often goes by contraries, then, doesn't it, sir?''

"Perhaps so." Did that explain his own intense, wayward feelings for Felicity? Thorn wondered. "By any chance, did my sister or Mr. Armitage mention where they might lodge once they reached Gloucester?"

The innkeeper's smile widened further. "As it happens, sir, they asked if I could recommend any place that might offer them a warm welcome even if they arrived at a late hour.''

"Did you?" Thorn strove not to sound as desperately interested in the information as he felt.

"I should say so, Mr. Greenwood. The wife's cousin keeps an inn in the old part of town between the cathedral and the shirehall. It don't get as busy as the big posting inns on the roads to London and Bristol. I told Mr. Armitage it would be a rare night he and his fair bride couldn't find a bed there, no matter what hour they knocked.''

"I appreciate your advising them." Thorn fished out a shilling from his card winnings. He offered it to the innkeeper, who made a token show of refusing before sliding the coin into his own pocket.

"I'll just see to the rooms for Lady Lyte and her servants, Mr. Greenwood.''

"One more thing, if I may?''

"Aye, sir. What might that be?''

"We ran into a spot of trouble on the road from Bristol—a highwayman.''

"My life, sir!" The innkeeper's eyes grew wide. "No one hurt, I hope. That scoundrel's been making a right nuisance of himself all spring. You're not my first guests to have been molested by him."

"I hope we may be the last." Thorn nodded toward the door. "We fetched the bounder along with us to give an account of himself before the magistrate. Whereabouts should I dispose of him?"

"I'd fetch him over to Berkeley, Mr. Greenwood." The innkeeper cocked his thumb in a direction Thorn took to be northeast. "They can deal with him there and be obliged to you for the taking of him, I should think."

As the innkeeper bustled off, Thorn turned back to Felicity, who had sunk down onto a nearby chair. He knew better than to comment on how she looked, but a qualm of guilt rolled low in his belly. She might have slept better stretched out on the carriage seat opposite him than awkwardly nestled on his lap.

He knelt before her and took one of her hands in his. It had warmed a little since he'd touched it a few moments earlier, but not much.

"The innkeeper tells me they can deal with our highwayman over in Berkeley. Will you be all right until I get back?"

"Of course I will." Felicity sat up straighter. "I'm neither a child nor a tottering old dowager, Mr. Greenwood. I do not need a keeper. You're quite welcome to cart that awful creature off to London for all I care. I can manage quite well on my own."

The gall of the woman! Dismissing his concern for her as if he held no higher standing in her life than her driver or her footman.

The notion sent Thorn leaping to his feet again. "As well as you managed last night on the heath?"

Felicity shot him a withering look. "Ah! Here is the

lecture you've been saving since last night. I doubt it will taste any less bitter, warmed over for breakfast.''

He had never seen this unpleasant side of her character during their time together. Thorn cursed himself. He'd been a fool to let himself fall under the spell of her wit, her spirit and her passion. Any man of sense might have guessed that such a vibrant rose could not lack for thorns.

Well, he was feeling the sting of them now.

"Last night you as good as owned you deserved a reprimand." Thorn struggled to suppress the memory of Felicity burrowing into his embrace, sweetly repentant. "I tried to show a little forbearance, believing you'd already learned your lesson in more forceful terms than any words of mine could match.''

Felicity surged to her feet, a welcome color returning to her face. "Why, you pompous... How dare you scold me as if I was one of your flighty little sisters?''

"My sisters have more sense than—'' Thorn choked back the rest of his words as another party of inn guests descended into the posting hall.

He forced himself to pitch his voice lower, though his anger had not abated. "We can resume this discussion in private when I return from Berkeley. In the meantime, I suggest you rest and take some food.''

"I told you, I'm quite capable of looking after myself.''

If he stood there a moment longer, Felicity's stubborn opposition might goad him to shake her. Worse yet, her nearness and the strange stirring friction between them might make him sweep her into his arms for a kiss so fierce and brazen it would fuel juicy gossip at the King's Arms for years to come.

* * *

As Thorn Greenwood executed a crisp pivot on his heel and strode away from her, Felicity struggled to subdue the storm of emotions that raged inside her.

How could she have taken the man into her bed night after night without ever guessing his true character? She'd thought him quiet, gentle and amiable, not the sort to demand more than she could give him or make a nuisance of himself in her life.

That was part of the reason she'd chosen him as her lover over a number of other candidates who had far more to recommend them. How could she have guessed Mr. Greenwood's accustomed mild manner masked an iron will that vexed her beyond bearing even as it excited a grudging respect?

The only thing she detested more than being bossed and bullied was being manipulated.

Perhaps some good had come of Oliver's foolish elopement if it had opened her eyes to aspects of Thorn Greenwood's temperament that she had either overlooked or willfully ignored. Now she could cast him off without any troublesome qualms of guilt.

Glancing out the window, Felicity spied the highwayman. Now that she got a good look at him in the belittling light of day, she could see he was no more than a spotty-faced youth. Damn his callow hide for giving her such a fright!

His hands were tied and bound to the pommel of his saddle. He appeared to be pleading with Thorn not to turn him in.

Quite against her will, a twinge of pity tugged at Felicity. The lad would almost certainly hang for his petty crimes—mischief that had probably sprung from some rash devilment of youth with no pause to consider the consequences. Just the kind of impulse that had propelled her to the altar with Percy Lyte at that age.

At least she'd survived her youthful mistake and learned from it. Felicity forced herself to look away. She gave a start when she discovered the innkeeper hovering nearby.

"We have a room ready for you, Lady Lyte." He beckoned her toward the staircase. "Nothing grand, but it's a quiet one at the back of the house. If you mean to rest, you'll not be disturbed by noise from the road."

"Thank you, Mr. Mobley." Felicity smothered a yawn. "I could do with a nap."

Even before she'd set out from Bath last night, she'd found herself unaccountably weary during the day. Now she could scarcely keep her eyes open.

"A very agreeable gentleman, that Mr. Greenwood," the innkeeper remarked as he led Felicity up the stairs. "You'll be pleased to welcome him into the family, no doubt."

"Family?" Were her feelings for Thorn that transparent?

"Aye, ma'am. With your nephew wed to his sister." The innkeeper glanced back at her with a knowing grin. "Did you and Mr. Greenwood contrive the match, by any chance?"

Felicity resisted an urge to laugh. "Quite the contrary, Mr. Mobley."

Either the innkeeper missed her meaning or he pretended to. "A love match, was it, then? Can't say it surprises me to hear it. A body could tell just by watching the way she hung on his every word."

Just as she had once paid such rapt attention to Percy Lyte? The thought made Felicity wince. It also made her wonder what had drawn the vivacious Miss Greenwood to a quiet young man like her nephew, if not the fortune he stood to inherit.

"Here we are ma'am." The innkeeper halted before the last door along the passageway and pushed it open for her. "Shall I send the wife up with a tray of breakfast for you?"

Just then the scent of food drifted upstairs, sending Felicity's stomach into rebellion. "Tea and rusks will be fine. I never sleep soundly after a full meal."

"Tea and rusks." The innkeeper chuckled to himself, shaking his head. "The wife lived on 'em when she was breeding."

When he realized what he'd said, the poor man went as red as a radish. "Tea and rusks. Tea and rusks, indeed. I'll have them sent up directly, ma'am. Be sure to ring if you need anything else."

"I'm sure I'll be quite comfortable, Mr. Mobley, as always." Felicity found herself only slightly less flustered than the innkeeper.

She ducked into the room, barely resisting the urge to slam the door behind her. "He didn't mean anything by it," she whispered to herself as she wilted onto the bed. "He can't possibly have guessed."

Though she knew it was true, the innkeeper's offhand remark had unnerved her all the same. In some curious manner, it suddenly made her condition more real to her.

A baby was growing in her womb—the child she had longed for and despaired of ever bearing. In some ways this would be even better than if she'd borne Percy's child, for this little one would not carry all the dynastic ambitions of the Lyte family. It would be hers, and hers alone, to raise and to love. To nurture and protect.

The intense conflicting emotions of the past few days slowly loosened their grip on her as Felicity pictured herself launching a toy sailboat with a small boy, holding a little girl on her lap while they played a duet on the pianoforte. She would finally know the untainted joy of childhood that had eluded her during her own youth.

Then her dream child turned its sweet young face toward Felicity, lavishing her with the tender, earnest gaze of Thorn Greenwood.

Chapter Six

Felicity's eyelids fluttered, then slowly opened.

On his seat by the door, Thorn fought to keep his own eyes from sliding shut. He had stolen into this room at the King's Arms some little while ago to let Felicity know he'd returned from his errand in Berkeley and to advise her they ought to set off for Gloucester soon.

When he'd found her fast asleep on the bed, all soft and loose-limbed, he could not bring himself to wake her. Instead, he'd subsided onto the one chair these modest quarters afforded and drunk in the delicious sight of her.

Now she opened her eyes and looked back at him.

In that first hazy moment of waking, her gaze fixed on Thorn with the promise of a thousand springtimes shining in her eyes. Some dry, wizened bulb, buried deep in the loam of his practical heart unclenched itself then, sending a slender green shoot straining toward the sun's life-giving warmth.

If he hadn't been half-asleep himself just then, Thorn would have known that soft look was a mistake, a passing fancy too sweet to last. Just like everything else about his romance with Felicity Lyte.

In the space of a heartbeat, her eyes widened and she sat up on the bed with a gasp.

"What are you doing here?" One hand raised to her bosom, as if to quiet a thundering heart. "How long have you been sitting there?"

Her tone, sharp with…hostility?…fear? sliced through the fragile sensation that had begun to blossom inside Thorn.

He might have barked out a sharp reply, but he was too weary. "Don't look so alarmed. I was just watching over you while you slept. I haven't been here above half an hour. I meant to wake you, but you looked so peaceful I hated to disturb you."

He neglected to mention how hard he'd fought the urge to stretch out beside her on the narrow bed. If she'd woken to find him there, she might well have boxed his ears.

Perhaps it would have been worth it, though.

His soft answer did appear to turn away Felicity's wrath. She rubbed her eyes and stretched, pulling the muslin bodice of her traveling gown tight against her breasts. The palms of Thorn's hands and his fingertips tingled with the physical memory of touching her bare body.

He reached up to loosen his neck linen which had grown tight all of a sudden.

Felicity fixed him with a gaze that lay somewhere between her first soft look and the hard emerald glare she'd fired at him when she'd come fully awake. "Did you manage to get our juvenile criminal properly disposed of?"

"In a manner of speaking." Thorn braced himself

for a row he felt too tired to fight. "You got a good look at the young bounder, I take it. Barely old enough to shave. His pistol wasn't even loaded."

"You let him go?" Felicity rubbed her eyes harder and stared at Thorn as if wondering whether she might be dreaming.

"Of course not." How could she imagine he'd ever do such a thing? "The fool boy committed a serious crime, robbing and frightening people like that. All the same, I hadn't the stomach to let him swing for it."

"What did you do?"

"The local regiment was recruiting in Berkeley this week. I gave the young scoundrel a choice of being turned over to the magistrate or enlisting in His Majesty's infantry. They need every man they can get if General Wellington is to put a stop to that troublesome Bonaparte fellow once and for all. The lad had sense enough to choose the army."

Felicity sprang from the bed and flew toward Thorn. He prepared to defend himself yet again.

But what was this? Instead of the blow he'd expected, her arms went around his neck. She pressed her lips to his in a kiss quite different from any she'd previously given him.

The others—light and teasing, deep and sensual or fierce and hot—had all been exclusive to their lovemaking. This one had an intriguing air of innocence, beneath which Thorn sensed a greater depth of feeling.

A sweet, soft warmth infused him from head to toe, as though he'd tossed back a large snifter of distilled sunshine.

When Felicity finally let him go, looking almost as shocked as he by what she'd done, Thorn recovered his breath enough to ask, "What on earth was that for?"

As soon as he found out, he'd be sure to do it again.

"That..." She bestowed a gossamer kiss on his brow. "...was for being such a wise, compassionate man."

If he'd been half as wise as Felicity seemed to think him, Thorn would have held his tongue. But something in her kiss set free the question that had throbbed in his heart for the past few days.

He reached out to graze the tips of his fingers against hers. "If I'm such a paragon, what made you so anxious to be rid of me all of a sudden?"

Flinching as though he had struck her, Felicity looked vulnerable in a way he had never seen her. The shadowy compound of wariness and regret that glistened in her eyes almost made Thorn wish he hadn't spoken.

But he had to know, and this might be his only chance to get an honest answer from her. "I thought we had an understanding, you and I. It all seemed to be going so well. Then, from out of the blue, I got your letter, ending it all. Do I not deserve an explanation, at least?"

"You deserve more than that, my dear Thorn, but I cannot give you more." Her voice wavered.

Felicity pressed her lips tightly together and drew several deep breaths before continuing. "My decision was not due to any *fault* of yours. I should have taken greater pains to assure you of that in my letter."

Her tone of gentle pity riled him. "I'm not a child, Felicity! You needn't lie to spare my feelings."

"Men!" she shot back with equal fervour. "You

are all alike. Thinking everything must center around you.''

"If I am not the problem—then what?" Thorn threw up his hands. "You admitted I deserve an explanation, so give me one that makes some sense."

For a moment that seemed to stretch on for hours, Felicity stared at him without speaking.

Thorn's ample supply of patience had nearly run out by the time she murmured, "Very well. Perhaps you are the problem, though not in the way you imagine. Did you never consider I might have grown *too* fond of you during the time we've been together?"

If he'd been standing, Felicity's admission might have rocked Thorn back on his heels. Of course he hadn't considered that possibility. He might not have believed it now, but for the look in her eyes and the blissful echo of a kiss that still tingled on his lips.

"I don't understand." His weary mind struggled to make sense of it. "Why does that present…a problem?"

Felicity shook her head, clearly exasperated. "Perhaps you are not as wise as I thought, Mr. Greenwood. Tell me, how did you feel when you received my letter, the other day?"

"Well…I…" Thorn sputtered. He wasn't used to giving his feelings much thought, let alone putting them into words. The deeper those sentiments ran, the more difficult he found it to frame them properly.

"Did it make you…happy?" Felicity prompted him, like an impatient governess simplifying her question for an impossibly dull scholar.

In just the way a baffled, embarrassed schoolboy might have done, Thorn scowled and shook his head.

"You may not believe this." Felicity's voice fell to

a whisper. "But it made me even less happy to write that message."

Greatly as Thorn was tempted to doubt it, a wistful edge in her voice persuaded him it might be true.

Felicity stepped to the room's one window, where she stared out over the green Vale of Berkeley. "I had no choice, though. If parting now makes us unhappy, imagine how much worse it would grieve us in a month's time, if we'd continued on the way we were."

Put that way, it did make a kind of sense, though Thorn shrank from acknowledging it aloud.

In fact, as the midday spring sunlight shimmered through the casement, gilding Felicity's exquisite profile and burnishing frets of warm chestnut in her rich dark hair, he found himself questioning why they should ever have to part.

Would Thorn believe her? Felicity wondered as she gazed out over the soft green countryside that sloped toward the mouth of the Severn.

Why should he not? Everything she'd said was true.

It *had* pained her to write that letter, breaking off their affair. In spite of her best efforts to keep their liaison free and easy, she *had* grown to care for her earnest, reticent lover far more than she'd ever expected or wanted.

And the longer she tarried in his company, the harder it would be for both of them to say goodbye.

But Thorn Greenwood was no man's fool—no woman's, either. True, he made no great pretensions of wit or genius, but his opinions were sound, honest and open to change. While he might not see fit to pass comment on everything that took place around him, little escaped his vigilant notice.

If she gave him time enough to consider, Thorn might realize she was holding something back...something of importance.

Reminding herself of all that hung in the balance, Felicity drew a deep breath and squared her shoulders. There would be plenty of opportunity later for looking back with regret. Now she must take decisive action to safeguard her future.

"So now you understand." She made herself turn to face Thorn. "You and I have sense and experience enough to recognize when a romantic connection is unworkable. My nephew and your sister are too young and impetuous to reckon how badly this elopement could end for both of them. I cannot let them put any farther distance between us if I hope to intercept them before they reach Scotland. Now that we have rested, I must set off after them at once."

"Agreed." Thorn got to his feet with stiff, halting movements that betrayed his deep weariness. "Knowing my sister, I doubt she and Oliver can have got away from Gloucester much earlier than this, so we've already narrowed their lead by a good deal. With luck and fair weather, we might catch up with them before they get through Hereford."

"*We* will not catch them anywhere." Felicity chided herself for not having the foresight to hire fresh horses and steal off to Gloucester while Thorn was away disposing of the young highwayman. "Please behave like the sensible fellow you are and head back to Bath once you've had a decent sleep. I mean to continue this journey on my own."

"You're a fine one to talk of sense." Thorn raked his long deft fingers through his hair. "Did last night teach you nothing? If you insist upon pursuing Ivy and Oliver, you need me with you.''

How could one man make her yearn for him one moment, then vex her beyond bearing the next? Her powerful contradictory feelings for him set Felicity off balance when she most needed to be in control.

''Of course I learned from what happened last night,'' she snapped. ''Though not the moral you appear to have drawn from it. In future, I will take care not to drive over stretches of deserted road after dark. When we reach Gloucester, I will hunt up a gunsmith from whom I can purchase pistols for Ned and Mr. Hixon. Does that satisfy you?''

''It does not.'' Thorn's slow-burning temper gathered power. ''There are plenty of other dangers on the road north that a brace of pistols won't do you the least good against. Storms, floods, problems with the carriage or the horses. Your footman is only a boy and a slight one at that. Your driver is well past his prime.''

Thorn's flash of anger had spent itself. He shook his head. ''I cannot understand why you are so set against having me accompany you.''

A black bottomless void opened in the pit of Felicity's stomach. She could not risk having Thorn reflect too deeply upon that subject.

Before she could stammer out a reply, his expression softened further. A crooked, self-deprecating smile tugged up one corner of his mouth. ''Haven't I proven myself useful to have around in a pinch?''

How could she resist such an entreaty? ''Of course you have, only—''

Thorn took one swift stride toward her then pressed the warm pads of his fingers to her lips. The token gesture itself did not silence Felicity. But the memories it conjured of his gentle, coaxing touch on her breasts and between her thighs made her mouth go dry and her breath catch high in her throat.

"Now, now, my lady, don't spoil your compliment by tacking on a miserable *only*."

Training a level gaze upon her, Thorn spoke with calm, quiet conviction. "I am coming and there is nothing you can do to prevent me. I have a horse and money to pay my own way. I swear I'll be no bother to you, but I will be there to provide assistance if the need arises."

He lifted his fingers from her lips. "Now, can we please act like the adults we are, rather than two bickering children? You and I have a common goal, one we'll accomplish far more quickly if we join forces than if we squander our time quarreling with each other."

The fact that he was right, and so maddeningly reasonable about it, did nothing to endear him to Felicity. Then again, she didn't want anything further endearing Thorn Greenwood to her. The man had already gained far too deep a foothold in her affections.

"Very well." She heaved a sigh of grudging surrender. "I suppose it won't do any harm to declare a truce until we run Oliver and your sister to ground."

Felicity hoped with all her heart it would not take them too long.

Her words of concession prompted a slow-blossoming smile to spread from that first wry twist of Thorn's lips, lighting his strong, solemn features. "Don't look so glum, then. It won't be as bad as you think, I promise."

Felicity cast him a dubious look. Every further hour

she spent in Thorn's company placed her future and her heart in greater peril.

"It will only be for a few days at most." Thorn grazed her chin with the fingers he had lifted from her lips. "Then you'll be rid of me. In the meantime, I give you my word I will be on my best behavior."

Felicity fought to keep her gaze from straying to the bed behind him. She fought even harder to keep from reaching up and running her hand over Thorn's side whiskers to let him know how desperately she longed to lie beneath him one last time.

It was not the prospect of his behavior during the next few days that worried her.

It was her own.

Chapter Seven

"Are you certain you don't want anything to eat before we get on the road again?" Thorn asked Felicity as they prepared to leave The King's Arms.

She shook her head with some vigor. "I had an enormous breakfast while you were off to Berkeley this morning. What about you, though? You haven't eaten yet today nor have you had a decent sleep in who knows how long."

Was she about to suggest he stay behind and catch a nap, then arrange to meet up with her carriage at Droitwich or Bromsgrove? Thorn had no intention of taking that bait.

"I'll manage," he muttered.

He put masculine pride aside long enough to let Felicity settle the bill with the innkeeper. After all, he hadn't done more than occupy a chair in one of the rooms to watch her sleep. The time might come when he'd need every twopence of his small hoard.

A few moments later, while the young footman stowed Felicity's portmanteau, Thorn helped her into the carriage. Once he had closed the door of the barouche box behind her, he mounted the horse Weston St. Just had loaned him.

The door flew open again, and Felicity called, "Why don't you tether your horse to the carriage, or let Ned ride post on it? That way you can catch a few winks of sleep in here while we drive."

Why was she suddenly offering to share her carriage with him, after she'd been adamant to the point of insult against having him accompany her?

"I told you, I'll manage."

If he was able to ignore her tantalizing nearness long enough to fall asleep, her scent would only haunt his dreams. Besides, he'd promised to mind his behavior. Alone with her in the intimate cocoon of the carriage, he might be hard pressed to honor that vow.

"Suit yourself." Felicity patted the dark-green hat which set off her striking eyes so well. "But do let me know if you change your mind. I had no idea what a stubborn man you could be, Mr. Greenwood."

He tried to fight off a grin, but failed. "I suppose that makes you and I a well-matched pair, Lady Lyte."

Clicking his tongue at the gelding, Thorn gave the reins a little jog and set off along the road to Gloucester. Behind him, he heard the carriage door slam shut. Harness jangled and hooves clattered as the horses began to move.

Gradually the carriage picked up speed until it drew alongside Thorn. In that tandem they continued through the pleasant spring afternoon, along a stretch of road first engineered by the Romans. It ran between the rolling splendor of the Cotswold Hills and the wide lower reaches of the Severn River flowing westward to the ocean.

As he rode, Thorn strove to keep his gaze from

straying toward the window of Lady Lyte's carriage. It was no mean feat, especially after one wayward glance happened to catch her watching him.

For a slow shimmering moment, their eyes met, held, searched and touched. A strange hot shiver ran through Thorn. He could not help feeling they had exchanged something more truly intimate than during any of the times he had bedded Felicity.

They might have remained locked in that silent, invisible embrace but for the sudden appearance of a toll gate. Thorn wrenched his gaze away from Felicity and dismounted to pay the toll.

As he handed over the coins, he asked, "I don't suppose you noticed a hired coach come through here last night carrying a newly wed couple? You'd remember the bride if you glimpsed her—pretty little thing with red-gold curls."

"You're right enough about that, sir," the man in the toll booth answered. "A lively creature. Pleasant way about her, too. I expect she could charm the birds out of the trees if she had a mind to."

"Indeed." Thorn could feel himself puffing up with an almost paternal pride. "That sounds very like my sister."

He had good reason to know it. How often in her younger years had Ivy gotten into some mischief, only to deflect her just punishment with a look that mingled winsome repentance with cheerful impudence?

Her brother had been helpless to resist it.

"One thing, though, sir." The toll clerk's brow furrowed. "It was only this morning they passed through here, not last night."

"Are you certain?"

"Aye, sir. They had a bit of trouble with their carriage, you see, so they stopped here awhile. It took the young gentleman a good three hours to get it repaired.''

''Did it, indeed?'' Thorn passed the man an extra shilling. ''I'm obliged to you for the information. How long ago did they leave?''

The man consulted a battered pocket watch. ''I'd say they've been gone as long again as they were here. A bit less, perhaps, but not above three hours. I do hope they aren't in any trouble, sir.''

''Trouble? Not a bit of it.'' With the likelihood of catching his sister and young Armitage by sundown, Thorn did not need to counterfeit a happy humor. ''I have some news to deliver they'll want to hear as soon as possible—good news.''

''You won't be long overtaking them with that, sir.'' The toll collector pointed toward Felicity's carriage. ''Whatever the young gentleman repaired on their rig, it still wasn't up to any kind of speed when they left.''

Thorn thanked the man again, then hurried back to the carriage, towing his mount by the reins.

''What a long time you've been.'' Felicity gave him a sharp look. ''Whatever were you gossiping about with that toll clerk? You look positively smug.''

''I was getting word about my sister and your nephew, as a matter of fact.'' Thorn tried not to look quite so smug—without success.

Neither could he resist the temptation to get in a little dig. ''If you'd come ahead without me, you might never have found out this valuable bit of information.''

His earlier fatigue forgotten, he relayed everything he'd learned from the toll collector.

Felicity listened in silence. One fine dark brow arched gradually higher, a barometer of her interest.

When Thorn had finished, she smiled rather too sweetly and inquired, "Do you mean to say we'd have caught up with them by now if we hadn't stopped in Newport this morning?"

"I...that is..." As Thorn sputtered and scowled, Felicity began to laugh.

He had heard her laugh before, of course, but never quite like this. Warmer and more robust, it was a most contagious sound.

Perhaps lack of sleep had made him giddy, or perhaps he just felt the need to laugh at himself after years of taking everything a little too seriously. Whatever the reason, Thorn began to chuckle, then laugh with greater and greater gusto until he could hardly catch his breath.

"I suppose...that sets us even," he was able to gasp at last, "for being wrong. What do you say we come to a true agreement on how to proceed next?"

"It hardly needs a decision, does it?" Felicity dabbed away a tear that her hearty laughter had provoked. "If we are that hot on their heels, we must make all speed until we run them to ground."

Thorn nodded. "You'll get no argument from me on that."

"It is very queer, though...."

"What?"

"If Oliver and your sister left The King's Arms last evening bound for Gloucester..." Felicity glanced back down the highway toward Newport as if she expected some explanation to arrive from that direction. "Why did it take them all night to get this far?"

"A good question." Thorn chided himself for not

thinking of it first. "Further trouble with their coach, perhaps? Or do you suppose they spent the night at Newport, after all, then bribed the innkeeper to mis-inform us?"

Felicity shrugged. "I suppose we'll be able to sat-isfy our curiosity once we catch them. Now, for the last time, can I not persuade you to ride the rest of the way in the carriage with me? A few more hours of each other's company isn't likely to harm either of us…especially if you're sound asleep."

Sorely as the invitation tempted him, Thorn shook his head. "I'll sleep soundly once I've recovered my sister. Until then, we'll make better time if I ride ahead to pay tolls, open gates and the like."

Her look of disappointment almost made him re-cant, but her brisk tone contradicted it. "Very well, then. If you're sure?"

Perhaps he had misread that glance, and she had only tendered the offer out of courtesy. Or to assert her control over their self-appointed mission.

Thorn mounted his horse. "Should I call *Tally-ho?* This is beginning to have the feel of a fox hunt."

His quip coaxed another chuckle from Felicity. "I only wish we had a good pack of hounds to pick up the scent of our quarry."

With that she closed the door of the carriage box, and they started off again at a good brisk pace along the road to Gloucester.

As the sun dipped lower behind the Welsh hills to the west and the miles galloped by, Thorn fell into deeper and deeper thought about himself and Felicity and their future.

If they had one.

What was Thorn musing about with such grave concentration? Felicity wondered as she watched him
through the carriage window. Was he, perhaps, re-
gretting his insistence that they stop in Newport?

Though she enjoyed being proven right, Felicity
could not bring herself to be sorry for the chance to
rest. Both the nap and the light breakfast had revived
her. In fact, she felt better now than she had in days.

She'd heard this phase of biliousness when a
woman was breeding did not last. Might she have put
it behind her already? If so, she could probably afford
to resume her affair with Thorn Greenwood and let it
run its natural course to the end of the Season, safe
from the fear that he would catch her in one of her
sick spells and guess its cause.

The prospect of taking up with Thorn where they
had left off brought a fleeting smile to Felicity's lips
as she admired his confident seat in the saddle and his
crisp patrician profile. The paltry few days since she'd
last welcomed him into her bed felt much, much
longer. She found herself craving his touch the way
women in her condition were inclined to crave strange
foods.

As her carriage rolled and swayed over the final
miles of the coastal highway between Bristol and
Gloucester, and the spring sun cast longer and longer
shadows, Felicity watched Thorn Greenwood with increasingly avid eyes. She felt herself slipping back in
time to the mild March night when he'd first become
her lover.

She hadn't reckoned on his lack of experience,
though perhaps she should have. Unlike her, Thorn
had never been married, and he was not the type of
man given to casual encounters with the fair sex. Upon

reflection, Felicity marveled that he had made an exception in her case.

To her vast surprise, his lack of experience had proven endearing...even piquant.

After all, her late husband had been a skilled lover. Which meant he'd honed his amorous technique on a long parade of other women. It made a refreshing change to be fondled and kissed by a man as though her body was some rare treasure and the act of mating with her a sublime rite.

In subtle ways, she had tutored her unseasoned lover in the arts of pleasure. He had proven a very apt pupil, indeed. The knowledge that he had limited scope for comparison had freed her to explore some novel avenues of lovemaking...with most gratifying results.

Her mouth grew moist as she recalled how the flicker of candlelight had caressed Thorn's naked lean-limbed frame and kindled rich, warm hues of polished wood in his unbound hair.

Ah, the delicious repertoire of touches he had cultivated... Some light as a summer night's breeze through the leaves, drawing her desire ever more taut until she quivered with anticipation. Others slow, deep and sensual as warm oil, that set her passion smouldering. Still others, fervent and fierce, provoking a fiery tempest that threatened to consume her.

Thorn Greenwood could arouse her without having to lay a finger on her, Felicity realized as the gallop of her heart outstripped that of his horse. Her breath came in hot, sharp little gasps, and she squirmed on the gently bouncing seat of the carriage.

She would not be sorry to continue their liaison for a little longer. In fact, once they apprehended Ivy and Oliver, perhaps she and Thorn could steal a brief tryst

at some Gloucester inn before they all returned
to Bath.

Even as the prospect made Felicity tingle with anticipation, the words she had spoken to Thorn back at
The King's Arms returned to plague her.

*"If parting now makes us unhappy, imagine how
much worse it would grieve us in a month's time."*

For herself, the promise of pleasure might be worth
the risk of pain...but what about Thorn?

When she'd written him that letter, it had never occurred to her that their parting would distress him.
Except, perhaps, for the loss of regular physical
gratification.

Yet, from the moment he had burst into her town
house last night, everything about his behavior had
betrayed a greater depth of feeling. Something beyond
the mere loss of carnal pleasure or even wounded masculine vanity. When she'd hinted that she might have
grown too fond of him, Felicity had sensed a poignant
echo of that feeling beneath his usual mask of resolute
composure. Would he agree to resume their relationship at her whim after she had already hurt him once?

It was all such a hopeless, distressing muddle!

Unshed tears prickled in the corners of her eyes.
Felicity despised herself for them. Ever since she'd
invited Thorn Greenwood into her bed, her emotions
had become heightened and dreadfully mixed up.
Worst of all, were no longer fully subject to her
control. Perhaps she would be better off to oust the
man from her life before he wreaked any further
havoc...no matter how much she yearned for him.

Because he made her yearn for him so.

With a sudden twitch and pounding pulse, Thorn came fully awake again after having fallen into a potentially dangerous doze. His growing exhaustion coupled with the lulling rhythm of the horse's gait seduced him to sleep. It became harder and harder to resist as his weary mind lapsed into deep thought.

He had been musing about Felicity and all the sound, logical reasons they could never be more to each other than transient lovers.

Her fortune, for instance. Plenty of men would have considered it a powerful inducement to marriage, but Thorn shrank from that notion in horror. Privately, he had vowed not to wed until both his sisters were happily settled and he had restored the Greenwood fortunes by his own efforts.

He recoiled from the prospect of what gossip would result if a man in his straitened circumstances married a woman with her wealth. It would paint him an unscrupulous exploiter and her a pathetic creature who must stoop to purchasing a husband. The latter fell so far from the truth as to be laughable, but Thorn was not the least inclined to laugh.

Felicity and he were both proud people in their way—not anxious to expose themselves to such humiliating tattle.

For all Thorn knew, Lady Lyte had no interest in marrying again, nor any need. She had both a title and a large fortune of which she would remain in control only so long as she remained unwed. If she wanted a child, she would be obliged to adopt one, whether she married or not.

And if she desired a man's company, the lady could simply take a lover. A woman of her wit and beauty would have plenty of eager candidates from which to choose.

The notion made Thorn's gorge rise and his hands clench and unclench around the reins. How would he bear it if Felicity discarded him for another man? One younger and better looking, with a facile wit to keep her amused. One canny enough to be satisfied with what she could give him in the bedchamber and not pine for more.

What had put the ridiculous idea of marriage in his mind, anyway? Thorn asked himself. Even if he'd been rich as Croesus and Felicity anxious to wed him, it would never do. When the time came for him to marry, he would need a bride capable of bearing him sons, which Lady Lyte was not.

Otherwise his beloved estate, Barnhill, would pass out of the immediate family to some odious distant cousin. Not for anything would he allow that to happen. Duty would not permit it, and he had long been a creature of duty.

With a jolt, Thorn had suddenly become aware of himself and his surroundings once again. He took a great gulp of air and shook his head to clear it. For a moment he considered signaling Felicity's driver to stop the carriage and accepting her offer of a seat inside. He discarded the idea almost as quickly as it had formed.

One way or another, they were bound to catch up with Ivy and young Armitage soon. If he and Felicity did not overtake the young lovers' coach on the road, they would likely find the pair spending the night in Gloucester. Then Thorn could surrender to sleep with the serene conviction of an important duty fulfilled.

What was that on the road ahead—another carriage?

All Thorn's faculties stirred to heightened alert, though his lingering fatigue gave him a queer sense of distance from himself. As the road took a wide bow to the northwest, he raised his hand to shield his eyes against the glare of the setting sun.

It *was* a carriage!

He glanced toward Felicity's rig to find her eyes trained upon him. Her beauty struck him anew, as though it had been months, rather than minutes since he'd last looked upon her.

"I think I see them!" Thorn shouted, exaggerating his words in case she could not hear him over the rattle of the carriage and the tattoo of the horse's hooves.

Felicity cocked her head and shot him a puzzled look.

"Up ahead!" He jabbed his forefinger in the direction of the other carriage. "Ivy and Oliver, I think!"

Her eyes widened and her brows shot up.

Again Thorn pointed. "I'll ride ahead to check!"

He nudged the gelding with his knees. Though it had been keeping up a brisk pace since they'd left the toll booth, the beast responded, surging forward. Yard by yard they began to overtake the other coach.

In his mind, Thorn began to rehearse what he would say to his sister. Impress upon her the folly of what she'd done, for a start, and the anxiety she had given him on her behalf. If Ivy fancied her usual half-cheeky expressions of remorse would win her brother's immediate forgiveness, the little chit had better think again!

St. Just's horse clearly enjoyed a chase, for the closer it drew to the carriage ahead, the faster it galloped. In another moment, Thorn would have a clear view of whoever was riding in the coach.

His impetuous little sister would not be the only one to catch the sharp edge of his temper, either. Thorn had a few hard questions to put to Oliver Armitage. The lad was supposed to be a scientist, after all. Could he not have predicted the consequences of eloping to Gretna with young Miss Greenwood? Did he not foresee what a bitter mistake marriage to a creature of Ivy's mercurial temperament might be?

With any luck, the past day's journey cooped up together in the close confines of the coach, might have shown the two young people exactly how ill-suited they were. Both Ivy and Oliver might feel secret relief at being rescued from their folly.

As Thorn drew level with the coach, he peered toward the window, hoping to see his sister.

Instead, the heavily-powdered visage of an older woman glared back at him. She motioned for him to be off and mouthed some words that Thorn was thankful he could not hear.

Fighting a twinge of disappointment, he prepared to slow his mount and fall back to report his mistake to Felicity.

Thorn wrenched his gaze away from the coach just in time to see a narrow stone bridge appear ahead of him. Fortunately, his horse saw it, too.

Before Thorn could gather his weary wits enough to rein the beast in, it veered to the right and plunged down a rather steep slope into a wide stream. The water immediately halted the gelding's progress, but not that of its rider.

Thorn felt himself jerked clear of the saddle and flung over the horse's neck in a high, lethal arc. His limbs flailed in vain for something to break his fall, but found only air.

   The water rushed up to meet him, driving the wind
from his chest in the instant before a burst of black
pain hurled him into the sleep he'd fought so hard to
resist.

Chapter Eight

The carriage slowed abruptly, jolting Felicity back into the upholstered seat. Outside, the horses whinnied as Mr. Hixon bellowed at them. They veered off the road, dragging the carriage in a drunken stagger over a bit of ploughed field. Thrown about the interior of the carriage like ivories in a gamester's box, Felicity shrieked.

What could be happening?

After a few tumultuous moments that seemed to go on forever, the carriage finally lurched to a halt. As Felicity tried to recover her wits after that fearful jostling, she heard her footman and driver scramble down from their perches. Their voices quickly retreated into the distance.

Why had they not checked at once to make certain she was unharmed?

Muttering under her breath about men and their entire lack of consideration, Felicity pushed open the carriage door and slid down to solid ground on very unsteady legs. She scanned the field, looking for some sign of Ned or Mr. Hixon and some clue as to what had just taken place.

The two servants were nowhere in sight, though Felicity could hear their voices, as well as the sound of water splashing. For a moment she stared at a narrow stone bridge, which stood not far from where her carriage had left the road.

All at once she recalled this place from her regular travels between Bath and her estate in Staffordshire. A deep stream ran beneath this bridge, its water flowing swiftly down from the Cotswolds, as if eager to merge with the mighty Severn.

A sense of alarm swelled in Felicity's breast until it seemed to hamper the workings of her heart and lungs. She scrambled toward the riverbank. Just as she reached it, Thorn's horse struggled up the steep incline, shaking water from its dark mane. Down in the stream, both Ned and Mr. Hixon were submerged up to their chests.

But where was Thorn?

The fear that had gripped Felicity when the highwayman accosted her carriage had been a mere twinge compared to the bottomless dread that now seized her in its ravenous jaws. How she hated being at its mercy!

Just then, the young footman dove beneath the water. He resurfaced a moment later with Thorn's arm around his shoulders. Bobbing above the surface of the churning water, Thorn's head hung slack.

Felicity clapped a hand over her mouth.

Mr. Hixon pulled Thorn's other arm around his shoulders. Then he and the young footman struggled toward shore, burdened by the larger, unconscious man.

She must do something to help.

Fighting down her distress, Felicity rushed back to the carriage and dug out the lap robes that were used when driving in cold weather. She scrambled back to the riverbank again just as her driver and footman wallowed the last few feet, burdened by the weight of their sodden clothing and the man they had rescued.

"Is he...alive?" Some superstitious dread made Felicity shrink from asking, but she *had* to know.

Too badly winded to do more than nod, her middle-aged driver gasped like a huge red fish landed by some angler after a hard fight. With a final great heave, he and the footman hauled Thorn onto the bank, then collapsed on either side of him, labouring for air.

"Are you sure?" Though she doubted she would receive an immediate answer, Felicity could not stop herself from asking.

As she wrapped one of the lap robes around young Ned, the boy strained to answer. "Aye...ma'am. He...retched up...a deal of...water...while we...was hauling him...ashore."

Perhaps so, but he lay frighteningly still, now, sprawled on his belly where his rescuers had dropped him.

"Thorn, can you hear me?"

She tugged the lap robe over his shoulders and ran a caressing hand down his cheek. Side whiskers, a warmer shade of brown than his hair, softened the sharp angle of his jaw. They looked much darker, now, and tiny beads of water clung to them. The skin beneath felt frighteningly cold to Felicity's anxious touch.

"Thorn?" Her voice grew more insistent as she shook his shoulder.

Then, as if it was the only answer he had the strength to give, more water gushed out of Thorn's mouth. He began to choke and gasp for air. Suddenly,

Felicity felt as if she, too, could breathe again. When a passing breeze chilled her cheeks, she realized they were wet with tears.

She swept the hair back from Thorn's face with trembling fingers as she glanced toward Mr. Hixon. Her driver's face was slowly subsiding from its alarming shade of red and each breath no longer sent a great shudder through his broad chest.

"Did you see what happened?" Felicity asked.

Of course he must, to have responded with such swift action and sound judgment.

"Aye, ma'am." Mr. Hixon pulled the lap robe tighter around him. Whether from the water's spring chill or the shock of what had happened, his teeth began to chatter.

"M-Mr. Greenwood rode like f-fury to catch the coach ahead of us. Then it was like he d-didn't even see the bridge in his path. His horse turned aside and w-went over the bank. I didn't get a good look at what went on after that, for I was t-trying to get stopped to go to his aid."

The other carriage—of course! The shock of what had happened had driven it from Felicity's mind. Had it been carrying Ivy and Oliver? Had Thorn been so preoccupied trying to flag them down that he hadn't noticed the approaching bridge until it was too late?

A low moan broke from Thorn, though he did not open his eyes. Felicity thought it one of the sweetest sounds she had ever heard.

She glanced from Mr. Hixon to Ned and back again. "What you did was truly heroic. I can scarcely thank you enough, but I will make certain that you're both well rewarded for it."

The driver gave a rueful grin, somewhat at odds

with his shivering. "I w-wouldn't refuse, ma'am, but I'm pleased to have been able to come to Mr. Greenwood's assistance. He's a fine man, Lady Lyte."

As the young footman nodded his agreement, an unwelcome heat rose in Felicity's face.

Of course, she knew her servants must be aware of Thorn's comings and goings from her Bath town house. But to hear one of them allude to her relationship, even in so roundabout a manner, made her feel ashamed in a way it might not if a less honorable man had been involved.

"Indeed." She shifted the subject as abruptly as her carriage had hurtled off the road. "Now, we must get all three of you to some place warm and dry before the sun sets much lower. And Mr. Greenwood must be seen by a physician straightaway. Are you able to drive, Mr. Hixon?"

"Aye, ma'am."

"Good," said Felicity. "Have you both a change of livery in the carriage?"

Her driver and footman gave ready nods.

"Then by all means go change clothes," she ordered them. "So we can get on our way at once."

Master Ned did not need a second invitation. The words were scarcely out of Felicity's mouth before he had scooted off to the carriage.

The coachman lingered a moment. "Begging your pardon, ma'am, but I often bring along a wee nip of spirits to keep the chill off during a long drive. If you could coax a drop or two into Mr. Greenwood, it might revive him some."

"A capital idea." Felicity barely refrained from admitting that she could do with a *wee nip,* herself.

"Send Ned with it once he's changed clothes. Now off with you before you catch a chill."

"Aye, ma'am." Mr. Hixon took the lap robe from around his shoulders and laid it over Thorn before dashing off to the carriage.

Her servants returned so quickly they would have done credit to a pair of experienced actors changing costume between scenes. Part of Felicity's judgment recognized and commended their haste. Yet in another way, every moment seemed to stretch and stretch, pulling her nerves taut along with them.

Though she'd continued to stroke Thorn's cheek and call his name, he had yet to open his eyes. Both the chill of his skin and its grayish pallor alarmed her. A memory alarmed her even more.

Her late husband had never regained consciousness after being thrown from a horse.

Cold, dark water had swallowed him.

Thorn could not tell whether he was rising toward the surface or sinking forever into oblivion. He tried to rally his wits and his strength, but both had deserted him, sapped by the heavy, soul-numbing chill that threatened to suck the very life out of him.

Perhaps he was a fool to resist it when he had nothing to resist *with*…except his will. Perhaps he should just surrender and be done with it.

Then, as if from a great distance, he heard a single word whispered by a voice that made his heart beat stronger. That word, he realized, was his name.

He could not summon an image of the whisperer, nor could he give her a name. Yet her voice dangled in the black, torpid depths that entombed him, like a fine filament of gold. He could not frame the thought properly, but he knew if he followed the slender thread, it would lead him back to himself.

Fearful that such a gossamer strand might snap or simply disappear at his touch, he grappled onto it with all that remained of his strength.

"Thorn. Thorn." It vibrated like magical music on the string of an enchanted harp. "Come back, my darling. Wake up."

A touch!

He had forgotten there could be any sensations but cold, heaviness and exhaustion. Now he felt pain that somehow defined the boundaries of his body. It made him want to lapse back into blessed numbness.

But he felt something else, as well. Something that persuaded him to brave the pain when a returning glimmer of sense warned him not to. The warm, gentle caress of a woman's hand on his face and through his hair.

Memories flooded his mind in a shimmering cascade. Of dark silken tresses splayed over a plump white pillow and over a rounded white breast. Of soft lips and nipples like sweet, red Madeira. Of a slick, sultry chasm, that...

What was this? His body could feel heat, as well as cold? Pleasure, as well as pain?

He tried to move...to reach for her. Even to wrest open one eye so he could see her again. But his body refused to obey. It remained trapped in the remorseless grip of that ponderous chill from which his spirit had barely managed to break free.

As something warm and very soft brushed down the side of his face, he caught her scent.

"Can you hear me, Thorn?"

This time the whisper came from so near, he wondered if it might only be a fancy within his own mind. Then he felt that touch against his face again, and he knew it could only be her lips.

Might her kiss restore him completely to himself? Thorn wondered.

When he'd been young enough to be cared for, rather than always taking care of others, his mother had liked to tell him whimsical stories of princesses wakened from deathlike sleep by the kiss of true love.

"So you see, my little hawthorn blossom, love holds great power if only we have the courage to use it."

He hadn't thought of those old stories in years. Nor of his mother in such an intimate way, lest it stir other memories that would riddle his heart with the kind of pain that now throbbed through his broken body.

Suddenly Thorn could picture his mother's face more clearly than he'd been able to in years—a good deal like his sister's, but without the faint shadow of sorrow Rosemary had worn until so recently. There had been a little of Ivy's looks in that beloved face, as well. All of the charm without the often maddening caprice.

Had there been something of himself there, as well? Thorn hoped so. Just as he hoped he'd cultivated whatever special qualities he'd inherited from his mother.

A great wave of weariness washed over him. It promised an escape from all his hurts, if only he would trim his sail and let it carry him away.

Again his mother's voice came to him with heart-breaking clarity. "I have to go away, my dearest boy."

He'd known she didn't mean to the seaside at Bournemouth or to take the waters at Bath, neither of which had ever effected more than a temporary improvement in her delicate health. He hadn't wanted her to speak of going away. He'd wanted to keep pretending she would soon be well again, though he could scarcely recall a time when she had not been ill.

"I feel so much easier in my mind knowing you'll watch over your sisters for me. The baby, especially. It won't be easy for her, poor wee thing."

He'd been strongly tempted to refuse. Perhaps, if he declined responsibility for Rosemary and Ivy, his mother would not be able to leave. At the very least, she might fight harder to remain with them.

He'd wanted to ask why she was placing the burden of his sisters' future on his young shoulders, rather than those of his father. Even though he'd known the reason as well as she did.

But he'd been a dutiful boy, so he had not refused. Nor had he questioned. He hadn't given in to tears, either, though he'd sensed they might ease the tight ball of fear and grief that had lodged deep in his belly.

Since that day he'd done everything in his power to rear his sisters into the kind of young women who would have made their mother proud. And to see them happy. When Rosemary had finally wed his old friend, Merritt Temple, Thorn had felt half the weight of that pressing responsibility lifted from his shoulders.

If he failed to rescue Ivy from her romantic folly, his sacrifices would all be for naught.

So he fought on when he would much rather have surrendered in the hope of mercy, clinging to the tattered remnants of consciousness with dogged persistence that was a useful virtue…if not a glamorous one.

The next voice Thorn heard belonged to a man— some administrator of torture, evidently.

"Nothing broken, so far as I can tell," the tormentor said in a jocular tone as he poked and prodded in a determined effort to break something. "He's not much bruised, either, thanks to the cold water."

"Sod off!" A harsh dry croak erupted from Thorn's throat as he flinched away from the prodding fingers.

At least his body was obeying him again. Would his eyes open if he willed them hard enough?

They did!

Expecting to see a stretch of Gloucestershire riverbank or perhaps the inside of Lady Lyte's carriage, Thorn started at the sight of a candlelit bedchamber. Was he truly conscious now, or still conjuring vivid fancies like the voice and face of his long-dead mother?

Heedless of Thorn's ungentlemanly language, the owner of the voice chuckled and took another poke at a very sensitive spot on Thorn's ribs. "Yes. I thought that might bring him 'round."

"Keep that bloody finger off me!" Thorn cuffed it away and tried to make his eyes focus on the speaker. "Unless you want me to remove it from your hand."

"His wits seem to be intact," the voice chirped.

Thorn's eyes decided to cooperate fully. At least he thought they did. The man he saw standing beside his bed, a stout little fellow with a hook nose and an old-fashioned periwig, looked less like a real person than like some figment of an overstimulated imagination.

The man thrust his hand toward Thorn's face. "How many fingers do you see?"

"Three." Resisting the urge to bite them, Thorn contented himself with a verbal snap instead. "Now will you please let me alone?"

"My examination is almost complete, sir, if you'll indulge me a few moments more."

"Make it quick," Thorn growled. "Anything that ails me won't be improved by your prodding. If you want to make yourself useful, fetch me a drink. I'm parched."

Which was strange, he realized, since the last thing he remembered with any clarity was pitching off his horse into the river.

"A drink?" The man considered Thorn's request. He half-turned to someone behind him and nodded. "I don't think it'll do him any harm. His vital organs don't appear to have suffered any damage."

"That's a mercy." Felicity peeped around the man to cast Thorn a reassuring smile quite at odds with the faint creases of worry etched around her eyes. "What sort of drink do you recommend, doctor? Fortified wine?"

The physician gave a dismissive gesture. "No intoxicants when the patient has so recently regained consciousness. Coffee might revive him further."

"I'll call for some." Felicity moved out of Thorn's line of vision, which was much obscured by the thick posts and heavy curtains of the bed on which he lay.

When the doctor reached toward him again, Thorn recoiled. But this time the man only clutched Thorn's wrist…which pained him less than most other parts of his body.

"Lie still, now, whilst I test your pulse." With his other hand the doctor consulted a watch suspended on a chain that spanned his broad middle.

After a few moments, he released Thorn's arm again. "As I suspected. Much stronger now."

Felicity returned to her place beside the doctor. "That is good news."

The doctor nodded. "He has a strong constitution in his favor. I expect he'll make a rapid recovery. Tell me, Mr. Greenwood, what's the last thing you remember before you woke to find yourself here?"

Thorn opened his mouth to reply, then hesitated.

He'd known a fellow once who'd lost consciousness for a time after a blow on the head. When he'd wakened, the man had no recollection of events for several days before his accident.

Doctors had warned the man's friends and family not to speak of that time or attempt to prompt his memory.

Thorn could not help wondering what might happen if he professed not to recall the past several days. Felicity looked quite anxious about him. Perhaps she would be willing to pretend she had not ended their affair, for a while at least.

But that would also mean feigning no memory of Ivy's elopement, giving her and young Armitage ample time to reach Gretna and come back again.

Besides, Thorn could not bring himself to deceive Felicity.

"I remember getting pitched into the water," he admitted. "After that, everything's a right muddle until I woke up just now."

Felicity pushed the doctor aside. Perching on the edge of the bed, she took Thorn's hand. "The other coach you were chasing, did you get a look at who was inside? Was it Ivy and Oliver?"

Though he hated to disappoint her, Thorn shook his head. "Some elderly woman. I hope I didn't give her too great a fright, tearing after her carriage like that."

Felicity pulled a wry face. "Oh dear."

The implication of what he'd just said might have knocked Thorn flat, if he hadn't been, already. He had a vague conviction, more nebulous than a memory, yet also more urgent, that he *must* find and rescue his sister from...herself. To fail would betray the trust his dying mother had placed in him.

"Ivy!" He forced himself up to a sitting position, though every muscle in his body screamed in protest. "Are we in Gloucester? I must go look for her!"

His bed spun and tilted in one direction while the room beyond whirled and pitched the opposite way.

"Hush now, hush!" Felicity pushed him back onto his pillow.

To Thorn's impotent frustration, he was unable to mount more than a token resistance.

"Since you ask, we're just on the outskirts of Gloucester." Felicity spoke in a soft, soothing voice as she brushed a lock of hair back from his brow. "I ordered Mr. Hixon to put in at the first inn we came to. This place wasn't far off. Fortunately, it turned out to be a well-run establishment."

"I'm sure it is." Thorn planted his hands wide to steady himself for his next attempt to sit up. "But I can't stay to enjoy its amenities while my sister may be within reach."

Felicity shot him a look that warned the less said about Ivy and Oliver in front of others, the better.

"What do you propose to do? If you haven't got sufficient balance to sit up in bed, there isn't much likelihood of your sitting a horse, is there?"

Though Thorn tried to concentrate on his original chain of thoughts, ideas seemed to flutter about his skull and fly out of his mouth of their own accord. "St. Just's horse—what happened to it?"

His question appeared to puzzle Felicity as much as it unsettled him. "It got…wet. The wretched beast is in much better shape than you are presently, I can assure you."

"I might be in worse shape, if that 'wretched beast' hadn't turned aside from the bridge in time."

Before Felicity could reply, a knock sounded on the door. She jumped most readily from her roost on the bed to answer it, as if she might be glad of a distraction.

Thorn cast a wary glance at the physician. If the prodding started again, he might have to throttle the little fellow.

Perhaps his intention broadcast itself on his face, for the doctor edged farther away from the bed and made a show of packing his satchel.

Thorn closed his eyes and willed his addled wits not to go astray. He had something important to think about, if he could only remember it and pursue it in spite of distractions.

Ivy! That was who he must concentrate upon.

Surely she and Armitage must be spending the night in Gloucester. Likely at that inn the keeper of The King's Arms had recommended. Thorn must go collect her straightaway.

Again he planted his hands on the bed at a good wide angle to steady himself. Then he pulled himself up by slow degrees, the better to keep dizziness at bay…even though the muscles of his abdomen protested painfully. This time he managed to raise his head without sending everything into a violent whirl.

After a moment of hushed talk, the door closed and

Felicity appeared in Thorn's line of sight again, bearing a tray loaded with a small mound of sandwiches and a pair of faintly steaming mugs. The rich, faintly bitter aroma of coffee pervaded the room.

A passing glance at the bed made Felicity start and nearly drop the tray. "For pity's sake, lie down, Thorn! You need time to rest and heal."

"I'll have plenty of time to rest once I have my sister back," Thorn muttered through clenched teeth as he prepared to swing his legs over the side of the bed. "I'm certain she must be passing the night somewhere in Gloucester. The sooner I find her, the better...for everyone."

Felicity set the tray of coffee and sandwiches down on a small table beside the bed with barely restrained force.

She glared at Thorn. "We can discuss this further once you've taken a little nourishment. If Ivy is in Gloucester, she'll be staying put until morning."

He could not properly explain his renewed compulsion to find his sister, not even to himself. How could he hope to make Felicity understand? Thorn set his mouth in a grim line and prepared to twitch back the coverlet, when it suddenly dawned on him that he was naked.

The realization almost knocked him back onto his pillows.

Meanwhile, Felicity had opened her reticule and taken out some money to pay the physician. It must have been a generous fee, for the little man thanked her heartily.

"I can see myself out, ma'am, while you attend to Mr. Greenwood. Don't hesitate to send for me in the night if his condition worsens."

"Thank you, Doctor." Felicity picked up one coffee cup from the tray and carried it over to the bed. "You've been most helpful."

Thorn managed to keep his contrary opinion to himself.

He took a sip from the cup Felicity held to his lips, hoping it would revive his strength and marshal his skittish wits into better order.

The physician gathered up his hat and satchel, then headed for the door. Perhaps because the lady had paid him such a handsome fee, he must have felt he owed her some parting advice to the patient.

"You'll recover all the sooner if you don't overtax your strength for the next day or two, Mr. Greenwood." He moved out of Thorn's sight. The door creaked open. "I suggest you rest and let your charming wife take care of you."

Wife!

The coffee in Thorn's mouth spewed out in a fine shower all over the bedclothes.

Chapter Nine

"Wife?" Thorn sputtered as soon as the doctor had closed the door. "What else took place while I was unconscious that you haven't told me about?"

Oh dear! A ripple of laughter burst out of Felicity. The buoyant relief of having Thorn awake, speaking and moving after what she'd feared had made her giddy. She'd struggled to maintain a sober appearance while the doctor was in the room. Now, Thorn's ridiculous assumption pushed her over the edge. She set his coffee cup back down on the tray, before she spilled it all over the floor.

In spite of the laughter that shook her until tears sprang to her eyes, it rankled that he would suspect her of such a thing. Not to mention showing such excessive dismay at the false prospect of having her as his wife.

"I'll remind you…" She gasped for breath, struggling to rein in her runaway levity. "…we are still hundreds of miles from Gretna Green…"

Really, it was too absurd! "…where I might haul you, unconscious, in front of a blacksmith and have

Mr. Hixon jerk your head back and forth to signify consent.''

The words rolled out of her very fast, borne on a fresh tide of laughter. She couldn't help herself. The whole scene unfolded in her imagination in such droll, vivid detail.

Thorn cast her a look that questioned whether he'd fallen into the clutches of a madwoman. ''Then, why did that doctor call you my wife?''

''What else *should* I have told him?'' Slowly, Felicity regained control of herself. ''What should I have told anyone? This inn only had one suitable room free, and it was clear you'd need someone to take care of you through the night. I didn't want to start a lot of scandalous talk that might get back to Bath.''

''You might have claimed to be my sister.''

His words jerked a mat out from under Felicity, throwing her more badly off balance than she'd been before.

''I—I suppose I might have,'' she admitted. ''I didn't happen to think of it, that's all.''

She wasn't anybody's sister, so she hadn't thought of pretending to be. Besides, she couldn't imagine herself related to Thorn Greenwood in that chaste way.

''Besides, what gives you the right to question what action I took in a moment of crisis?'' Felicity pulled herself taller and thrust out her chin. ''You're alive, aren't you?''

Her sudden shift from defense to attack seemed to catch Thorn off guard. ''Well…obviously.''

''You're alert, if not entirely reasonable.'' Felicity would not retreat. ''You have no hurts that a few days' rest won't cure. I'd say my servants and I did well by you. But do I get a word of thanks?''

At least Thorn had the manners to look chagrined.

Felicity supplied her own answer. "I do not. Instead you insist on courting further injury by proposing to ride all over town when you have barely regained consciousness. Then you question my innocent ruse of posing as your wife for one night."

"I'm sorry." Thorn pulled the coffee-soaked coverlet closer around his waist. "I didn't mean to sound ungrateful. The 'wife' business caught me by surprise, was all. As for the other, I only want to find my sister while I have the chance. Aren't you just as anxious to recover your nephew and bring the young fool to his senses?"

"Of course, but..." But she found herself even more concerned with Thorn's well-being.

Monumental idiocy when she would have to cut all ties with him. When this shared journey of theirs was meant to sever a potentially troublesome link.

"Of course." Thorn held out his hand, and for one sweet, mad moment, Felicity thought he was inviting her to join him on the bed. "Now be a dutiful wife and fetch your poor injured husband his linen and breeches."

It gave her a passing measure of vindictive satisfaction to inform him, "I wish I could, truly. But you pitched into the river, remember? Your clothes were sodden, and so cold I'm surprised you've warmed up yet. I shudder to think what state you might be in now if we hadn't removed them as soon as we got you settled here."

"We?" Thorn's countenance took on a bilious cast.

"Ned and I," Felicity replied. "While Mr. Hixon went for the doctor. Like most footmen, the lad's had plenty of experience helping a gentleman undress who's incapable of undressing himself.''

So had she, for that matter, though Felicity shrank from admitting it. Instead, she pointed toward the hearth, which Thorn probably couldn't see from the bed. ''Your clothes are drying before the fire, but they have a long way left to go. With luck they may be fit to put on by morning.''

''I don't care if they're wet.'' Thorn thrust back the coverlet, then twisted about to lower his feet to the floor. ''Bring them here.''

''I will not!'' Felicity told herself it was the heat of the fire, not the sight of Thorn splendidly naked that made her blush like a simpering virgin bride. ''You'd catch your death going off on a cool spring night in wet clothes.''

A fierce scowl overset Thorn's usual look of affable composure. ''Then I'll get them myself.''

Felicity put herself between the mantel and the bed. ''Take one step toward that hearth, and I'll toss your clothes on the fire!''

''What's gotten into you, woman?'' A grimace of pain twisted Thorn's features as he lurched to his feet. ''You're not my mother, for pity's sake. You don't even want to be my mistress anymore. So leave off trying to coddle me.''

He tried to take the threatened step, but the strength of his legs clearly failed to match the strength of his will. He staggered toward Felicity, who mustered all her strength to push him back onto the bed. At the last instant, his hand closed around her wrist and pulled her down on top of him.

The indignation she tried to summon, melted like summer hail on a sun-baked rock.

A bewildering sense of completeness stole over her as the fleet skip of her heart tangled with the strong, swift beat of Thorn's until it became one thrilling, intricate rhythm. The fear that had chilled Felicity from the moment she'd watched her servants drag Thorn ashore began to thaw at last—warmed by the sensation of his vital, solid body beneath her.

One part even more solid and vital than the rest.

The undeniable evidence of his desire held Felicity to Thorn when discretion urged her to pull away.

Perhaps she had been going about this all wrong. Instead of trying to force Thorn to remain in bed, might she fare better by enticing him to stay?

Slowly she raised her gaze to meet his, and her hand to brush against his side whiskers.

"Would you like me to be your mistress again, for one more night?" Her question came out in a husky whisper. Not only to tempt him, but because she feared her voice might break if she spoke any louder.

After all that had happened between them, what if Thorn refused her?

Had Felicity truly spoken the words Thorn thought he'd heard, or were his addled wits playing a cruel joke on him?

Even if she had made the offer and meant it, could he afford to risk his sister's future happiness to gratify his own transient desire?

"Of course I want you," he answered gruffly. "That much is obvious, isn't it? What I can't understand is why you're willing all of a sudden to let Ivy and your nephew get away when they're within our grasp."

A flicker of guilt shadowed the fiery intensity of her

gaze. "I'm *not* willing to let them get away. But neither am I willing to risk your health simply to keep my nephew from making a foolish mistake."

Felicity did care about him as something more than an instrument to gratify her desires. Curiously, the notion heightened Thorn's physical longing for her. Would it be so wrong to put his own needs ahead of his duty to others…just this once?

After a moment's thought, the subtle ridges of concentration disappeared from Felicity's brow. Her eyes sparkled like distant patches of dew-kissed clover at sunrise.

"What if I bid my servants to check the inns around town?" She spoke in such an eager rush, Thorn could scarcely grasp her words. "Once they locate my nephew and your sister, one of them can keep watch through the night, then fetch Oliver and Ivy here as soon as they stir in the morning."

Her plan tempted Thorn almost as much as the luxurious curves of her flesh beneath the flimsy layers of her muslin gown, or the passionate promise of her lips.

Felicity's glittering eyes challenged him. "If I do that, will you behave like the sensible fellow you are and stay here in bed?"

With the delicious warm weight of her on top of him, Thorn Greenwood had never felt less sensible in his life. "Here in bed…with you?"

"With me."

He angled his lips to engage hers, so his kiss might answer for him. As their lips touched, a strange energy surged through him—dark and rich as the coffee she'd offered him, with a bitter edge that only enhanced its potency. Thorn could not decide whether it truly soothed his pain or only made him cease to mind it.

Either way, he was grateful.

"You drive a hard bargain, Lady Lyte," he whispered before he began to suckle on her lush lower lip.

She gave no answer save for a sharp intake of breath, released as a lingering sigh.

Thorn sensed a shift in the connection between them. Though Lady Lyte had invited him to become her lover, until tonight he had approached her more as a servant or a supplicant making an offering of pleasure in hope of winning favor.

For this one last tryst, he would taste the heady elixir of mastery.

After one final deep draft from Felicity's sweet mouth, he reminded her, "Hadn't you better go despatch your driver and footman before they take to their beds for the night?"

"Ah…yes. Yes, of course."

She sounded almost as befuddled as he'd felt on first regaining consciousness. When Felicity pulled herself away from him with obvious reluctance and gained her feet, her legs appeared more than a trifle unsteady as she stepped toward the hearth.

"What are you doing?" Thorn asked.

She plucked his breeches from their drying place and waved them at him. "Taking *these* with me to ensure that you don't steal away while I'm gone."

Crawling back under the coffee-spattered coverlet, Thorn gave a rueful chuckle. "Is my word as a gentleman not good enough for you anymore, Lady Lyte?"

On her way to the door, Felicity peeped around one of the stout carved posts at the foot of the bed. "I suspect underneath all that stiff honor and gentlemanly virtue, you may have a spark of roguery in you, Mr. Greenwood.''

She wagged one slender forefinger at him. "I don't intend to take any chances that you won't be here when I return."

Thorn laid a hand over his fast-beating heart. "I swear to you, I shan't stir farther than to get myself a sandwich."

"You had better eat." Felicity tried to maintain an expression of innocent concern, but a flicker of mischief danced in her eyes. "To keep up…your strength."

"You had better be on your way." Thorn narrowed his eyes in a mocking pretence of menace completely at odds with his character. "Before I pull you back into bed and say to blazes with my sister and your nephew."

Felicity shook her head and chuckled at his impudence as she headed for the door.

He didn't mean it, of course—about letting Ivy and Oliver go to blazes—though part of him wished he could take such a cavalier approach to his responsibilities.

"Don't stay away any longer than you have to, Felicity."

She glanced back over her shoulder. "Not a moment longer. I promise."

Felicity dashed up the back stairs after ordering her servants to track down Ivy and Oliver.

Part of her haste was born of eagerness. The image of Thorn waiting naked for her back in the room quickened her steps. He had surprised her with his playful banter, and she could scarcely contain her anticipation of what other delightful surprises this night might hold in store.

Something else hastened her, as well, though Felicity was loathe to admit it, even to herself. Doubts nipped at her heels like a brace of those horrid little dogs with their incessant high-pitched barking that some dowagers of her acquaintance kept for pets.

Resuming her affair with Thorn would make it that much more difficult to break with him later…for both of them. Of the two, much to her astonishment, Felicity found herself more concerned on Thorn's account than on her own. After all, she would have their child to rear and love.

What would Thorn have?

"Mrs. Greenwood, ma'am?" a young woman's voice sounded behind Felicity.

For a moment, she was too preoccupied with her own thoughts to realize she'd been addressed by a name she could never hope to bear.

The voice spoke again. "Do you or your husband require anything else, ma'am?"

Her husband. The word sent a contrary mixture of feelings brewing in Felicity's heart. All the bitterness and betrayal that were the barren legacy of her marriage swirled like a raw Cornish wind around her fragile new sprout of trust and affection for Thorn.

She glanced back to see the servant girl who'd delivered the tray of coffee and sandwiches to their room earlier. "We have everything we require, thank you."

"Do the gentleman's clothes need laundered, ma'am?"

Following the maid's gaze, Felicity realized she was still holding Thorn's breeches!

"Ah…no…thank you." She hoped her sputtering

and the guilty blush that burned in her cheeks would not provoke the girl's suspicion. "I noticed…a button…hanging by a single thread. So I took it down to our footman to sew back on. He was apprenticed to a tailor before he went into service, so he's very clever with a needle."

What was one more falsehood on top of the tottering tower of deception she'd already piled up? Felicity asked herself when her conscience gave a bothersome twinge. If she kept at it, she might almost equal the number of lies she'd been told in her lifetime.

"Very good, ma'am." The girl's bland countenance betrayed no doubt that all was as it should be with Mr. and Mrs. Greenwood. "If you need anything else, just ring. I hope you pass a pleasant night here, ma'am."

The heat of Felicity's blush intensified. "I'm certain we shall."

That much was true, at least.

In case the maid's gaze might follow her, Felicity forced her steps to a sedate pace as she proceeded down the corridor back to their room. Letting herself in, she quickly shut the door behind her, slamming it in the faces of those pestering little doubts.

The room was darker than when she'd left it, bathed only in the rosy flickering glow of the fire.

"When I told you to hurry back, I didn't mean you should exhaust yourself running all over the place." Thorn's deep, mellow voice reached out from the bed like a strong but gentle arm pulling her into an embrace.

Felicity bolted the door behind her for good measure. Then she returned Thorn's still-damp breeches to the hearthside, stirring up the coals and tossing another large stick of wood onto the fire.

"You didn't eat any of the sandwiches." She nodded toward the breakfast table.

What was it about Thorn Greenwood that inspired her to take care of him in the way a woman who employed a small army of servants had no need to do?

"I thought it would be more enjoyable to share them. Besides, my hands are a trifle shaky. Would you think me a great sook if I asked you to feed me one?" A rare hint of levity bubbled beneath Thorn's words.

"A very great sook," she teased, selecting two triangles of bread and ham from the plate. "Just like I was, sitting on your knee in the carriage last night, blubbering my eyes out. I don't see why we can't indulge one another now and again."

She kicked off her slippers and climbed onto the bed, holding one sandwich out to him while she took a bite from the other.

Thorn gave an approving nod. "A very enlightened attitude, my dear."

He held her in a gaze as warm as the glowing coals in the hearth, peppered with provocative golden sparks. As Thorn took a bite of the sandwich she offered him, his lower lip brushed against Felicity's finger, sending a delicious ripple of sensation up her arm, all the way to her throat and down her breasts.

She barely managed to swallow what was in her mouth without choking. "They make very good sandwiches, here, don't they?"

The bread was fresh and soft, the ham flavorful and generously cut, enlivened by the piquant tang of mustard. But the zest of Thorn's company and the prospect of a night unlike any they had shared before, made the most toothsome condiment of all.

"Mmm." Thorn nodded as he swallowed his own bite. "The best I've ever tasted."

He snapped the remainder of the sandwich out of her hand, gnashing his teeth to make her squeal and laugh.

"You must be very hungry." Felicity fetched two more sandwiches off the plate.

When she settled beside him on the bed, Thorn leaned closer. But instead of nibbling on a sandwich, as Felicity expected, he nuzzled her neck. Every particle of sensation in her entire body seemed to cluster on that small patch of skin over which his lips hovered.

They began a sweet lingering climb upward. First his tongue glided, hot and wet, over the sensitive flesh, then his lips created a moist seal with her skin for a slow, easy suckle. Just when Felicity felt her bones begin to melt, Thorn ventured the lightest possible touch with the sharp edge of his teeth, setting her deliciously ashiver.

When he finally reached her ear, he whispered a single word.

"Ravenous."

Felicity had to swallow twice before she could coax any words out of her arid throat. "So am I."

Suddenly remembering the two sandwiches in her hand, she glanced down to find them squeezed to an unappetizing pulp.

What did it matter? She tossed them onto the floor. They were not what she hungered for. She doubted Thorn would miss them, either.

Forsaking self-control just as readily as she had dropped the sandwiches, she wrapped her arms around his neck and sought his lips.

They collided with almost savage urgency, as Thorn's hands found their way to her hair and began to pluck out the pins that held it in a sleek coil high on her head. True to his word, his hands did tremble. But that did not seem to hinder him.

Felicity's hair tumbled free, down her back and over her shoulders. Her body yearned to be equally at liberty. Equally available to Thorn's eager hands and lips.

He must have sensed what she wanted, for his fingers fumbled with the row of tiny buttons down the back of her gown while he continued to kiss her. His tongue coaxed her lips farther apart, then tasted her with a power and authority he had never before demonstrated.

With every touch, every taste, every mingled breath, Thorn Greenwood made her want him with a fervor that frightened and roused her in almost equal measure. A ravenous hunger built within her, to consume every crumb of pleasure he could grant her. And be consumed by it in turn.

And yet...

"Must we go so fast?" she pleaded in a breathless murmur as Thorn tugged the short sleeves of her unbuttoned gown off her shoulders and began to kiss his way down her neck, where he had earlier kissed his way up. "There's no need to rush when we have the whole night ahead of us."

"Oh, but there is need, my lady." He nuzzled the cleft between her breasts with his unshaven cheek.

"This need." He led her hand down the flat plane of his belly to wrap around him.

Felicity could never remember touching him...or

any man in such a way. It filled her with a heady sense of power.

"And this need." Leaving her to explore, Thorn thrust his hand up beneath her gown. Before she had time to guess what he would do—or having guessed, to object—he delved between her thighs to the slick, hot welcome awaiting him.

"Yes, but…" Behind Felicity's closed eyelids, the moist heat of tears hovered. She could not fight the urgent demands of her own body, even when they tormented her heart.

"Then it will be over." The words sighed out of her.

With a scarcely audible chuckle, as comforting as the soft patter of raindrops on a window, Thorn shook his head.

"Then…" He spoke in a delicious husky whisper as he lowered her onto the pillows and pulled her muslin bodice down to uncover the breasts that craved his attention. "…it will have just begun."

The breath she hadn't realized she'd been holding wafted out of Felicity in a gasp of understanding followed by a purr of sweet anticipation.

Too impatient to undress her completely, Thorn raised her skirt until it bunched around her waist with her bodice. Parting her stocking-clad legs, he eased himself into Felicity on a crest of sensation that carried her to the brink of bliss and held her there.

Chapter Ten

It seemed to Thorn as if he'd again plunged over a steep bank and felt the wonder of flight for a lingering instant before shattering and losing himself. Only this time passion and pleasure replaced panic and pain.

He lazed in the dark, sultry depths for what seemed like a very long time, more free than he could ever remember from the demands of his life. Nothing could tempt him back to consciousness...except the sweet prospect of making love to Felicity all over again.

This time, *slowly*.

The sensation of her lips on his stubbled chin, lured him to open his eyes. He couldn't bear to waste a single moment of this night not drinking in her beauty.

"I must say, you have phenomenal powers of recovery, sir."

She treated him to a bewitching grin as she wriggled out of her gown and stockings and tossed them to the foot of the bed. "Who would ever guess that not an hour ago you scarcely had strength enough to hold a sandwich?"

Thorn could not let such impudence pass without exacting the penalty of a kiss.

"A patient would be far gone, indeed, not to improve under your tender care, my lady." He cupped her breast, passing the pad of his thumb over the rosy-brown peak. "As for my recovery—you have seen nothing yet."

She cast a glance up at him through the fine dark fringe of her lashes. "From any other man I would call that a boast, but you are the least boastful fellow I have ever met, Mr. Greenwood."

"I have a good deal to be modest about," he replied, only half in jest.

The faint light of the fire gilded her features, suddenly fierce and ardent. "A good deal to be proud of, you mean. There's not a person of your acquaintance who does not speak of you with respect. Even Weston St. Just, who holds almost nobody in esteem."

Tiresomely respectable. Thorn swore he could feel the bonds of convention and propriety weighing him down. He had made a temporary escape from them to take up with Felicity, but it was madness to think of abandoning them altogether. Without his reputation, what identity did he have?

"If nothing else, you must be proud of your sisters," Felicity insisted. "Ivy once told me you practically raised them both."

"We raised each other." With a sigh Thorn subsided onto his back with Felicity's head pillowed in the hollow of his shoulder. "They are fine girls, both. You're right—I am proud of them, though I take little credit for how they turned out."

He gave a rueful chuckle at his own expense. "You see? I'm hopeless. What proper sort of man talks about his *sisters* while he's lying in bed with his beautiful mistress in his arms, after he's just made love to her and means to again?''

For the last time.

Thorn clenched his lips to imprison those wistful words. Why could he never allow himself to live in the moment instead of brooding over the past or worrying about the future?

Thorn wasn't certain what reaction he'd expected from Felicity. What he did not expect was for her to reach up and slide her hand down his cheek in a lingering caress.

''A very good sort of man, I would say.''

Perhaps she did not intend to add anything more, but further whispered words trickled out of her, just the same. ''I wish I'd been brought up by people who'd put my welfare ahead of their own aims.''

She didn't intend to reproach his behavior, Thorn knew, for she had done everything possible to prevent him going in search of Ivy and Oliver, as he'd meant to do. Her words stung him just the same.

True, he'd been a trifle unsteady when he first woke up. That had passed quickly, though. If he'd insisted, as he ought, Felicity could never have detained him here against his will. But he'd wanted this one, last night with her, and he'd been prepared to sacrifice his sister's future happiness to satisfy himself.

Bemused by his shame, it took Thorn a moment to realize the significance of what Felicity had just told him.

By mutual unspoken consent, they had never talked much about their pasts. Knowing this brief reprieve would soon be over, Thorn found himself suddenly greedy to find out everything he could about Felicity Lyte.

Where had she come from? Who were her family? What were her dreams and fears? What experiences had made her the passionate, fascinating woman she'd become?

"How old were you?" He ran a strand of her lustrous dark tresses between his thumb and forefinger, savoring its rich, smooth texture. Comparing Felicity's hair to mere silk didn't begin to do it justice.

She did not answer him right away. Thorn wondered if he should frame his question more clearly or continue to honor their tacit agreement to avoid discussing their pasts.

"Thirteen," she said at last in a hushed voice, "when my mother died. I barely remember my father. I didn't have a responsible elder brother to take charge of me, and my grandfather was off making piles of money."

"It could have been worse," said Thorn. "The old fellow might have been off losing piles of money, like my father."

"I'll grant you that." She glanced up at him then. Her gaze held neither the pity nor censure Thorn half expected to see. "I wish I'd had someone sensible on hand to tell me so at the time. It might have helped me accept my privileged lot with a little better philosophy."

"I'm sorry, Felicity. I didn't mean—"

"I know what you meant, Thorn." Yet she did not appear to resent it, for which he was grateful. "No doubt there were plenty of girls who'd readily have changed places with me. I doubt either of your sisters would have, though."

She looked away from him, then, but not before Thorn thought he had seen a faint film of tears in her eyes. "Fortune is all very well, but there's a good deal of truth in the old saying that you can't buy happiness."

"Perhaps that's what my father tried to do after my mother died," Thorn whispered to himself.

For the first time since he was a very small child, Thorn thought of his frequently absent, increasingly desperate father with something other than resentment. It felt strange, yet somehow...liberating.

Felicity appeared not to have heard him. "My grandfather left me in the care of a lot of beastly governesses who were bent on turning me into a milksop miss."

Thorn pressed his cheek against the top of her head. "I'm delighted they failed so miserably."

"They certainly made my life miserable in the attempt, with all their rules and lectures and punishments."

The plaintive bitterness in Felicity's tone made Thorn ache for the high-spirited child she must have been.

"Though your sister is not the sort of wife Oliver needs, her vivacity does you credit. You must have been tempted to break her of it—to make her more respectable, less apt to embarrass you."

"Now and then," Thorn admitted, warmed by Felicity's approval. "Though it wasn't quite the struggle you make it sound. I've always rather envied Ivy her exuberance. Who knows but a little of her daring may have rubbed off on me?"

With the delicate pressure of two fingers under Felicity's chin, he tilted her face toward his for a kiss. "For instance, I wonder what my respectable acquaintances would say if they could see me now?"

"No doubt we'd provide the Pump Room with entertaining gossip for a week." A mischievous chuckle escaped Felicity's lips as she parted them to welcome his. "Perhaps even two."

The corners of Thorn's mouth curved upward. No woman had ever buoyed his sober spirits the way Felicity could with no more than a look or a word. No woman had ever kindled a storm of passion in his tranquil heart the way she did.

The hot wind of that tempest roused within him once again. "In that case, don't you think it would be our civic duty to provide them with something truly worth tattling about?"

"Indeed?" Felicity ran one smooth slender hand over his bare flank. "What did you have in mind, my dutiful darling?"

As sternly as Thorn warned himself not to interpret her playful banter as anything more, the word *darling* still caressed his ears like warm liquid velvet.

"You're a good deal more imaginative than I am," he teased her back. "Have you any suggestions?"

Her hand blazed a trail up his chest, then along his shoulder. The dying firelight cast bewitching shadows over her face as it stirred the verdant embers of desire in the depths of her eyes.

"I believe you have already overtaxed your strength for one night." She gave a gentle push against his shoulder, tipping Thorn onto his back again.

Before he could protest that he had strength enough to make love to her at least once more, Felicity canted herself up on one elbow until she hovered over him. Her hand began a provocative slide from his shoulder, down the ripple of his chest to the flat plane of his belly and lower.

Any words Thorn might have spoken rolled into a resonant growl of arousal instead.

From deep in Felicity's throat came a husky, sensuous chuckle in answer. "I know you promised to make love to me again...slowly. But I think you should conserve your energy while I amuse us both."

She played her hand over him, running her fingers like a fleet, delicate scale on the pianoforte that set a drumroll of pure hot lust coursing through him.

Her lips poised above his—ripe and sweet as temptation. "Let me truly be mistress of you."

"With pleasure," he whispered.

Her dark hair fell forward, creating a silky veil around their faces.

"With pleasure," she promised.

Felicity proved as good as her word, and better. Using not just her hands and mouth, but every delectable part of her, she coaxed him again and again to the very peak of delight. Each time easing away at the last instant, then beginning the delicious ascent afresh.

She finally welcomed him into her sultry sanctum before he broke down and begged her, a favor for which Thorn was grateful. He had not guessed how much rousing him would rouse her. Scarcely had they joined when she gasped his name and her body clenched in sweet spasms around him, sending Thorn on a swooping cartwheel into ecstasy.

He returned to awareness with a mixture of eagerness and reluctance. Eager to cradle Felicity in his arms until morning. And more reluctant than ever to let her go again.

From the moment she had challenged him to become her lover, he had begun to admire this woman, with her full-blooded zest for life and her daring penchant for denying society's often rigid expectations. She was his opposite in those respects, and while it vexed him at times, being with her made him feel whole in a way nothing else ever had.

The prospect of losing her from his life brooded on his horizon like a day when the sun would disappear from the sky and never shine again.

The obstacles between him and Felicity were many and none admitted of an easy solution. He'd overcome obstacles before, though—both in raising his sisters and in recovering his family's fortune. Anything worth winning demanded hard work and sacrifices.

Felicity Lyte was worth winning.

His unexciting virtues of patience and persistence had stood him in good stead before, Thorn assured himself, and they would again.

Somehow he knew that the key to any future for he and Felicity lay buried in her past. But could he delve for it, without driving her away?

Her head pillowed on the solid swell of Thorn's chest with the steady rhythm of his heart beating a lullaby in her ear, Felicity had never felt more safe…or more free. Somehow his reliable strength and quiet constancy gave her a secure perch from which to fly.

Tonight for instance. She had never taken so active a role in lovemaking before, never put concerns for her own satisfaction aside in a single-minded quest to give pleasure. The result had catapulted her higher than she'd ever soared, to wheel and glide among the stars.

Perhaps it was fitting that her most sensually fulfilling encounter with a man should be her last. Hard as she tried not to let that regret mar this wondrous, peaceful moment, a faint chill quivered through her, as though a splinter of ice had pierced her heart.

Alert as ever to her unspoken needs, Thorn reached down to twitch the coverlet over them. If only he knew—a mountain of blankets could not substitute for the dependable warmth of his embrace or the mellow timbre of his voice.

"Did you ever *try* to buy happiness, Felicity?"

Though asked in tones of warmest sympathy, Thorn's question made her insides clench tight. Much as she wanted to dismiss it with some wry half jest, she couldn't.

Perhaps the shadowy intimacy of the moment seduced her, or perhaps the secret she was keeping from Thorn required all her powers of discretion, leaving her ill-equipped to guard herself in other areas.

She gave a brittle, mirthless chuckle. "How do you suppose I learned the folly of it? After my grandfather died, I purchased the handsomest, most well-bred husband money could buy. I thought I was buying my freedom, as well. But it turned out to be as elusive a commodity as happiness."

If Thorn had made any reply at all, Felicity would have found a way to change the subject. But his understanding silence would not be denied.

Words seeped out of her like blood from a tiny, unnoticed wound. "I had this ridiculous notion that being married would let me escape all the people who tried to control me—governesses and trustees and grasping relatives. Then I met my mother-in-law."

She shuddered. "The woman was like the worst of my governesses all rolled into one. She never missed an opportunity to insinuate that my filthy trade fortune besmirched her family. All the while her son was spending it like water to keep Trentwell from falling down around our ears.''

''The rotter!'' Thorn's indignant anger sounded so sincere.

How easy it would be to convince herself that her heart was safe in his keeping, because he was nothing like her late husband.

She'd been fooled before, Felicity reminded herself. ''Oh, Percy was quite nice at first, taking my part against his mother. I did try very hard to be a good wife to him. Much harder than I'd ever tried at anything before.''

Her voice grew more and more quiet until she could scarcely hear herself above the soft crackle of the dying embers in the hearth. ''It was no good, though, since I failed in a wife's prime duty.''

No word, sound or movement betrayed Thorn's reaction to what she'd said. Felicity sensed it just the same. If anyone could understand the shattering humiliation of failing in one's duty, he would.

''My mother-in-law took such grim delight in being right about me. Until she came to realize what that would mean for her precious family.'' More than anything, that had probably contributed to her rapid decline. Felicity had taken no satisfaction from it. ''Percy didn't take my part then.''

She shook her head slowly, acknowledging a deep regret. ''If only I'd known...''

''Known what?''

The quiet, earnest question slapped her out of the fuzzy half dream into which she'd slipped.

Her insides felt like some strange manner of engine, with her hurtling heart agitating her stomach and squeezing the air out of her lungs. Did she need any further proof that she could not trust herself around Thorn Greenwood?

His quiet sympathy seduced her wary spirit just as his tender caresses seduced her yearning body.

Part of her wanted to change the subject or kiss him cross-eyed again. Anything to rescue herself from the treacherous waters into which they'd drifted. But if she didn't soon make a clean break from him, she might end up telling him about the baby. Then, knowing Thorn's overdeveloped sense of duty, she'd never be able to rid herself of him.

"If only I'd known that widowhood is the most advantageous state for a lady of fortune." She could not bring herself to look her lover in the face as she delivered this tart pronouncement. "She can still enjoy all the pleasures of marriage without losing her independence."

Thorn flinched. Felicity did not have to see it to know.

She hardened her heart against the pity that would leave her vulnerable. He deserved a little sting, after all, for making her dredge up all those distressing memories and making her feel their forgotten pain all over again.

She braced herself for Thorn to sting back. It would give her a reason to peel herself off of him and go find out how her servants had fared in their mission. Once morning came and the two of them parted ways once and for all, perhaps fewer regrets would plague her. Not likely...but perhaps.

Instead, Thorn enfolded her with one arm, while his other hand passed over her hair in a comforting caress.

"Oh, dear heart," he sighed. "No wonder you rebel against any bid to dictate your actions."

His unexpected insight struck Felicity speechless. There was something exhilarating about being understood so well. Something frightening, too.

"No wonder you refuse to give up control in the smallest aspect of your life," Thorn murmured. "Even if it meant undertaking an uncomfortable journey to recover your errant nephew, when I'd have willingly gone in your stead."

Though she longed to surrender to his tender siege, Felicity could not. The man was too damned perceptive for his own good—or hers. What other secrets might he ferret out if he tried? And how could she be certain he would never use his dangerous knowledge of her vulnerabilities against her?

Thorn seemed too lost in his new realizations to recognize the shift in her emotions.

"No wonder you've been content with transient love affairs," he whispered, as if thinking aloud, "rather than submit to the tyranny of a husband."

"How dare you, Thorn Greenwood?" She struggled out of his arms, her eyes stinging furiously. "How dare you presume to judge me or pity me?"

"But, my dear, I didn't mean…"

He looked so hurt and bewildered, it was everything Felicity could do to keep from hurling herself back into his stalwart arms in the absurd hope that he would fix everything that had gone wrong in her life. Another part resented him for tearing aside the rose-colored curtain of her self-delusions to expose all that was wrong with it.

"Oh, save your earnest speeches!" She grabbed her gown and stockings from where they lolled wantonly around the bedpost. *"Transient love affairs* can be almost as tiresome as marriage when they carry on for too long. And lovers can be quite as tyrannical as husbands when they refuse to keep a permissible distance.''

"See here." Thorn pulled himself up from the pillows. "I was only trying to say that I understand and that I care about you. Is that so wrong?"

Felicity dove behind a dressing screen in the far corner of the room.

"Did I ever ask to be understood?" she cried, more to stop Thorn from filling her ears with further simple, heartfelt declarations of his feelings than anything else.

"Did I ever ask…" An unuttered sob caught in her throat. "Did I ever ask you to care about me?"

Spying an ewer full of water in the washstand, she poured it into the basin. Perhaps the running water would drown out Thorn's reply. It might well have, for she heard nothing more from the direction of the bed.

She wet a wash cloth in the cold water and began to scour the subtle musk of their lovemeking from her body. Despite the rosy glow of the dying fire, her skin took on a bluish-white cast as it rose in gooseflesh.

Felicity welcomed the bracing chill. Perhaps it would cool her delirious fever of desire and bring her to her proper senses.

As she reached for her gown, she glanced up to find Thorn standing beside the screen, naked as Adam. At the sight of his tall, lean frame, a hot blush seared through her body, undoing whatever good her cold scrubbing might have done.

Though her gaze was inclined to linger on his splendid body, Felicity forced it upward, half afraid, half eager to confront the furious outrage she expected to see on his face.

What she found instead she could not fathom. Was it calm, icy wrath? Mute anguish? Bitter disappointment? Or a little of all three, as well as something else that affected her far more than she wanted it to.

He did not shame her by gawking at her naked body. Instead he stared deep into her eyes, asking a wordless question she could not understand and seeking an answer Felicity knew she must not give him.

"I told you once before, we cannot choose who will care for us." He didn't sound angry...exactly. Just very certain. "I'm not asking anything of you, Felicity, and I will never take anything from you. But you cannot dictate to my heart...any more than I can."

He had every right to rage at her, Felicity acknowledged as a bilious tide of shame rose within her. Every right to withdraw the priceless gift she must pretend to spurn. Everyone else in her life had turned away from her when she could not do or be what they wanted.

Why should Thorn Greenwood be any different?

Because he *was* different, whispered her heart. Because he did not give or show love easily. But once given, his affections would be as constant as the earth—fallow in some seasons, but always ready to bloom afresh.

At that moment, she wanted nothing more than to step into his arms and claim what he offered her.

Except, perhaps, to vomit her guts out.

The nausea that suddenly gripped Felicity made all her previous spells of illness seem like robust health by comparison. Not daring to speak, in case more than words should spew out of her, she wriggled into her gown and pushed past Thorn.

Out the door of their chamber. Up the corridor and down a flight of stairs. Through a back door.

It was too dark outside for her to make out more than vague shapes and shadows, but Felicity knew she must be near the stables. The reek of horse muck slammed into her, and she began to retch, surge after bilious surge, until it seemed impossible there could be anything but a gaping void left inside her.

A void as empty as her life had been before Thorn Greenwood had begun to fill it in his quiet way.

Perhaps, thought Felicity, as she huddled shivering in the dark, she needed to reconsider her plans for the future—plans in which there had been no place for a man, least of all the father of her unborn child.

First, though, she must put some distance between them, so she could think things through clearly and come to a decision without any influence from others. There was so much at stake, after all. Not only her own well-being, but her child's. She could not afford to have her judgment thrown awry by the squall of contradictory feelings Thorn set brewing within.

Nor could she risk his discovering about the baby and insisting he wed her out of duty. If anything could blight the constancy of his feelings for her, that would.

She deserved better. So did her child. So did Thorn.

For all their sakes, she must retrieve Oliver, then go into seclusion for a time to reflect and assess her choices. If, in the end, she resolved to gamble her heart on Thorn Greenwood, she would know where to find him.

Hearing soft, rapid footsteps approaching, she had

only enough time to scramble to her feet before Thorn barreled out the door.

"Felicity?" He clasped her tight and planted his feet wide to keep them both from falling. "What are you doing out here? Why did you run off like that?"

Quickly, before he smelled the sour scent of vomit, she pushed him back inside. "What are *you* doing out in these clothes? They're still damp."

He chuckled. "I thought it preferable to risk a chill than to court scandal by strolling the corridors naked." His tone turned serious again. "Do come back and get warm. Dress yourself properly. I won't make a nuisance of myself, I promise. I'll vacate the room if that's what you'd like."

"Thorn, I—"

As she searched for words to justify her recent contrary behavior, Felicity heard more footsteps. Outside, this time and accompanied by a soft murmur of voices.

Voices she recognized.

"Mr. Hixon, Ned, is that you?" she inquired as the door swung open.

A startled oath. "Lord-a-mercy, ma'am, you gave me a turn," whispered her driver. "Have you been waiting up for us? Here now, is that Mr. Greenwood on his feet again?"

Felicity countered his questions with a pressing one of her own. "Have you found Miss Greenwood and Mr. Armitage? Where are they lodging? We must go at once."

After a disquieting hesitation, Mr. Hixon heaved a weary sigh, "We've been to every inn in Gloucester, ma'am."

"Twice," added Ned in a plaintive voice.

Her driver scarcely needed to add, ''There's no sign of them, ma'am.''

Felicity had already guessed.

Now what would she do?

Chapter Eleven

"They aren't here?" Felicity repeated in a dazed murmur. She swayed toward Thorn, who caught her around the waist and held her secure.

As a dutiful brother charged with protecting his sister from her own ill-considered impulses, Thorn knew he should be distressed by the news that Ivy and Oliver were nowhere in Gloucester.

Instead, as he stood in the dimly lit corridor of the inn, conferring in hushed tones with Felicity and her servants, Thorn struggled to mask his delight at the prospect of continuing their journey together. Once they recovered his sister and her nephew, Thorn knew Lady Lyte would disappear from his life as quickly and completely as she had entered it.

At the moment he couldn't figure how to reconcile duty to his family with the untenable passion that had taken root in his heart. And if he did manage to untwist that riddle, he questioned his ability to win Felicity for something more than a passing clandestine liaison. The only things he knew for certain were that he must try on both counts and that he must stick close to her if he hoped to succeed in either.

Felicity's driver cleared his throat. Thorn sensed the man was about to deliver more bad news to his mistress.

"The last place we inquired, ma'am…"

"For the second time," the young footman added, in case there should be any question of their diligence.

The driver continued as though he hadn't noticed the interruption, "At the main posting inn, ma'am, one of the hostlers told us a lady and gentleman had arrived around suppertime and hired a fresh coach to replace one that was in a bad way."

"Did this hostler say which way they were headed?" Felicity asked. Thorn could feel her shivering.

"No, ma'am, just that they went off again as soon as the coach was hitched. He said the young gentleman gave it a good looking over before they left."

"Where can they have gone?" Felicity whispered to herself. "What will I do now?"

She needed him.

The notion swept through Thorn with a strange vital energy, driving chills, aches, fatigue and doubts before it. "We can't do *anything* for a few hours. So let's make certain we put that time to good use."

He addressed Felicity's servants, "Go catch a little sleep while you can, both of you. Thank you for your efforts tonight. You did well."

The men hesitated, perhaps expecting their mistress to countermand his orders.

But she did not.

As the pair shuffled down the corridor toward the small room that had been hired for them, Thorn called softly, "And thank you for saving my life, today, with your bravery and quick action."

"Glad we were on hand to help, sir." The coachman lapsed into a deep yawn. "Good night, sir. Good night, ma'am."

Felicity did not stir or speak as her servants' footsteps retreated down the darkened corridor.

Once Thorn heard a door open and shut in the distance, he nudged her toward the stairs. "Come back to bed, now."

"To sleep, this time," he added, to forestall any protest. "And to lay our plans for tomorrow."

Felicity made no reply, though perhaps she nodded. In any event, she did not resist when Thorn took off his coat and wrapped it around her. Without another word, they fumbled their way up the unlit stairs and back to their room.

While Thorn built up the fire and set his clothes back in front of it to finish drying, Felicity retired behind the dressing screen, emerging a short while later in a nightdress with her dark hair plaited into a single braid.

She cast a wary look toward the bed, where Thorn lay with the covers drawn up to his chest.

He patted the empty space beside him on the mattress. "Come along, now. On my honor as a gentleman, I'll leave you be."

With halting steps, she approached, as though something propelled her forward, while something else tried to hold her back. This subdued silence wasn't anything like her usual temperament. Though Thorn preferred it to a stormy clash of wills in which he was too weary to engage, Felicity's sudden change of manner made him uneasy.

"Much as I might fancy enjoying your favors again, I'm afraid you have done me for the night, my dear."

Thorn pulled a droll face at his own expense, which Felicity rewarded with the barest flicker of a smile as she climbed into bed with him.

Tugging the sheet and blankets up over her, he tried not to flinch when her icy feet came in contact with his leg. "All I'm good for at the moment is to wrap you in my arms until you're warm again."

A spark of her usual spirit returned. "Don't undervalue such a worthwhile service."

She turned her back to him, but when Thorn nestled against her, she did not object or pull away.

By rights he should offer to continue their pursuit of Ivy and Oliver on his own, Thorn reflected as he rested his cheek against Felicity's hair. Now that she'd got a taste of the discomforts of the journey, she might be inclined to accept. Especially since it now appeared likely they would have to chase the evasive young pair every mile of the way to Gretna Green.

For perhaps the first time in his life, Thorn could not bring himself to pursue the responsible course of action. The situation alarmed and exhilarated him in equal measure.

Felicity told herself not to enjoy the novelty of sleeping in Thorn's arms, nor the comforting prospect of waking there. But it was no use.

She wasn't accustomed to denying herself—quite the contrary. Perhaps money couldn't buy happiness, but it could purchase independence and pleasure. Until recently, she'd been content with those.

"I suppose we ought to decide how to proceed next." The mellow murmur of Thorn's voice sounded in her ear, almost as close as her own thoughts.

The absurd but disturbing fancy that he might overhear all the bewildering questions abuzz in her mind sharpened Felicity's tone. "I confess I'm at a loss. If I didn't know better, I'd think those two young fools were deliberately leading us a goose chase."

Perhaps she should simply wash her hands of Oliver Armitage. Leave him a bit of money, but otherwise cut him out of her life when she disappeared to raise her baby. The young man was no blood relation to her, after all.

Thorn heaved a sigh, followed by a low chuckle. "That will be my sister's influence, no doubt. I can't recall a time when Ivy ever did what anyone expected of her. By now your poor nephew is probably hoping someone will intervene to save him from having to marry the little minx. He seems the sort of young fellow who was probably a nurse maid's dream—regular and methodical in his habits straight from the cradle."

"You may be right." Though Felicity tried to stifle it, a little smile, more brooding than amused, played at the corners of her mouth. "It's difficult for me to picture Oliver as an infant. Even when I first met him, as a schoolboy, he seemed far too solemn and seasoned for his young years."

Somehow the quiet, neglected child had slowly worked his way into one of the empty corners of her heart. A place that might have remained sealed against a jollier, more exuberant lad. She could not expel him now, no matter how much trouble he might cause her.

"I remember Percy bringing Oliver to Trentwell on the first school holiday after we were married." She could picture it so vividly. "I could tell the poor little fellow was happy to be there, though he didn't seem very well acquainted with the feeling. As if he liked it...but didn't trust it."

The Harlequin Reader Service® — Here's how it works:

Accepting your 2 free books and gift places you under no obligation to buy anything. You may keep the books and gift and return the shipping statement marked "cancel." If you do not cancel, about a month later we'll send you 6 additional books and bill you just $4.47 each in the U.S., or $4.99 each in Canada, plus just 25¢ shipping & handling per book and applicable taxes if any.* That's the complete price and — compared to cover prices of $5.25 each in the U.S. and $6.25 each in Canada — it's quite a bargain! You may cancel at any time, but if you choose to continue, every month we'll send you 6 more books, which you may either purchase at the discount price or return to us and cancel your subscription.

*Terms and prices subject to change without notice. Sales tax applicable in N.Y. Canadian residents will be charged applicable provincial taxes and GST.

If offer card is missing write to: Harlequin Reader Service, 3010 Walden Ave., P.O. Box 1867, Buffalo NY 14240-1867

NO POSTAGE
NECESSARY
IF MAILED
IN THE
UNITED STATES

BUSINESS REPLY MAIL
FIRST-CLASS MAIL   PERMIT NO. 717-003   BUFFALO, NY

POSTAGE WILL BE PAID BY ADDRESSEE

HARLEQUIN READER SERVICE
3010 WALDEN AVE
PO BOX 1867
BUFFALO NY 14240-9952

GET FREE BOOKS and a FREE GIFT WHEN YOU PLAY THE...

SLOT MACHINE GAME!

YES! I have scratched off the silver box. Please send me the 2 free Harlequin Historicals® books and gift for which I qualify. I understand I am under no obligation to purchase any books, as explained on the back of this card.

349 HDL DRRQ

246 HDL DRR6
(H-H-01/03)

Just scratch off the silver box with a coin. Then check below to see the gifts you get!

FIRST NAME	LAST NAME

ADDRESS

APT.#	CITY

STATE/PROV.	ZIP/POSTAL CODE

7	7	7	**Worth TWO FREE BOOKS plus a BONUS Mystery Gift!**
🍒	🍒	🍒	**Worth TWO FREE BOOKS!**
♣	♣	♣	**Worth ONE FREE BOOK!**
🔔	🔔	🍒	**TRY AGAIN!**

Visit us online at www.eHarlequin.com

DETACH AND MAIL CARD TODAY!

Offer limited to one per household and not valid to current Harlequin Historicals® subscribers. All orders subject to approval.

© 2000 HARLEQUIN ENTERPRISES LTD. ® and TM are trademarks owned by Harlequin Enterprises Ltd.

"So, young Armitage was…your husband's nephew?"

Felicity nodded. "Percy's sister's child. His parents had sent the boy home to school from India. Then his father was killed in some beastly colonial war and his mother perished in a shipwreck on the voyage back to England."

"I had no idea," said Thorn. "Poor little chap. My brother-in-law, Merritt Temple, was in a similar case when I first met him at school. Little money. No family. I invited him to spend summers with us at Barnhill because he had nowhere else to go."

The offhand mention of his kindness to an unfortunate schoolmate convinced Felicity that Thorn would have taken a more tangible interest in Oliver's welfare than the boy's uncle ever had.

"My mother-in-law didn't pay Oliver much mind." That was one of the first things that had drawn Felicity to the studious little fellow. "Some nonsense about Percy's sister marrying against her wishes. I don't think the boy's father had any fortune to speak of."

She shook her head. "There was no pleasing that woman. Oliver's father didn't have enough money to suit her, while I had too much…or perhaps the wrong sort."

"It sounds as though she'd have got on well with my father." Though Thorn tried to affect a tone of jest, Felicity detected an edge of indignation in his voice.

"Poor Merritt fell in love with my sister Rosemary during those summers at Barnhill. When my father paid enough heed to realize what was happening, he persuaded my sister to rebuff Merritt's attentions, even though it was obvious she cared a great deal for him."

Rosemary must be like her brother, Felicity decided, too dutiful to refuse.

Thorn's tone sharpened. "At the time, I thought Father was only trying to look out for my sister's future happiness. Later I began to suspect he had ambitions of her snaring a wealthy husband who could rescue him from his debts."

"How did it all work out in the end?" Without thinking what she was doing, Felicity turned toward Thorn. "You called this fellow your brother-in-law."

Thorn gathered her into his arms. "You might say Fate gave Merritt and Rosemary a second chance, which they were wise enough to seize...with a gentle nudge from Ivy and me."

He smothered a yawn. "It has been one of the greatest joys of my life to see my sister so happy again."

It couldn't have been easy for Rosemary Greenwood and her husband to find their way back to one another, Felicity reflected as she savored the tender strength of Thorn's embrace, and wondered why the happiness of two strangers mattered so much to her.

A proud young man who'd been spurned by his first love and a woman who must have doubted his willingness to forgive her. Yet they had come together again in a happy ending...or a happy beginning.

Could Fate be offering her and Thorn a similar opportunity? Felicity asked herself as the gentle slowing rhythm of his breath lulled her toward sleep.

If only she could have the luxury of a little time and distance to think things through, away from the sweet but confusing distraction of Thorn's constant presence, she might sort out her feelings. A quiet week or two at Trentwell, perhaps, once this business with Oliver and Ivy was settled....

"Trentwell, of course!" Felicity sat up so quickly, she almost bumped heads with Thorn.

"What's the matter, my dear?" he struggled up from the pillows to put his arms around her.

"It's all right," she reassured him. "I just figured out where we can intercept Oliver and your sister—at Trentwell. I'm certain Oliver would not pass so close without stopping there."

"Oh? Good." Thorn didn't sound quite as pleased as Felicity had expected. Perhaps he was still disoriented from being woken so abruptly. "Whereabouts is this Trentwell? How soon can we get there?"

"In Staffordshire." Felicity reviewed past journeys between Bath and Trentwell in her mind. "If we get away from here early tomorrow and make good time, we might be able to reach there before nightfall."

The prospect of eating at her own table and sleeping in her own bed appealed to Felicity vastly.

"We missed them at Newport and Gloucester." Thorn fell back onto the pillows again. "Let us hope the third time's a charm."

"You know what they say, men—third time's a charm." Thorn strove to inject a note of hearty confidence into his voice as he looked from Felicity's coachman to her young footman and back again, not long after sunrise.

"Indeed, sir." Mr. Hixon exchanged a glance with Ned. "So we'll press all the way through to Trentwell today, Mr. Greenwood?"

Forcing himself to ignore the signs of weariness on their faces, Thorn nodded. "Apart from stops to change horses. We'll contrive to get a bit of refreshment and whatnot then, as well.''

"I reckon we'd better get moving, then, sir." Felicity's driver jammed on his tricorn hat. "There's many a long mile between here and Trentwell."

"I'll take your word on that," Thorn replied. "I know what with checking all the inns for some sign of Mr. Armitage and my sister, neither of you got much sleep last night."

Felicity emerged from the inn just then, looking distinctly the worse for her own sleepless night. At least the two of them might be able to catch a bit of rest in the well-upholstered, well-sprung carriage box.

"I'd be glad to spell you at the reins for a while this afternoon," Thorn continued, to the coachman, "so you and Ned can close your eyes for a few minutes, at least."

"It's kind of you to offer and all, sir, but I couldn't hear of it. I'll manage well enough."

"Nonsense, man." Thorn ignored the look Felicity shot him. "We've all seen the unfortunate result of someone handling horses when they haven't got their proper wits about them. I'm sure Lady Lyte doesn't want her fine traveling coach landing in the middle of some river."

"Well, of course not..." Felicity sputtered.

Thorn smiled. "There, you see? That's practically an order from your mistress. You and Ned would be doing us a favor, taking our places in that stuffy box so we can get a bit of fresh air and sunshine."

"I suppose, when you put it like that, sir..." The coachman climbed aboard while Ned held the carriage door open for Thorn and Felicity.

They were a good mile or more on the road to

Tewkesbury when she finally demanded, "What's got into you? Offering to exchange places with my coach-man so he can sleep in the middle of a journey? I never heard of anything so ridiculous!"

"What's ridiculous about it? Those men saved my life, Felicity. Just because they're servants doesn't mean they deserve no consideration."

Aware of his voice growing louder and his tone sharpening, Thorn asked himself why this mattered so much to him. It had to do with more than her footman and driver, he realized. It had to do with seeing people for who they were, rather than for what they owned or what they did for a living.

He looked her in the eye and made a conscious effort to speak more quietly. "When you can no longer afford to employ as many servants as you've been accustomed to, you soon learn to appreciate ev-erything they've done for you. Would it do either of us any harm to drive your coach a few miles on a fine spring day?"

Another lady of fortune might have dismissed the notion out of hand, but Felicity seemed to heed what he was saying—perhaps even the deeper meaning be-neath his words.

"I suppose it wouldn't be all that different from tooling around Sydney Gardens in a phaeton."

A beam of sunshine penetrated the carriage window just then, making the tiny dust motes sparkle like flecks of gold. A ray of hope shimmered in Thorn's heart, as well, gilding the warm smile he lavished on Felicity.

"Capital! It'll be a lark—you'll see."

One of her fine dark brows lofted in a dubious look. "Very well, then. On one condition."

Now it was Thorn's turn to raise his brows.

"I want to hear more about this Barnhill of yours," said Felicity. "About growing up there with your sisters and the summers Merritt Temple came from school with you for holidays."

"That's not much of a condition." Thorn settled back into the corner of his seat and stretched his legs out. "I'll be glad to give you a full account, though I warn you I'm not half as diverting a storyteller as Ivy."

"That's not all." Felicity made herself more comfortable in the seat opposite him, bringing her feet up to rest on his out-stretched riding boots. "I want to hear everything about your sister's second courtship with her future husband. For instance, what sort of *little push* did you and Ivy give them toward the altar?"

"Very well, I'll tell you all about that, too."

Her request stirred a curious image in his mind. Before he had a chance to think better of it, Thorn heard himself say, "Shall I be like that sultan's bride in the Arabian Nights—as long as I continue to amuse you with stories, you'll keep me around?"

The look that came over her face made him wish he could take back the awkward jest that had strayed too close to his true feelings. Her eyes seemed to hold a conflicting mixture of apprehension and wistful longing. Or did he only fancy a reflection of his own confused emotions?

Before he could stammer out an apology, she confounded him with a flirtatious little smile. "You never know. Perhaps I might."

His thoughts buzzed with the implications of what she'd just said, though perhaps he was fooling himself and she hadn't meant anything beyond a little banter.

He was powerless to stop a daft grin spreading

across his face, just the same. "I'd better get started then, hadn't I? Hmm, what can I tell you about Barnhill? It's very old, but not very grand, I'm afraid. Greenwoods have lived there for time out of mind. There's a good beech wood nearby, which is probably where the family came by our name."

If he kept on at this rate, he'd put Felicity to sleep, rather than induce her to continue in his company. Thorn plundered his memory for any curiosities about Barnhill that might pique her interest.

"A brook cuts through the estate to empty into the Ouse. When Merritt came to stay with us in the summers, he and I used to fish and swim there. Once, Ivy dared Rosemary to spy on us. To see whether we wore our breeches in the water."

"Did you?" A lively challenge sparkled in Felicity's eyes.

"Of course not!" Thorn lofted his reply toward her. "Lady Rose paid for her carnal curiosity when she lost her footing and tumbled down the hill into the water."

Thorn began to chuckle. "If you knew my sister, especially as she was then." He shook his head. "Very beautiful and elegant. Not to mention overly conscious of her dignity. I wish you could have seen her cartwheeling down that riverbank, then plopping into the water!"

"The poor child!" cried Felicity as Thorn's laughter gathered momentum. "Was she hurt?"

"Only her vanity." Thorn gasped for breath. "But that took a terrible bashing. All her perfectly curled hair sodden and bedraggled around her face and her dress a ruin. It's a wonder Merritt and I didn't drown. We were laughing so hard, we kept falling down into the water. Rosemary flounced off with her nose in the air and refused to speak to either of us for a week.''

"I'd have made it a fortnight," insisted Felicity, though she appeared more amused than indignant on Rosemary's behalf. "What else did you do for entertainment in the summers, besides cavorting naked in the brook and laughing at the misfortunes of your poor sister?"

"Let me think. Battledore and shuttlecock matches when the wind was calm. Ivy and I played against Merritt and Rosemary. Sometimes we'd pack up a lunch and go off picking berries. Endless card games and chess matches on rainy days, or each curled up with a book in the sitting room, reading the best bits aloud to each other."

With a jolt, Thorn roused from his reminiscences. "Sounds tedious, doesn't it?"

Felicity shook her head. "Not at all. I'd have given most anything to be part of such goings-on when I was that age. Tell me, did you ever go to parties?"

"Once in a great while the girls would coax us to squire them to the Assembly Hall in Lathbury. And I seem to recollect Sir Edward Faversham hosting a grand fete at Heartsease."

"Heartsease?"

"A big estate not far from Barnhill. After Sir Edward died, the place went to some distant relation of his who put it on the market."

His voice trailed off. Happy as he'd been when Merritt Temple had come to Lathbury and bought Heartsease, Thorn had hated to see it pass out of the Faversham family.

Might the same thing happen to Barnhill one day, if he had no sons?

Chapter Twelve

"There's something I still don't understand," said Felicity a while after she and Thorn had taken over her coachman's accustomed perch. "How did your brother-in-law come to own a large estate like Heartsease? I thought you said he hadn't any money."

"He hadn't when we were young." Thorn kept his gaze on the horses and the road before them. "At least not much. Enough to put himself through school and buy a modest commission. However, my old friend returned from his time in Spain with General Wellington something of a hero. As a result of his fame, he caught the eye of..."

For an instant Thorn's hesitation puzzled Felicity. Then she understood. "A lady of fortune? Your friend married an heiress?"

Thorn nodded.

"Pity." Her stomach clenched. "I had rather liked the sound of your Mr. Temple...until now."

"Merritt did not wed the woman for her fortune, if that's what you presume." Thorn's hands tightened on the reins. "He loved her...or thought he did. At first."

A Royal Mail coach overtook them just then with

a great clatter. It must have been behind schedule, for the maroon-liveried coachman did not spare his whip. Two young men, who occupied the cheapest places on the outside of the vehicle, shot curious looks at Felicity, perched up on the driver's seat of her carriage. She barely resisted the childish temptation to stick her tongue out at them.

The mail coach finally gained a great enough lead that Felicity could hear herself speak. "I take it the first Mrs. Temple failed to meet your friend's expectations."

When love died in a marriage, no amount of money could provide a remedy. Unlike Merritt Temple's first wife, at least she had survived her marriage to reclaim her independence. The thought of having gone to her grave unwept by her husband, then having him use her fortune to attract a second wife made Felicity's gorge rise along with her temper.

They rode on for a time, an awkward silence falling between them until at last Thorn broke it.

"The truth is, Merritt failed to meet his wife's expectations. He has never said an ill word about the first Mrs. Temple in my hearing, but Rosemary has let the odd remark slip. And I know my friend well enough to guess what his first marriage must have been like."

"And how do you guess it must have been?" Her question came out in a sharper tone than she had intended.

Thorn shrugged and slanted a fleeting glance toward her. "The lady assumed she'd purchased him. For his fame, I suppose, and perhaps for his looks. From an ill-fed youth, Merritt had matured into quite a handsome fellow. His wife probably thought she had a right to order him around like a servant or some sort of lapdog.''

If Thorn had turned and thrashed her with the coachman's whip, which he hadn't once touched to the horses, Felicity could not have taken a deeper cut. She had never treated Percy the way Merritt Temple's wife had treated him. Had she?

Did Thorn believe she would treat him in that high-handed fashion if he was fool enough to wed her?

Pulling her cloak tighter about her, she stared off at the Midland countryside where the county boundaries of Shropshire, Worcestershire and Staffordshire got hopelessly mixed up.

Almost as mixed up as her emotions.

''Unequal fortunes can place a grave strain on a marriage.''

Was she trying to excuse her past actions or to caution Thorn and herself against flirting with dangerous fancies? Felicity hardly knew.

Thorn's shoulders appeared to slump a degree or two—or had she only imagined it? ''Merritt told Rosemary much the same thing when he first returned to Lathbury with his infant son, after his wife died.''

Those words gave way to a wry chuckle—the last sound Felicity had expected to hear from Thorn just then. ''The poor fellow almost ruined his chances with my sister then and there. He had no idea how our fortunes had fallen in recent years, and Rosemary was too proud to tell him. When he finally found out, Merritt assumed the worst—that Rose had kept the truth from him intentionally while she pursued him for the fortune he'd inherited.''

''How awful!'' Felicity's heart warmed in sympathy for both Merritt and Rosemary. In either of their places, she might have done or believed just as they had.

"A bad business, keeping secrets," said Thorn. "Especially from those we love. Somehow whatever we're trying to hide always comes out at the worst possible moment. Then it makes the situation ten times worse than it was before."

All the air seemed to rush out of Felicity's lungs, as though she'd been clouted by a low-hanging tree branch. For a moment she feared she might pitch off the carriage.

How would Thorn react if he found out the secret she'd been laboring to keep from him?

That wasn't hard to guess. He'd hate her for not telling him, but that wouldn't stop him from insisting they wed—for the sake of respectability and duty. As grounds for a lasting union, those would be as inadequate as the exchange of wealth for fame or title that she and Merritt Temple had endured in their first marriages.

She must have swayed or given some other subtle signal of her distress, for Thorn gathered the carriage reins in his left hand, then slipped his right arm around her shoulders.

"Is something the matter?" He held her steady, with both his firm grip and his tone of fond concern. "I know the height and the motion can set one dizzy. Shall I stop and let your driver take over again?"

"I'm fine," Felicity insisted, praying she sounded sincere. "I only thought how awful for Mr. Temple and your sister. How did it all work out in the end?"

"I had a hand in that as a matter of fact." Thorn tugged on the reins to slow the horses as they approached a village. "The most devious bit of thinking I've done in my life."

He sounded touchingly proud of himself. "I knew that neither Merritt nor Rosemary could abide the slightest suspicion that she had wanted to wed him for his fortune, so I suggested he pretend to have lost his money in bad investments."

"That *was* devious." A week ago, Felicity would not have believed him capable of hatching such a scheme. But since the night he'd stormed into her town house in search of Ivy, Thorn Greenwood had proven himself a man of hidden depths. "Did your sister believe him?"

"Why would she doubt it after what had happened with our father?" Thorn spared Felicity a quick side-long glance. "Just as I'd hoped, Merritt's pretended loss of fortune did nothing to lessen Rosemary's feelings for him. They were married shortly afterward and have been happy ever since. I'd be dead envious if I didn't love them both so well."

The wistful craving in Thorn's voice echoed one that gnawed at Felicity's heart.

"What did Rosemary say when she discovered her husband had lied to her about losing his money?" Felicity asked. "Wasn't that every bit as bad as her keeping the secret of your family's financial reversal?"

"Perhaps so." He considered for a moment. "Rosemary may have decided that Merritt's innocent deception set them even. I gather she forgave him most readily."

Thorn's sheepish grin ripened into a rather devilish one. "Or perhaps it was because he told her the truth just after he'd made love to her on their wedding night."

"Indeed?" Felicity found herself laughing, though a quiver of unease went through her at the same instant. Was there anything she might not forgive Thorn if he asked during the lazy weightless warmth after lovemaking?

Only half in jest, she inquired, "What if I was to tell you I'd lost *my* fortune?"

Thorn greeted her question with a hoot of laughter. But after a moment's reflection, his answer sounded as solemn and sincere as Felicity had ever heard. "I would tell you what Rosemary told Merritt and just as truly. It would make no difference to me."

Easily said under the circumstances. But how she longed to believe him.

"Wait," said Thorn. "Let me amend that. It *would* make a difference. I would prefer you without a great fortune. For then you could be certain my feelings are genuine. And there'd be no odious gossip about me wanting you for your money or you having to buy a husband."

He made the calamity of losing her fortune sound almost appealing. Except that it would also mean the loss of her hard-won independence. Felicity could not give that up.

"And what if I told you the matter of my inability to breed was all a mistake and that I was quite capable of bearing children after all?"

The instant those words left her lips, Felicity wished she could take them back. The question had seemed to ask itself against her will. "Would *that* make any difference to you?"

She held her breath as she listened for Thorn's answer. If only it did not matter so much to her...

"I wish I could assure you otherwise, my dear."

His arm tightened around her for an instant, then he drew it back to grasp the reins more securely. "But I'm afraid that *would* make a difference."

To Felicity, it felt as though her heart had fallen beneath the carriage wheels and been ground into the unyielding surface of the road.

It was all well and good for Thorn to preach about the folly of keeping secrets, as if her conscience didn't trouble her enough already. Even putting aside the whole distasteful question of fortune, she could never again wed a man who valued her only as a broodmare on whom to sire offspring.

Not even if his offspring was growing in her womb that very moment.

He had hurt her.

Not that it was easy to tell with Felicity, for she didn't pout or pine. Instead she donned a mask of mocking amusement, keeping up a steady banter about their mutual acquaintances in Bath. If he hadn't known better, Thorn might have thought he was conversing with Weston St. Just.

Early in the afternoon, they had stopped in Wolverhampton to tend the horses, after which Mr. Hixon and the young footman had resumed their posts, looking somewhat better for their improvised nap. Thorn and Felicity had returned to the relative comfort and quiet of the carriage box for the final leg of their journey to Trentwell.

Thorn had started to relate another story about the escapades of he, Merritt, Rosemary and Ivy during their summers at Barnhill, but Felicity had been quick to divert him with talk about Bath.

He could not escape the sense that she was pushing

him back to arms' length, after having made the mistake of allowing him to get too close.

The subtle rebuff stung him at first, even as he found himself laughing at her tart quips.

Gradually, however, he began to pay less heed to her words, other than to nod or chuckle when Felicity appeared to expect it. Instead, he drank in the sparkle of her eyes and the rich, dark lustre of her hair. The way she held her head when she spoke and the graceful manner in which she moved her hands to emphasize what she was saying.

Each of these touched him with a fond familiarity that had grown over the weeks since they'd begun keeping company. They also touched him with a sweet sadness when he realized they might soon be nothing but an elusive recollection, slipping from his memory the harder he tried to hold them.

A week ago, her present performance might have fooled him. But the time and confidences they had shared since setting out on this journey had given him fresh insight. What he'd said, about her barrenness making a difference, had wounded her. Now she was creating a diversion to cover her retreat. She could not risk allowing him close enough to strike another blow.

"Was I wrong to tell you the truth?" Thorn wanted to protest.

Another man might have reassured her with a diplomatic evasion or an outright lie. He had never mastered the knack of deception. Besides, he cared for Felicity too much to offer her anything but the truth.

He wanted children of his own. Not as dynastic pawns or to carry on the family name, but to raise and to love. To infuse his practical, workaday life with their unique wonder.

The way his sisters had done in their younger years, only better. For this time he would embrace his responsibility for them from the moment they were born, and even before, rather than having it thrust upon him. He would be ready to nurture and guide them as they needed, not preoccupied with trying to grow up himself.

If it were possible to barter Felicity's fortune for the chance to have children with her, Thorn knew he would do it without a second thought. Unfortunately, some things in life were too precious to be purchased.

And this was one of them.

"I thought it a most diverting story." Felicity's voice broke in on Thorn's musings. "Perhaps I told it badly."

"Not at all." Thorn struggled to recall what she'd been talking about. "You always have a witty way of putting things."

"One would never know it from the grief-stricken look on your face." The set of her features and her airy tone declared she was only teasing him, yet a trace of tightness around her eyes suggested something more.

Thorn shrugged. "I have not your flair for masking my true feelings, my dear."

"Masking?" Her eyes widened, while her smile stretched taut. "I have no idea what you're talking about."

"Of course you do." Thorn hunched forward until his elbows rested on his knees. "Though perhaps it's impolitic of me to mention it. I wouldn't say I felt grief-stricken. Regretful, perhaps."

"Ah, regrets." Felicity caught her bewitching lower lip between her teeth for an instant. And for that instant her mask crumbled like an eggshell and fell away. "Who of us doesn't have those?"

"Do you regret taking up with a tiresome, fortuneless fellow who refuses to keep a permissible distance and can't recognize when a transient affair has gone on too long?"

Without recrimination, he repeated the sharply barbed words she had flung at him the previous night as a curious sort of peace offering.

She made a valiant effort to repair her mask and slip it into place again. Perhaps his soft steady stare told her it was no use, that he'd only see past it anyway.

"I will never regret what we have shared, Thorn." Felicity reached forward to rest her fingers over his folded hand. "I do regret what I said to you last night. And I regret very much if I've given the impression that I don't *want* to be with you anymore."

Her hand closed over his in a tremulous caress and by some unlikely intuition Thorn knew that the truth came as hard to her as deception came to him. "I wouldn't blame you for having regrets about taking up with a spoiled heiress too selfish to care about anyone's feelings but her own."

"Not selfish." Thorn shook his head. "Self-protective, perhaps."

"Do you think so?" She gazed at him with a soft, vulnerable look that made Thorn ache to gather her into his arms. "I suppose it is possible. From as far back as I can remember, I have felt the need to protect myself."

Her voice fell to a whisper, as if the truth of what she was saying frightened her. "Often from those closest to me."

"Never from me, Felicity."

Abruptly she drew back from him, releasing a brief tinkle of laughter that reminded Thorn of winter wind through tree branches laden with icicles.

"You most of all, Thorn Greenwood. You understand me too well, which makes you harder to safeguard against. And you persist in making me care about you more with each passing day."

Never had he believed it with the certainty that now took root in his heart. The realization rocked Thorn backward and left him speechless.

"I don't regret what we have shared." Felicity spoke the words as if they both elated and terrified her. "But I fear I may come to regret it very much if I'm not careful."

Before Thorn could summon any words of reassurance, the carriage slowed and took a sharp turn to the right.

"That will be the road to Trentwell." With an obvious effort, Felicity once again donned the poised, charming demeanor of Lady Lyte. "Another half hour should see us there, I believe."

She stared out the window, perhaps to distract or collect herself. "See that wood? It's part of Cannock Chase. Percy used to hunt there often."

Thorn cast an absent glance toward the broad expanse of forest. He tried to recall a remark Weston St. Just had made shortly after introducing him to Felicity. Something about her husband having been killed while riding...or hunting. Had Percy Lyte died here at Cannock Chase?

"I'm so looking forward to sleeping in my own bed tonight." Felicity stretched and yawned. "Not to mention enjoying all the other amenities of a well-run household.''

''Indeed.'' Thorn had no illusions that the most luxurious bed in the kingdom would afford him the peaceful hours of rest he'd savored last night at that little inn on the outskirts of Gloucester.

Unless he could once again hold Felicity in his arms—which didn't seem likely.

''You and your sister are welcome to stay on for a day or two before you head back to Bath.'' Felicity did not take her eyes off Cannock Chase as she tendered this gracious, but stilted, invitation. ''And you're welcome to take your choice of rigs from the coach house for your journey.''

She wanted to be rid of him, and the sooner the better. Thorn strove to keep in mind Felicity's vulnerable admission of only a few moments ago—that she needed to protect herself from her growing affection for him.

Faced with the aloof beauty who spoke in so offhand a manner of their imminent parting, he found it easier to believe she'd simply grown tired of his company.

''Will you and your nephew not be returning to Bath, as well?'' he asked. ''It would save a great deal of bother if we all travel together.''

Felicity's nose wrinkled in a look of distaste. ''I fear that might prove impossibly awkward. Besides, there isn't much left of the Season. I believe I'll remain at Trentwell.''

Clearly, she didn't want to run the risk of bumping into him at Sydney Gardens or the Upper Assembly Rooms in the coming weeks.

Though he lacked Felicity's skill at acting indifferent, Thorn made an effort not to let his dismay show. "In that case, *if* we find Ivy and your nephew at Trentwell, I believe it would be best for all concerned if she and I leave at once. We could probably get as far on our way as Wolverhampton before nightfall."

Was it only his wishful fancy, or did Felicity's face suddenly turn pale?

Thorn felt compelled to explain. "Given the way they've eluded us time and again, I wouldn't put it past that pair to steal away from Trentwell during the night, if Ivy and I stayed on."

"I see your point."

"Thank you for the offer of a carriage." In truth it would gall him beyond bearing to accept her charity. "But I'd prefer to hire the coach Ivy and Oliver have been using. We may not return to Bath, either, but head straight home to Lathbury. Ivy would probably be better off under Rosemary's supervision, and there's less apt to be gossip in Bath if she doesn't return. Out of sight, out of mind, and all that."

"Very sensible of you." Felicity's expression softened. "As always."

Though he knew she'd meant it kindly, Thorn still flinched. Part of him longed to abandon sensibility and respectability and all those other tedious virtues. But did he dare risk becoming like his father?

Never.

"It isn't very sensible to talk as if our finding Ivy and Oliver at Trentwell is a foregone conclusion." Thorn knew he sounded stern and pedantic, but he didn't care. He'd show Lady Lyte *sensible*...with a vengeance. "We should plan some contingency in case they never arrived or have been and gone again."

Deep in his heart, a most preposterous bud of hope

quickened. If he and Felicity were forced to continue with their journey, perhaps all the obstacles that stood between them would magically fall by the wayside with each mile they traveled north.

"That's not possible." Felicity's words echoed the harsh verdict of Thorn's own reason. Then he realized she was talking about Ivy and Oliver. "They must be there. Oliver would never pass so close to Trentwell without stopping. I expect they're as anxious for proper rest and meals as we are. More, perhaps, if they've been traveling at odd hours and lodging at only the cheapest inns."

"I hope you're right," Thorn lied.

For all the inconvenience, discomfort and turmoil of the past three days, he would rather face many more days of the same than bid goodbye to Felicity and ride out of her life forever.

Oliver Armitage was a clever chap. If he had any inkling that he and Ivy were being pursued, as surely he must, his aunt's estate would be the last place he'd risk stopping.

So Thorn told himself as he glimpsed a magnificent silvery-gray mansion off in the distance, nestled among massive spreading oaks. The carriage slowed even more, turning onto a long broad lane with a row of tall arching elms standing sentinel on either side.

No wonder Sir Percy Lyte had needed to marry one of the wealthiest heiresses in the country to keep this place up, Thorn acknowledged as he surveyed the impeccably kept grounds and the marble swan fountain in the forecourt. Revenues from the estate farm and other such income would barely make a dent in Trentwell's ruinous maintenance.

As the carriage rolled to a gentle halt before the

stately eight-columned portico that fronted the vast house, Thorn realized that his jaw had gone slack, permitting his mouth to gape open.

He shut it with such savage force, his teeth rattled.

A middle-aged footman in full wig and livery pulled the carriage door open. "Lady Lyte, what a pleasant surprise, ma'am."

"Thank you, Dunstan." Felicity dismissed the servant's greeting with the graceful flutter of one gloved hand. "Tell me, have you seen anything of my nephew in the past day or so?"

No. No. No! The word beat an insistent tattoo inside Thorn's skull.

Even with the vast edifice of Trentwell now added to the other barriers between himself and Felicity, he clung to the ridiculous illusion that a few more days in her company might make a difference.

"Master Oliver?" the footman exclaimed in a hearty tone that rang in Thorn's ears like the death knell of his foolish hopes. "Why, he arrived just this morning with his young lady, ma'am. I believe the pair of them are taking a stroll 'round the garden with Master Rupert at the moment."

"How fortunate," replied Felicity as the footman helped her down from the carriage box. "We've been most anxious to catch up with them."

A plaintive tightness in her voice belied her careless declaration. Or perhaps Thorn conjured it up out of the dark choking chasm inside his own heart.

Without waiting for any assistance from Lady Lyte's servants, he scrambled down from the carriage and strode over to the fine marble fountain. There he pretended to inspect the trio of exquisitely carved swans which spewed water from their bills in graceful arcs.

Unlike Felicity, he needed some time and effort to fabricate a mask of cheerful indifference with which to cover his naked despair.

Chapter Thirteen

For a moment the footman's words refused to make sense to Felicity. She had fully expected to find Oliver and Ivy here. She had cautioned herself repeatedly to distance herself from Thorn Greenwood, while she still had some choice in the matter.

All the same, the news that her nephew and Thorn's sister were presently strolling the grounds of Trentwell brought her neither the satisfaction nor the relief she'd hoped.

"Notify me the moment Master Oliver and Miss Greenwood return to the house, Dunstan. And make sure the stable master knows my nephew is not to take any of the horses without my permission."

"Not even the hired team he came with, ma'am?"

"Especially not them." Felicity glanced around for Thorn only to find him contemplating the swan fountain. "Make certain I'm advised if Master Oliver tries to do anything of the sort."

"Very good, ma'am." Dunstan hustled off to carry out her orders.

"Lady Lyte, ma'am," Ned called down from the boot of the carriage, "shall I fetch your luggage in?"

A sharp retort sprang to Felicity's lips. Of course her luggage should go in. Even if she hadn't found Oliver at Trentwell, she would not have set out after him until she'd enjoyed at least two good meals and one decent night's sleep.

Before Felicity could say anything, the young footman smothered a yawn.

Words of Thorn's resonated in her mind as clearly as if he'd stood beside her and repeated them.

"Just because they're your servants doesn't mean they deserve no consideration."

And later, speaking of Merritt Temple. *"His wife probably thought she had the right to order him around like a servant."*

Felicity glanced up to find Ned waiting patiently for his orders.

"I would like my valise brought in, thank you," she said. "Once that's done, you and Mr. Hixon must hie yourselves off to the kitchen and tell Cook I want her to prepare you a rattling good tea."

Over the roof of the carriage, the coachman and footman exchanged broad grins.

"Very good, ma'am," they answered in chorus.

With a nod of acknowledgement, Felicity turned away from the carriage and sauntered over to the fountain with carefully cultivated poise.

"Beautiful, aren't they?" She kept her eyes trained on the three swans at the center of the fountain. "Percy's great-grandfather brought some famous sculptor all the way from Italy to carve them."

"Skilfully done, indeed," Thorn agreed, though in a somewhat absent tone, as if his thoughts were otherwise occupied.

An urge to capture his full attention took hold of

Felicity, though she scolded herself that it was pointless.

"The sculptor took long enough." She forced a bright, animated tone, quite at odds with what she felt. "He stayed and stayed until Percy's grandfather threatened not to pay him, saying the fellow had received free bed and board long enough to equal a fat fee for his services. At least that's the story I was told when I first came to Trentwell."

She couldn't resist a brief glance to see if Thorn was paying any attention to her. Her spirits leapt when she caught his steadfast gaze upon her.

"What happened then?" he asked. "Did the sculptor finish the job?"

"He was gone the next morning." Felicity savored the story's saucy conclusion. "And the master's eldest daughter gone with him."

"Well, well." Thorn pulled a wry face. "I've heard of people paying vast sums for works of art…but a daughter? That is very dear."

Felicity could imagine it all. The lady and her lover meeting for stolen trysts around the estate. Why, there were dozens of spots on the vast grounds of Trentwell that would make piquant venues for romantic interludes.

In spite of her herself, Felicity began to picture Thorn and her making love in some of those places.

"Let's go inside." Her anxiousness to distract herself from such thoughts made the words burst out of her. "We can take some refreshment while we wait for Oliver and Ivy to return from their walk in the garden."

More images rose in her mind. Of Percy's great-aunt wringing her hands as the day of her lover's departure approached. Perhaps the sculptor had begged her to come away with him. How torn she must have been—to leave behind her family and a life of restrictive privilege for a free but uncertain future with the stranger she'd come to love.

"Well, Lady Lyte...are you coming?"

She stirred from her fancy to find Thorn several steps ahead of her.

"Yes, of course." She breezed past him just as a tiny drop of rain landed on her neck. "We had better get inside before the skies open on us."

They crossed the forecourt and climbed the broad marble steps to the front entrance. Felicity pulled off her gloves and cloak, passing them to the footman who waited inside the lofty oval entry hall.

"Shall I send some of the grounds keepers to fetch Master Oliver and his lady in, ma'am?"

She should give the order, Felicity knew. Yet she shrank from bringing her last few private moments with Thorn to an end. "No need to make a fuss. I'm certain they'll return quickly enough once the rain begins to fall in earnest."

The footman nodded his acknowledgement of her wishes in the matter. "Is there anything you'd like, ma'am?"

"Indeed there is. Tea for Mr. Greenwood and me in the Rajah sitting room, please."

"Mr. Greenwood?" The footman murmured.

"Yes. Mr. Greenwood is the brother of the young lady my nephew brought with him." Felicity's regal tone dared the servant to make anything of it. "By the by, tell Cook to make certain the tea tray is well laden. I'm starved and I expect Mr. Greenwood is, too."

When the footman had bowed and withdrawn below

stairs, Felicity turned to Thorn who was staring around him with some wonder and perhaps a little dismay. Those certainly had been *her* first reactions to Trentwell when she'd come here as Percy's bride.

She glanced from the massive sweeping staircase to an imposing portrait of the first Lord Lyte, who glowered down upon all who entered his house. "A bit imposing, isn't it?"

"Enormous, too." Thorn swallowed hard. "I always thought Heartsease was a very grand place, but it would barely serve as Trentwell's gatehouse. As for poor old Barnhill, you could put half a dozen of it in here and still have plenty of room to spare."

"That sounds a far more reasonable size." Felicity beckoned him toward the south gallery. "I'm not sure anyone really *owns* a place of this magnitude. It owns them."

Trentwell wasn't going to own her much longer, she vowed to herself. Once this business with Oliver and Ivy was settled, she'd find a buyer for this elegant monstrosity, then acquire a nice cozy spot in the country to raise her child—one far from Thorn's country house in Buckinghamshire.

"So what is this Rajah room?" asked Thorn as they made their way down a long windowed gallery hung with more portraits of Lyte ancestors.

Felicity stopped before an open set of double doors. "*This* is the Rajah sitting room. Percy's great-grandfather made his fortune from the East India Company. Later in life, he imported all sorts of curios from India."

That was why she'd chosen to take tea here. The room itself would provide plenty of fuel for conversation, preventing those awkward silences that cried out to be filled with words she had no intention of uttering.

Thorn obliged her, wandering around the exotic room asking pleasant, impersonal questions about the tiger skins draped over the back of the rosewood settee and the slender open-shelved teak cabinet with elaborate ebony inlay that housed ivory statues of elephants and multiarmed goddesses.

"What about this basket in the corner?" he asked at last. "The weave is very intricate, but it seems rather modest compared with all these other treasures."

"Oh that!" Felicity chuckled, beginning to relax. She had become so engrossed in their conversation that she'd almost forgotten how soon Thorn would be gone from her life.

"They say Percy's great-grandfather kept a live snake in there for years, until it bit one of the servants who was assigned to feed it."

Thorn's eyes widened as he took a step back from the basket. "For a house so much newer than Barnhill, this one certainly has its share of colorful stories."

Before Felicity could relate any more of them, a footman entered, bearing the tea tray. He set it on a low table formed by a round slab of tawny marble resting on top of four green terra-cotta elephants.

Felicity's mouth watered at the comforting aromas of tea and seed cake.

Through the open doors of the sitting room, a flurry of movement in the south gallery caught her eye. It looked like a young man hurrying past.

Without wasting a second, Felicity brushed past the servant and called to the person in the gallery, "Oliver? Come here at once, please. Mr. Greenwood and I have a few things we wish to discuss with you.''

The young man halted abruptly, then turned on the toe of one of his highly buffed riding boots.

For a long moment Felicity stared at his face, unable to recognize it, apart from knowing it did not belong to her nephew...and realizing it had been injured. Three bright red lines scored one swarthy cheek, while the opposite jaw bulged as if from a severely ulcerated tooth. The young man cradled his left hand in a way that suggested it was also wounded.

"Rupert Norbury?"

Felicity had never seen the most importunate of her late husband's illegitimate children looking so unkempt. Children whose mothers *claimed* they'd belonged to Percy, she privately amended.

"What happened to you? And what are you doing at Trentwell? You're supposed to be in Ireland."

For the first time since she'd caught him swaggering around the estate as a boy and come to realize who he was—or who everyone thought he was—Felicity had never seen Rupert Norbury quite so chastened.

"Ah, Lady Lyte, what brings you to the country so early?" His attempt at bravado fell short.

Felicity's patient stare, waiting for an answer to her questions, appeared to rattle him.

"What happened to me?" He grimaced. "Oh, this. Difference of opinion with a horse."

Felicity sensed Thorn Greenwood hovering behind her a moment before he spoke.

"Do horses in Staffordshire sport claws?" he asked in a jesting tone subtly whetted with mockery. "If so, I'll make sure to avoid the stables."

The young dandy's scowl darkened further. "Rode

into some beastly branches,'' he muttered as he raised his sound hand to cover the scratches on his cheek.

He'd been up to no good, as usual. Felicity could see it as clearly as the angry red swelling of his forefinger. Fighting with one of the grooms, perhaps. Or taking liberties with a scullery maid, more likely.

For all the contradictory emotions her present situation provoked, Felicity knew she would take singular satisfaction from evicting this odious pup from Trentwell once and for all. But first things first...

''Have you seen anything of Oliver Armitage or the young lady he brought with him from Bath?''

The young scoundrel looked eager to distract them from the subject of his injuries. ''I did as a matter of fact. 'Books' said something about showing her the old dovecote and the wild garden.''

He gave a sidelong nod toward the high gallery windows and the vast estate park that lay beyond. ''I shouldn't expect them back much before dinner.''

Against all sense, the weight on Felicity's heart lifted. She half turned to Thorn. ''Oliver must have assumed we'd given up the chase and gone back to Bath. By the time they return it'll be too late for you and Ivy to get any distance on the road.''

Thorn replied with a doubtful-sounding rumble deep in his throat.

''You really needn't worry about Ivy and Oliver running off in the night.'' Out of the corner of her eye, Felicity watched Rupert skulk away to tend his wounds. ''I'll post armed guards outside their doors, if need be. You deserve at least one decent night's sleep before you head away. Then you and Ivy can make a fresh start in the morning.''

Those words sounded so pleasant—*a fresh start.*

She would be making a fresh start tomorrow, too. Hard as she tried to summon up the necessary enthusiasm for it, Felicity could not.

As he watched the battered dandy disappear down the gallery, Thorn tried to subdue the squall of emotion that gathered force inside him. It threatened to erupt unless he gave it some outlet.

"Who is that young coxcomb?" he demanded, half-afraid of the answer he would receive. "And what business has he striding about your house as if he owned the place?"

Thorn cringed at the pitiful bluster of jealousy he heard in his own voice.

Felicity rounded on him, her eyes flashing like summer lightning filtered through a thick canopy of woodland foliage. "What business have you quizzing me in such a peremptory tone, sir?"

None at all, Thorn admitted to himself. That was the problem.

Out of the corner of his eye, he saw the young footman who had delivered the tea tray steal out of the sitting room and slink away up the gallery.

Thorn lowered his voice. "I make it my business, the same way I made it my business to follow you from Bath. Because I care about you."

Felicity's expression softened, and for a moment Thorn feared she was about to weep. If that happened, he might complete his humiliation by joining in her tears.

He clung to his possessive anger like a lifeline. What did it matter if he offended Felicity, now? She had cast him off once, and he would soon be out of her life forever.

Stabbing the innocent air with his forefinger, he pointed in the direction Felicity's *young man* had gone. "A swaggering puppy like that will bring you no end of trouble."

"Why, you righteous hypocrite!" Felicity flounced past Thorn into the sitting room.

He followed, shutting the door behind them. The strange room, with its draperies of violent scarlet and provocative bare-breasted statues, did nothing to soothe him.

Felicity stood before the mantel, looking fierce, yet curiously vulnerable at the same time. And so beautiful, Thorn ached anew imagining her in the arms of any other man.

"How dare you question what company I choose to keep?" She looked ready to grab one of the heavy curios off the mantelpiece and hurl it at his head. "When you'll be traipsing off in your own good time to wed some apple-cheeked virgin of good family and pump her full of babies to inherit your nonexistent fortune!"

"What would you have me do?" Thorn strode toward her, but she did not flinch. "Give up any chance for happiness in the future and spend the rest of my days pining for you? I'm a practical, unromantic fellow, Felicity. You know that. I've spent my whole life making the best of what Fate has dealt me, and I will do it again."

His conscience smarted, though, imagining his poor *second best* bride, and children who would carry the unfair burden of consoling their father for the great disappointment Fate had dealt him.

Perhaps the time had come for him to put aside his accustomed practice of resignation and salvage. Time to risk his heart and his pride in a fierce struggle for what he wanted.

Felicity gazed up at him, the protective armor of her indignation shattered. "You make it sound so...bleak."

The word brought Thorn to his knees. "A life without you *will* be bleak, Felicity. Now that I have seen Trentwell, I understand why you can never trust a man to value you solely for your own charms...considerable though they are."

She replied with a rueful nod that made Thorn yearn for her more than ever. In the beginning she had enthralled him with her wit, her verve and her confidence.

His growing awareness of the self-doubt and vulnerability she took such pains to conceal had not dimmed his fascination with her—only tempered and deepened it. He loved her imperfections, for each one made her a little more accessible to a man like him.

Felicity made no protest when he took her hands in his. But her long slender fingers felt damp and cold to his touch.

For an instant, Thorn's voice caught in his throat, but he managed to force it free. "No doubt it is even more difficult to believe from a man in my straitened circumstances, but it is the truth. I care about *you*, Felicity. Not your estate. Not your fortune."

He pressed his lips to her hand. "Only your touch. Your voice. Your smile."

The corners of her mouth curved upward, but her eyes did not crinkle in the manner of a true smile.

"My dear Thorn," she murmured, "of course I believe you care nothing for my fortune. I have never doubted it."

An unexpected surge of hope propelled him to his feet again and sent his lips seeking hers to kiss away that wistful mockery of a smile.

He sensed reluctance and eagerness battling within her as her lips melted against his, froze for an instant, then melted again. Emboldened by Felicity's declaration of her faith in him, Thorn suckled her lower lip in the way he knew she enjoyed. After a final moment's hesitation, she returned his kiss with a desperate fervor, as though she meant to devour him. The blood roared through Thorn's veins in a fast, fevered rhythm.

Though he recalled making love with her twice during the previous night, his body now ached for Felicity as though they'd been long parted. Had it not been for the likelihood of someone blundering in on them, he might have tossed one of the tiger skins on the sitting room floor and seduced the mistress of Trentwell, then and there.

"Please be sensible, Thorn." She averted her face and made a token effort to retreat from his embrace. "Don't make this any harder than it must be. And don't pretend my fortune is the only thing that stands between us."

Deprived of her lips, Thorn set about the delightful occupation of drizzling kisses up and down her slender, sensitive neck.

"I'm tired of being sensible," he whispered as his lips ravished one delicate ear. "I want to make it so hard for us to part that we'll do *anything* in order to stay together. I don't care what stands between us. I can't abide the thought of any other man in your life. Nor can I abide the thought of *my life* without you."

Felicity drew back from him, just enough to let their gazes meet.

The quickening wonder of a thousand springtimes glowed in her eyes. Yet Thorn sensed something else, too. The bated hope of a child watching a beautiful but flimsy soap bubble waft on the breeze.

At last she risked shattering their fragile moment with a few quiet words. "The young man you saw me talking to in the gallery, he's not what you think he is."

Thorn struggled to retain his composure. "What is he to you, then?"

A shadow of old pain and humiliation darkened her features. "Rupert Norbury's mother was one of my husband's many mistresses."

If she had brained him with the heavy jade tortoise carving from the curio cabinet, Thorn could not have been more dazed.

He remembered the flippant reference Felicity had once made to her late husband's illegitimate progeny. Seeing one of them, and sensing a faint echo of the anguish she had suffered on their account was another matter entirely.

"Y-you let him stay here?" Made him some sort of allowance, too, if the young rascal's wardrobe was any indication.

Felicity gave a reluctant nod. "Mister Norbury seems to think he has a better right to Trentwell than I have."

"Preposterous!" For reasons he could not fathom, Thorn found himself no less indignant for understanding Rupert Norbury's true position in Felicity's household. "Why, the fellow's a walking, talking insult to you."

"This is the only home he's known for many years. I hadn't the heart to deprive him of it." She made it sound as though she was admitting a vice. "Beneath my show of sophistication, I'm rather a sentimental ninny."

"I warn you, madam." He gave her nose a delicate tap with his forefinger. "I won't stand idly by and hear the woman I love maligned."

"The woman you love." Felicity savored the words on her tongue and appeared to find their flavor very sweet. "She is a fortunate creature, indeed."

"Not half as fortunate as I, if she could return my feelings."

"She fears she does return them, Mr. Greenwood." A faint sigh escaped Felicity's exquisite lips. "But she fears so much else besides. You may have no designs on her fortune, but there are those who would claim you do. Could a respectable man like you abide being the subject of vicious gossip?"

Before he could stop himself, Thorn flinched.

"You see?" Felicity raised her hand to brush against his side whiskers. Not as their usual signal for lovemaking, Thorn sensed, but as a gesture of endearment and wary trust. "I would feel the same about malicious tattle that the trade heiress had bought herself another man."

Thorn shook his head vigorously. "No one with any sense would believe that a woman of your beauty and charm needed to purchase a husband."

The sweet beginning of a genuine smile lit Felicity's face with a soft, rosy glow. "And no one with any judgment would believe you capable of dishonor."

"In that case," said Thorn, "if all the people with

sense and good judgment know better, who are we to care what spiteful fools may speculate?''

When he moved to claim a kiss, Felicity drew back. ''There is still the matter of children, my dear. Don't pretend you can shrug that one off so easily.''

''No, I cannot.'' Thorn hadn't consciously weighed his decision, but the problem had brooded in his heart. Now he knew what he must do. ''I won't deny wanting a family of my own, very much. I believe I have it in me to be a good father.''

Was that part of what made him care so much—the need to be the kind of father he had lacked?

''Yet, weighed against the prospect of losing you from my life... I fear even that falls short.''

Felicity stared at him, her eyes blinking furiously to dispel a faint but persistent mist in them. ''W-what are you saying, Thorn?''

What else could he say? ''I know these aren't the only things that stand in the way of a future for us. But if we weigh each one as I have done, I believe the scale will always fall in our favor.''

He dropped to one knee. ''Don't let us part, Felicity...ever. Please say you'll marry me.''

As the silence between them swelled like the heavy hush before a storm, Thorn watched fondness and faith war with doubt and distrust for possession of Felicity's heart.

Why had he blurted it out like that—so bald and colorless? What self-respecting woman would accept such a proposal, let alone a woman who had reason to doubt the sincerity of any marriage offer?

At that moment, Thorn would have sold his birthright to borrow Weston St. Just's glib tongue for five minutes. Just long enough to ask the most important question of his life with persuasive eloquence.

As he steeled his spirit in vain against the anguish of her rejection, Felicity gave him her answer.

The second most beautiful word in the English language.

"Perhaps."

Chapter Fourteen

Perhaps.

A soft, seductive echo of her answer to Thorn's un-expected proposal whispered through Felicity. Not just in her thoughts, but in her heart and along her veins, it made a kind of bewitching music.

Perhaps he had bewitched her.

She hadn't meant to give him false encouragement. She'd intended to reply with a firm, unswayable *no*. But his words had sounded so reasonable, his voice so sincere. The glow of passion in his eyes and the tender ardor of his touch had worked an innocent magic over her. One that had proven too potent to resist.

If she had not exercised the waning strength of her will at the last moment, the answer that passed her lips might have been a thoroughly impossible *yes*.

The look on Thorn's face was enough to prevent her from dashing his hopes.

"I'll be content with *perhaps*." He spoke softly and without haste, all the while making a determined effort to curb his smile. As if he feared any show of eager-ness might change her mind.

Yet he could not keep himself from adding, "For now."

He would kiss her, Felicity knew, if she gave him even a crumb of encouragement. Once he began, she might never summon up the resolve to stop him.

"The tea!" she cried. "We should have some before it grows cold."

Thorn glanced toward the well-laden tray. "We haven't exactly been taking regular nourishment since we left Bath, have we?"

"We must compensate for that." Felicity tugged him toward the settee.

The familiar rituals of pouring and serving might give her a welcome opportunity to regather her tattered composure. It would be futile to discuss matters of consequence between bites of dainty sandwiches and sips of tea, when a weighty remark might be countered with an offer of cake or a query about how many lumps of sugar Thorn preferred.

Felicity craved the sanctuary of polite, meaningless table talk, during which she might sort out her new, uncertain feelings. She reached for the teapot as if it were a lifeline, and she were atoss in a stormy sea.

Her hand trembled a little as she poured the steaming amber liquid. "Cream or lemon?"

"I never took anything but cream for the longest time." Thorn spoke with an intensity that scarcely befit such a commonplace remark.

Curiosity prompted Felicity to lift her gaze from the tea tray and meet the compelling look he focused upon her. He was talking about something more than the tea....

"Lately, I find the piquancy of lemon much more to my taste."

A peculiar sensation crinkled along Felicity's shoulders and up her neck.

"Lemon." The flesh of her mouth tingled as if she had just bitten into that tart fruit. Employing a pair of tiny silver tongs, she lifted a slice from the bowl and deposited it in Thorn's tea.

"Sugar or honey?" she asked. "We keep our own bees at Trentwell."

"Trentwell honey?" Thorn seemed to savor a drop of it on his tongue. "That sounds too sweet to resist."

Just like every word out of this man's mouth, Felicity mused as she drizzled a measure of thick golden syrup into his cup. Whether remarking about the refreshments, beguiling her with stories of his family or urging her to make a permanent place for him in her life, Thorn Greenwood appealed to her in a way no other man ever had.

Their fingers brushed as he took the delicate cup and saucer she offered him.

How ridiculous to feel a tremor of suppressed excitement over a chaste, casual touch, when she'd taken the man into her bed on a regular basis for many weeks. But there it went, all the same—unbidden. Overpowering her carefully cultivated self-control in a way that both roused and frightened her.

An odd but potent fancy rose in her mind. Of she and Thorn sitting in this very room taking tea thirty years hence, with a large family gathered around them. The kind of family Felicity had never known but for which she'd secretly yearned her whole life.

She could almost hear their laughter and good-natured quarreling. It did not take much imagination to picture Thorn's hair thinner on top and liberally frosted with silver. Nor the deeply etched lines that would fan out from the corners of his eyes whenever he smiled. She imagined herself a bit stouter with a wrinkle and a white hair to match every one of her husband's.

Two things did not change in her wishful glimpse of the future. One was the steady glow of affection in Thorn's eyes, and the other was the giddy spark of desire that leapt within her whenever they touched.

Was not the promise of such a future worth braving whatever obstacles might rear up between now and then? Like Trentwell honey and Thorn's fond assurances, the notion was too sweet for Felicity to resist.

"Eat up." She held a plate piled with tea sandwiches. "Then I'll take you for a look around the rest of the house. We can discuss what we'll say to Oliver and your sister when they return."

What would she say to her nephew, Felicity wondered? In good conscience, could she advise him to resist the powerful lure of love, when she was on the verge of surrendering her own heart?

Thorn nodded toward the window where fat raindrops beat a muted tattoo against the glass, driven by a brisk southwest wind.

"I suppose the first thing we'll say is, 'Go change out of those wet clothes, the pair of you.'" He glanced at Felicity. "I expected they'd be back long before this. Hadn't we ought to send someone out to find them and fetch them home?"

Her thoughts had already turned in that direction. Before Thorn had finished speaking, she pulled on the bell cord to summon a footman from the servants' hall.

If Oliver and Ivy looked suitably contrite and sufficiently in love, Felicity decided, she might intervene on their behalf. If Thorn agreed to let them undertake a proper courtship, away from tattling tongues in Bath, the young lovers might well be relieved to abandon this elopement nonsense in favor of a family wedding in a few months time.

A double wedding…perhaps?

He was going to have the devil's own time looking properly severe when he reproved his scapegrace little sister and her beau, Thorn decided some time later while Felicity conducted him on a tour of the great house.

If not for the necessity of chasing down the young runaways, he and Felicity would now be going about their separate lives in Bath. He, nursing a broken heart and trying without success to forget her, wrongly convinced that she'd never cared twopence for him.

In one elegant salon, he caught sight of his reflection in a looking glass framed with gold filigree. Thorn scarcely recognized the fellow staring back at him with a daft-looking grin on his face.

"Don't tell me you're growing vain, Mr. Greenwood." Felicity's face appeared in the mirror with Thorn's.

For an instant he gazed at the image of them together and savored the wonder of it. Felicity's reflection cast him a flirtatious little smile.

"Like something out of a French fairy tale, isn't it?" She nodded toward the ornate looking glass. "Do you suppose if we ask it who's the fairest in the land, it will tell us?"

Thorn wrapped his arms around her and bestowed a kiss on the base of her neck. "It's already showing me the fairest one."

"I might accuse you of flattery." She inclined her

head toward his, nuzzling his hair with her cheek. "But I've never known you to exaggerate the truth."

"Nor am I now." He'd have been perfectly content to stand there for hours, sating his senses on the sight, sound, touch, scent and taste of her. In a state of complete…felicity.

No doubt about it, the woman was aptly named.

"Wasn't there another magic mirror?" Felicity mused, raising her hand to rest against his cheek in a proprietary caress. "One that showed a person their heart's dearest desire?"

"A remarkable object, this glass of yours." Thorn gazed into it and beheld his heart's dearest desire— the two of them, together. "It scores on both counts."

Even better, he decided, for this was no magical illusion.

"Would you like to see the library next?" Felicity asked in a high, breathless tone that roused Thorn from his modest flight of fancy.

He steered his lips toward her ear, watching her face and his own as he whispered, "Is there any way I might persuade you to conduct me on a tour of…the bedchambers? A magnificent house like this must have some very fine ones."

A delicious blush rose from her bosom, gathering intensity as it climbed toward her brow. "Mr. Greenwood, I see I have had a most devilish influence upon you."

"Are you sorry?"

The lush sparkle of her eyes mocked the absurdity of his question. "Not in the least. There is nothing I like half so well as a dash of mischief in a respectable man. I only hope you do not repent it."

"Never!" Thorn quite liked the look of himself

hovering behind her in the glass, one eyebrow cocked at a roguish angle. For the first time in his life, he thought his unremarkable features almost handsome. "Now, about that inspection of the bedchambers..."

Before Felicity could answer, the sound of hurrying footsteps made them both start and draw a decorous distance apart.

"Excuse the intrusion, ma'am." A sodden footman hung back in the doorway, clearly reluctant to drip water on the elaborate parquet floor.

Felicity beckoned him in. "You have something to report, I take it. Have Master Oliver and Miss Greenwood been fetched home?"

The servant shook his head. "Not a sign of 'em anywhere on the grounds, ma'am. We've searched high and low."

"Everywhere?" Felicity demanded. "Are you certain? What about the dovecote?"

"First place we checked, ma'am."

"The shell grotto? Lady Elizabeth's pagoda?"

At the mention of each place, the footman nodded. "Master Oliver and the young lady weren't at any of them, ma'am. Not the west tower, neither. Nor the dairy."

"They must be somewhere. Did anyone see them come back to the house?"

"Dunstan thought of that, ma'am. Had the maids take a look about in their rooms when they laid the fires."

"And...?"

"Neither of them was about, ma'am. But their bags was gone."

Felicity looked ready to curse. "I left orders that Master Oliver was not to be given a horse."

"He wasn't, ma'am," the footman assured her. "Nobody at the stables seen hide nor hair of 'em— just Master Rupert. He took a gig into the village a while ago."

Thorn didn't like the sound of that. "It's not a very pleasant evening for a drive. Do you suppose Norbury helped Oliver and Ivy give us the slip?"

Felicity pondered the suggestion, then shook her head. "I can't think why he would. He and Oliver have never had much use for one another."

"The fellow was obviously lying about his injuries." Thorn cursed himself for not getting to the bottom of that when he'd had the chance. "Perhaps that has something to do with it."

"So it might." Felicity caught her lower lip between her teeth, her brow furrowed.

After a moment's consideration, she turned back to the footman, who'd been patiently awaiting her orders. "Go make some inquiries in the village. Find out if anyone's seen Master Oliver and Miss Greenwood, then report back to me at once. If you find them, do what you can to detain them while you send word back here."

"Very good, ma'am." The footman headed off.

Thorn opened his mouth to speak, but before he could get the words out, Felicity called after the young man, "Make sure you change into dry clothes before you go anywhere."

The lad glanced back, acknowledging his mistress's order with a self-conscious nod before continuing on his way.

Felicity made a wry face as she caught Thorn's hand in hers and gave it a squeeze. "If I'm not careful, you'll soon have me coddling all my servants."

"It seems we've each been having our own influence upon the other."

"Perhaps so." Her teasing look turned earnest. "Only, don't expect to change me altogether, my dear. I'm a selfish creature at heart, and I mean to keep it that way."

Thorn considered reminding her that there was a difference between selfish and self-protective, but decided against it. He remembered how angry she'd become the last time he'd shown a particular insight into her character.

It was enough for him to recognize the difference and act upon it. Once Felicity understood that she could always depend upon him to guard her happiness, she would be able to relax her own vigilance. Then she'd become the warm, winning woman he had so often glimpsed behind her defences.

He shrugged. "Neither must you believe you can turn me into a charming rogue."

"Why would I want to commit any such folly?"

Though she spoke in a jesting tone, Felicity's voice also carried a sweet ring of sincerity. The transparent affection in her gaze made him feel as if he'd suddenly grown several inches in stature.

Could it be that in his modest, responsible way, he was the perfect partner for her?

Thorn and Felicity had just finished the second course of their dinner when the footman returned from the village. The look on the lad's face told Felicity he had no good news to report.

"Out with it, man. They've gone, haven't they?" Frustration sharpened her voice. She'd been looking forward to a pleasant interlude at Trentwell with Thorn, once they'd chastened Oliver and Ivy.

The footman gave a reluctant nod. "They had been at the Fox and Crow, ma'am. I only missed 'em by an hour. The innkeeper said they arrived on foot, then a while later Master Rupert called to collect them."

Thorn bolted the last mouthful of wine from the bottom of his cup. "Did the innkeeper know which way they were headed?"

"No, sir. He thought Master Rupert might be fetching them back to Trentwell."

Under her breath, Felicity muttered, "Heaven forbid that young scoundrel should ever do anything to oblige me."

"Pardon, ma'am?"

She waved him away. "That will be all, thank you."

As the footman withdrew, Felicity turned to Thorn. "A slippery pair of fish, aren't they? I should have sent the servants out to round them up the moment we arrived. It never occurred to me they might steal off to the village on foot, and I didn't—"

When she hesitated, Thorn shot her a questioning glance.

Felicity stared down at her lap as she folded and unfolded her napkin. "I didn't...want to part from you any sooner than I had to."

When she finally gathered the courage to look Thorn in the face, she saw pleasure and chagrin vying for control of his features. "That makes two of us. I could have searched the grounds for Ivy as soon as I found out she and Armitage were here. Should have, obviously."

If, in the years to come, Ivy suffered any regrets

about her elopement, Thorn would hold himself responsible, because he'd followed his own inclinations rather than his brotherly duty. Felicity had no doubt of it.

"What shall we do now?" she motioned for the serving maid to remove their plates.

Thorn held his tongue until the maid had replaced their empty dishes with a fresh course and gone below stairs again.

"What else can we do but take up the chase? The circumstances between you and I may be altered, but that does not make this elopement of Ivy and Oliver's any less a mistake."

He was right, of course, Felicity realized as she nibbled at her fillet of turbot with a greatly reduced appetite. Their errand had lost some of its urgency for her, since she'd almost made up her mind to accept Thorn's proposal.

Still, she must not forget her nephew's future happiness.

"If you'd rather stay here at Trentwell," Thorn offered, "while I carry on the chase...?"

His suggestion tempted Felicity.

Sleeping in her own bed. Taking regular meals from her own good kitchen. Not cooped up inside a bumping, rattling carriage...

...with Thorn.

Somehow, that consideration made all the bother seem positively attractive.

Besides, if she stayed behind at Trentwell, filled to the rafters with reminders of how her first marriage had gone wrong, her usual wariness might reassert itself. She might fall prey to all manner of doubts she didn't want to entertain.

"I'd rather come along, if you don't mind."

Before Thorn could protest, she reached out and laid her hand on his. "Not because I don't trust you to manage on your own or any nonsense of that sort. It's just that, in spite of all our misadventures, I've rather enjoyed the past few days with you."

Wasn't the kind of man who made such things possible worth keeping in her life?

Thorn's brows shot up, as if he'd just discovered something surprising. "I've enjoyed them, too. Apart from nearly drowning."

"And being accosted by that dreadful highwayman." Felicity shuddered.

She gave Thorn's hand a parting squeeze before returning to her dinner. "That's all settled, then. We'll go together."

"If you insist," said Thorn, who didn't look as though he'd needed much persuasion. "I'll tell you, though, I've had my fill of chasing after Ivy and your nephew only to miss them by minutes. I suggest we press on for Carlisle with all speed and wait there for them to come to us."

"An ambush?" Felicity savored the notion. "Yes. It would serve them right after the bother they've put us to. I'll tell Mr. Hixon to be ready first thing in the morning."

Thorn shook his head vigorously. "We shouldn't delay. They have only a few hours' head start on us, if that. We've never been so hot on their heels."

He thought for a moment. "At least not that we've been aware of. I believe we should go as soon as we've finished eating. Can a carriage be readied for us in the meantime?"

"Possible." Felicity tapped her fork against the side

of her plate. "But not advisable. Really, Thorn, there are times a little self-interest is not such a terrible thing."

"But if we don't reach Carlisle and prevent them from crossing the border into Scotland, all our efforts until now will have been wasted."

Under the table, she ran the toe of her slipper down his booted leg. "Not *entirely* wasted, I hope."

The color rose in Thorn's face.

Though she knew she should not take such amusement in teasing him, Felicity couldn't help herself. There was something curiously endearing about a man who could blush.

"The word *waste* was badly chosen, I'll admit. But you know what I mean, Felicity. Unless we intend to do whatever we can to stop this elopement, perhaps we had better stay put at Trentwell and enjoy ourselves."

She lowered her chin, casting him a mischievous, inviting look through the dark fringe of her lashes. "You mustn't tempt me like that."

"Felicity…" The pretended severity of Thorn's tone matched his look.

If she finally made up her mind to marry him, Thorn might try to curb her occasional excesses. But never too harshly and always for her own good. Always honest and open, never underhanded or manipulative.

To Felicity's surprise, the notion of such firm but loving limits kindled an unaccountable feeling within her. One so unfamiliar that she scarcely recognized it at first.

Could it be…security?

Chapter Fifteen

W as he mad to risk his heart and his future on such a passionate, headstrong woman? Thorn asked himself the next day as Felicity's carriage sped north, past the cotton and wool milling towns that huddled along the ragged edge of the wild Yorkshire moors.

Against his better judgment, he'd let Felicity persuade him to pass the night at Trentwell before continuing their journey. The sly minx had cajoled him into staying with veiled promises of lovemaking in one of Trentwell's enormous beds. During the few minutes it had taken her to steal down the gallery and into his guest chamber, however, Thorn had fallen so deeply asleep she hadn't been able to rouse him.

He found that all but impossible to imagine.

Yet something—her scent, perhaps, or the warmth of her body pressed against his—had trickled deep into his dormant mind. That sweet, twilight awareness of her had soothed and cheered his dreams, granting him the most restful night's sleep he could recall in a very long time.

Evidently it had been less so for her. When they'd rolled away from Trentwell that morning, it had been just light enough for Thorn to make out the dusky smudges beneath her eyes. Later, while they made swift progress through the flat, green plain of Cheshire, he had caught Felicity more than once rubbing her eyes or stifling a yawn.

By the time they passed the smoky sprawl of Manchester, her head had lolled against his arm at increasingly frequent intervals, and her conversation had gradually subsided into deep, easy waves of breath. Now, she rested against him, calm and quiet in repose as she would never be otherwise.

Long suppressed feelings for her surged in Thorn's heart, even as faint eddies of doubt lapped around the edges of his resolve. No matter how much he wanted to, *could* a man like him hope to make a woman like Felicity happy...for as long as they both should live? And if he failed, how unhappy would that make them both?

Thorn couldn't bear to answer either question, so he occupied himself with watching the changing countryside. All the while wishing Felicity would open her eyes, whisper his name and dispel all his foolish, reasonable doubts.

Good Lord, what was that? Thorn started when Felicity's hand, which had lain slack on his thigh, began to move, setting a hot, hungry plague of sensation swarming through his loins.

He glanced down at her face, expecting to find her staring up at him with a naughty little smile, eyes brimming with lusty mischief. Instead, he discovered her still asleep, though her eyes seemed to rove in a restless manner behind her closed lids.

Had he caught her in the midst of a sultry dream? Or was she only feigning sleep to bedevil him?

Suspecting the latter, Thorn slid his own hand between hers and the far too sensitive flesh of his thigh. It helped, but only a little. The sweetly suggestive motion of her fingertips made him ache to remove every barrier between them and his bare skin.

Exercising every ounce of restraint he could summon, Thorn shifted her hand back to her own lap. Though part of him yearned to rest his fingers there and give Felicity a taste of her own provocative medicine, he managed to resist.

In an effort to quench the impish flames of lust that nibbled at him, he forced his mind to the most tedious subjects he could imagine—summing columns of numbers, deciphering the fine print in legal documents, listening to pointless, repetitious gossip in the Pump Room at Bath.

Thorn could just imagine the furious buzz of tattle that would ensue if certain persons there knew what he and Felicity had been up to in recent days. Hard as he tried to dismiss such worries with the contempt they deserved, he could not quite manage it. Shame seeped into his spirit, cold and slimy as a bucketful of slops poured over his head.

What did he have, after all, besides his spotless reputation? No title. No fortune. It behooved him to preserve his good name. Not only for himself, but for the sake of his family.

However, when Felicity's hand returned to provoke his desire anew, propriety fell by the wayside, like an unsecured article of baggage off the boot of the coach. He angled himself around to engage her lips, while his hand fumbled beneath her cloak to brush against her bosom.

With a squeak of surprise, Felicity's eyes flew open. So she'd truly been asleep after all.

"I...didn't mean to wake you." What a fool he felt! "Only, you touched me, and I thought perhaps..."

Felicity salved his embarrassment with a low chuckle as sinfully rich and sweet as a cup of chocolate, a luxury in which Thorn Greenwood seldom indulged. "Pray don't apologize, my dear. Whatever you thought, I can assure you I heartily approve."

Then she shocked Thorn quite speechless by unfastening the buttons on the lap of his breeches and sliding her fingers in to investigate the effect her touch wrought upon him.

"One seldom wakes from such an agreeable dream," she murmured in a husky tone that stirred Thorn almost as much as the feel of her hand, "only to discover it is quite real."

Once she had thoroughly tantalized him, she withdrew her hand from his breeches and launched herself onto his knee. There she commenced to grapple with the buttons of his shirt, all the while kissing him into a frenzy.

"We...really oughtn't carry on like this," he protested in a passing moment of reason, even as his hands made a liar of him by roaming over the tempting curves of her body.

"Why ever not?" Felicity pulled his neck linen loose. "Can you suggest a more diverting pastime to idle away the hours until we reach Preston?"

"Hardly." Well, he couldn't lie, could he? "What if someone sees us, though?"

"You must be joking!" Her breath came in rapid spasms.

After she had kissed him breathless, as well, she

gasped, "The light is too dim and the carriage is going too fast for anyone to mark what we are up to."

"But…your servants…"

The husky chuckle that greeted his suggestion was laced with only a little bitterness. "I can assure you that after serving my husband for so many years, no one in my employ would be so foolish as to stop the carriage and fling open the door without warning."

Thorn recalled the blind eye all her staff had turned on their relationship. It had never occurred to him that they might be accustomed to such goings-on.

Propriety was not his only concern, though.

"There's only so much of this…a man can stand…" he stammered.

His face was probably glowing in the dark like a red-hot coal!

"Is *that* what you're worried over?" Laughter gushed out of her. "Well, there's no need to be. I haven't the least intention of working us up to a pitch of passion, then leaving us unsatisfied."

"But…a carriage…"

She silenced him with the tip of her forefinger pressed against his lips. "I can see we must begin to cultivate your imagination, dear heart."

The next thing Thorn knew, Felicity had hiked up her skirt and straddled his lap, her bare bottom warm and welcoming against the open flap of his breeches. Even if he could have phrased a coherent protest from the seething turmoil of his thoughts, he could never have forced the words out of his constricted throat.

She twined her arms around his neck and began nuzzling her way up his throat. With every delicate kiss and nibble, she tore great gaping holes in Thorn's token resistance. By the time she reached his lips, he could think of nothing but how much he wanted her.

Not only in his arms, but in his life.

All trace of restraint seared away, he cupped one hand beneath the soft rounding of her backside. The other he let dally between her parted legs while he kissed her with the pent-up ardor of a lifetime. When he felt her quiver in the grip of the same delirious need she had excited in him, he let Felicity push his breeches down over his hips. She expelled a shuddering sigh as he buried himself deep within her.

Every sway and lurch of the vehicle sent pleasure pounding through him on heavy hooves.

Thorn braced his feet against the opposite seat and gave himself up to the wildest carriage ride of his life.

A ride whose destination lay but one stop short of heaven itself.

Her late husband had been a skilled and considerate lover. Felicity would have been the last to deny it.

Even after other parts of their marriage had soured, on those increasingly rare nights when Percy had come to her bed, she'd still been able to fool herself into believing he cared for more than her fortune. Indeed, if it had not been so, she might never have felt the need to take a lover after her husband's death.

Yet in the time since she had first made the intimate acquaintance of Thorn Greenwood, she'd discovered a more profound fulfillment than she'd ever hoped to find. It made no sense, for she hadn't chosen him on the basis of an overwhelming attraction. From their very first night, she had tried to hold something of herself aloof. But the harder she had struggled, the deeper she had fallen.

Now, as she clung to him in the darkened carriage, spent in the most delicious way, Felicity knew she had fallen too far to turn back without an effort that might wrench her apart.

Before she could stop it, a sigh seeped out of her.

Thorn stirred. "Is something the matter, dear heart? I...this...didn't hurt you, I hope."

He touched his lips to hers with such tender restraint that she felt quite ashamed of herself for entertaining the slightest doubt about her feelings.

"Hurt me?" She endeavoured to mask her unease with a flippant answer. "No, indeed."

Nor never would he, either. Never hurt her, deceive her or betray her.

"If I had to stifle a cry, just now, it was for the opposite reason, entirely."

"I could say the same." Thorn pressed his cheek against Felicity's hair and inhaled deeply, as if to glut himself on the scent of her. "I fear you will make a wanton of me yet, woman."

Beneath his jesting tone, Felicity sensed a faint note of true disquiet. For reasons she could not fathom, it coaxed her to make her own admission, disguised in banter.

"And I fear I will become a slave to my desire for you."

There, she had voiced her anxiety. The sense of being powerless against her growing love for Thorn Greenwood made her uneasy. She had only known true power and control over her life since she'd become a widow. Before that, she had been prey to such unhappiness. Not even moments of ecstasy like she had just experienced would be worth so harsh a price.

Thorn gave a quiet chuckle, that wrapped around

her heart in a warm embrace. "I vow I shall be a kind master to you, if you'll be a kind mistress to me."

How could she resist such an entreaty? How could she entertain such foolish fears when Thorn held her in his strong, dependable arms? She must find some means to atone for doubting him.

Tell him about the baby, perhaps?

No. She could not yet bring herself to do that, even though she could guess how happy the news would make him.

Once Thorn knew of it, their child would bind her to him even more firmly than marriage vows. Though the prospect of parting from him had pained her, the notion of never being able to part from him, or any man, still haunted her.

The child was his, too! her conscience protested. Thorn had a right to know about it. A right to know that he was not giving up the chance for a family by wedding her.

She would tell him. Just not today—not this moment. Soon, though. Perhaps it could be her wedding gift to him.

Wedding…?

"It does seem a terrible waste…" Her voice gathered fresh conviction with every word. "…to travel all the way from Bath to Gretna Green, then come away with no wedding to show for it."

"All the money you paid for inns and tolls," agreed Thorn. "Not to mention the wear and tear on your carriage to make such a journey."

A silence fell between them, broken only by the muted hoof-beats of the horses, bearing them mile by mile closer to Scotland. Felicity willed them to gallop faster.

Fast enough to outstrip her silly doubts.

"Do you mean what I hope you mean, Felicity?" Thorn swallowed hard. "Or am I only dreaming?"

She lifted her face to him, unable to see more than a shadow in the darkness, yet somehow conscious of the dear, hopeful light in his eyes.

"The way I was dreaming a little while ago, you mean?" she asked. "Then woke to find it true?"

"Those are the best kind of dreams...when they're good."

"Shall I pinch you?" She let her hand rove down beneath his open waistcoat and unbuttoned shirt. "To make certain you're awake?"

"Oh, no you don't!" He flinched from her touch, his body shaking with soundless laughter. "I'm prepared to take it on faith."

"Does that mean you won't protest if I haul you in front of a parson when we reach Scotland?"

"Not a peep." He cupped her face in his large capable hands and drew it toward him for a deep, delicious kiss to seal the bargain.

"Do you suppose we'll be able to prevail upon Oliver and your sister to stand as our witnesses?" Felicity asked Thorn the next evening as their carriage drove the last few miles to the border town of Carlisle. "After we've forbidden *them* to get married there, I mean?"

Thorn shifted in his seat and flexed his shoulders to relieve the tightness in them. He'd be pleased to stretch his limbs soon and still more pleased to put these long days of driving behind them.

"They just might, you know," he said. "Especially if we make it clear we don't mean to prevent them *ever* marrying. We only ask that they slow down a little and make certain this is what they both want.''

Thorn could picture it all. "I'm certain that, given her choice, my sister would vastly prefer a nice church wedding in Lathbury with lots of guests and a pretty, new dress to a slapdash affair in Gretna Green.''

Realizing how that must sound, he began to stammer out an apology. "Not that *our* wedding will be a slapdash affair…it's just…''

There was something less than respectable about a Scottish elopement. It smacked of fortune-hunting. He'd assured Felicity he cared more for her than he cared what gossip would say about him, and that was true. But it didn't mean he'd ceased to care about his reputation altogether.

"I believe I know what you mean,'' said Felicity. "I've had one fine wedding with many guests. But I'd far rather have a quick, quiet ceremony in Gretna Green *with you.*''

"You're right, of course, my dear.'' All the same, he couldn't help feeling that if she'd been proud of their connection, Felicity might have favored a more public wedding.

Perhaps she guessed something of what troubled him. "At least taking part in our wedding would give Ivy and Oliver a valid excuse for having run off to Gretna. If people are busy gossiping about you and me, no one will have a word of censure to spare for them.''

Thorn could not resist the temptation to rally her a little. "That sounds like an unselfish scheme if ever I heard one.''

"A momentary lapse, I assure you!''

Though he doubted she could see him, Thorn shook

his head. "If I didn't know you better than that, my dear, I should not deserve to marry you."

An expectant pause.

"You deserve far better than me." All trace of laughter had deserted her voice.

He gathered her close to him. "Come now, you can't mean that."

"I do, though." She sounded more like a plaintive child than like the vibrant, forceful woman who had captured his heart.

Thorn doubted many people got to see this side of her character. He felt privileged to be among that few...possibly the only one.

"Nonsense." He had comforted and jollied his sisters out of similar moods over the years. He knew what to say. "You're tired out from all this—we both are. Things will look better tomorrow. See if they don't."

"Perhaps..."

"Of course they will. You can lie in as late you want tomorrow while I keep watch for coaches coming up London Road heading for Eden Bridge. Once we've rounded up Ivy and Oliver, we'll both be able to breathe easier."

"What if we fail, though? What if they've been a jump ahead of us the whole time? That seems to have been the way of it ever since we left Bath."

Much as he wanted to reassure her, Thorn could not gainsay the possibility. "Don't let's borrow trouble. We'll deal with that if we have to, but on a full stomach and after a sound night's sleep. Yes?"

He felt her head move in a tentative nod.

"Very sensible. I need a sensible man like you to keep me on an even keel."

"And I need an exciting woman like you to shake me out of my comfortable rut."

"We are good for each other, aren't we, Thorn?" She turned her face up to him. "Even though we seem so much at odds?"

The sweet moist warmth of her breath tickled his side whiskers. And made the fine hairs on the back of his neck raise in a faint chill.

"We *are* good for each other. We will be happy together." Surely if he infused his voice with sufficient conviction, Felicity would believe it...and so would he.

Chapter Sixteen

"Any sign of them yet, Ned?" asked Thorn as he emerged from the inn on Carlisle's market square after a restless night's sleep.

So many long days trundling north in Felicity's carriage had left him with a subtle but unshakeable sense of that movement. He'd kept waking up, expecting to find himself back on the road. Once awake, he'd had a devil of a time falling back to sleep. Despite his assurances to Felicity last evening, he could not help worrying that they might fail in their task.

This was, after all, their last decent chance to intercept Ivy and young Armitage before the young couple reached Gretna Green.

"No carriage traffic to speak of at all, Mr. Greenwood." Ned rose from the bench by the inn's front door. The brisk breeze blowing up Solway Firth had nipped his face to a rosy glow, and he had his hands jammed into the pockets of his coat. "A market cart or two and a couple of fellows on horseback. Nobody who could have been Master Oliver and your sister."

His report completed, the young footman failed to stifle a vast yawn.

"Glad to hear it." Thorn glanced back down the main road that led to Penrith. "If they haven't gotten ahead of us, which I doubt, they'll likely turn up sometime today. Now, go tuck into a good breakfast, lad, then get some rest. Or the other way around, whichever you feel greater need of."

"Bed first, I think, sir." The lad rubbed his eyes as he headed for the door. "Good luck on your watch."

"Thank you, Ned." Thorn beckoned him back. "And thank you for your patience and discretion in all this. Lady Lyte and I are most grateful."

"Glad to help, sir," replied the young footman, lowering his voice when two men who looked to be merchants of the town passed by. "I know how I'd feel if it was my sister."

As he headed off to bed, Ned muttered to himself, "Though not if she was with Master Oliver, of course."

Thorn wished he could be so sure.

On the few occasions they'd met, he had found Oliver Armitage a good sort of fellow, though rather preoccupied with his studies. Still, the young man must have more on his mind than books and experiments or he never would have run off to Gretna Green with a lively lass like Ivy.

From his own experience in the past few days, Thorn had reason to know passions could run high between a man and woman pent up for long hours in close contact.

Remembering how he and Felicity had made love in her carriage on the road to Preston, Thorn felt his face burn with a heat too intense for the raw spring breeze to cool. Until he'd met Felicity Lyte, Thorn had never been shocked by his own behavior.

He did not care for the sensation.

Perhaps he could tolerate being the butt of gossip and even accept a future without children, if these were the price he must pay for making Felicity a permanent part of his life. But his feelings for her shook up his cautious, methodical nature to the very foundation.

Part of him found the change as exhilarating as that wild ride into Preston. Another part feared the loss of control over his own actions. Where might it end? His father's imprudence with money had cost their family dearly.

Thorn shook his head to clear it of fatigue and his preoccupation with Felicity.

A small coach, drawn by a single pair of horses was approaching up London Road. It looked very much like the one Ivy and her beau had left behind when they'd slipped away from Trentwell.

Thorn stepped out into the street and flagged it down.

"Here now," cried the driver, "what's all this, then?"

Ignoring the man's inquiry, Thorn strode to the door of the coach and wrenched it open.

A young woman, who bore absolutely no resemblance to Ivy, screamed and shrank back into her seat.

Before Thorn could stammer an apology, a ruddy-faced young man with ginger side whiskers demanded, "What is the meaning of this, sir?"

"I beg your pardon!" If he'd woken to find himself sleepwalking stark naked in the market square, Thorn could not have been more thoroughly humiliated. "I thought this carriage belonged to friends of mine. Please accept my apologies."

The girl appeared ready to swoon. The young man looked far more vexed than the incident called for. Understanding hit Thorn with the force of a runaway carriage.

This young pair were bound for Gretna, too.

He'd probably given them the fright of their lives, thinking some of her relations had apprehended them at the last moment.

Thorn's mortification turned to amusement, which he fought to suppress. He continued to beg their pardon while the young man glared at him and called for the coachman to drive on.

As he watched the hired rig continue on up the square to where the road split into three separate streets, the bells of nearby Carlisle Cathedral chimed the early hour.

Shaking his head, Thorn muttered to himself, "This is going to be a damn long day."

A voice far too hearty for so early in the morning boomed out behind him. "Begging yer pardon, sir. Would ye be expecting a party this way?"

Thorn turned to find the inn's porter regarding him with the unmistakeable glint of avarice in his deep-set eyes.

"Expecting?" Thorn shrugged. "Hoping? Very much so."

Though he was not naturally inclined to take strangers into his confidence, what did he have to lose by it?

"Been chasing my sister and her young man all the way from Bath. I believe we overtook them somewhere between here and Staffordshire. I was rather hoping to head them off before they cross the border."

The man nodded over Thorn's account as if he'd

heard it every day for many years. Given where he worked, perhaps he had.

"I shouldn't flag down every coach that comes up the London Road if I was ye, sir." The porter screwed up his mouth to express his disapproval. "Could land yerself in no end of trouble."

"I'd prefer not to if I could help it," Thorn assured the man. "But it wouldn't have been worth my time coming all this way just to let them drive past into Scotland."

The porter gave a sympathetic nod. "So it would be worth a little something to ye, would it, sir, to have any northbound coaches stop for a moment for ye to have a look in at the passengers?"

"More than a little. Would such an accommodation be possible?"

Flashing Thorn a broad grin, the porter tapped the side of his nose with his forefinger.

"Folks coming to Gretna is a flourishing trade in these parts, squire. Everybody makes his little bit off it some way or other. It's mostly all the same lads drives this last leg of the trip up from the south, ye see. Year in, year out, we've got to know each other."

"I see," replied Thorn, for he was beginning to.

"A signal from me," continued the porter, "and the drivers will stop long enough for me to slip 'em two-pence or fourpence."

"Provided by me?"

"You do see, squire!" The porter beamed at him like a society hostess over her protegé. "While they're stopped, you have a quick glance in the window to see if you recognize anybody. If not, the coach drives on with none inconvenienced or any the wiser."

What would old Lord Hardwick say if he knew

what commerce his Marriage Act had generated here in the north? Thorn wondered.

Spin like a top in his grave, no doubt.

"And your fee for performing this signal service, my good fellow?"

"Guinea a day, flat," said the porter, "plus half again of whatever I pay out to the drivers. Most folks call it a bargain."

Thorn's eyes widened. "You must prevent a very good class of elopement."

"I do, squire, and proud of it." The man's smug countenance testified to that. "The niece of a peer, just last week. A Derbyshire heiress not long before that."

"My sister is not of that rank." Thorn commenced to empty his pockets. "Except to me. It would be worth every penny of that sum to secure her future happiness."

As he began to empty his pockets, he heard a vehicle clattering its way up the road behind him.

The porter gave a cheery wave of his hand. The carriage slowed, just as he had said it would, stopping long enough for the porter to snatch twopence from Thorn's palm and toss it up to the coachman.

The carriage door opened a crack and a querulous voice demanded, "Why have we stopped? What's going on, driver?"

Inside the coach, Thorn spied an elderly couple and a middle-aged woman.

The coachman winked at the porter as he called down to his passengers, "Just about to inquire which is the road to Kirkhampton, gov'ner."

"Humph! A queer thing to hire out as a driver if you don't know the roads." The carriage door slammed shut.

The porter made a show of providing directions, then the coach moved on.

"I take it neither of those ladies answered to yer sister's description, sir?"

"They did not." Thorn poured a jingling stream of copper and silver coins into the porter's large open palm. "But it provided a fine demonstration of your service."

He nodded toward the money. "That sum won't last long if any amount of traffic passes this way before I locate my sister. I can go get more, but…"

Would Felicity approve such an expenditure? And would this be the first of many occasions when he'd be obliged to go cap in hand to his wife for money?

True, her property would be considered his, by law, once they married. Yet Thorn knew he would never think of it as such. And he would never be comfortable with the disparity between their fortunes.

"Worried the young lady will pass by while yer gone?" asked the porter, ever helpful…for a price. "Don't give it another thought, sir. Tell me what she looks like, and I'll see to it any coach carrying a passenger of her description tarries until ye get back. Horses going a bit lame and such."

"Very well." Thorn glanced around the square and back down London Road. He could see no sign of anything but local market traffic. "You shouldn't have any great trouble spotting her, she's the kind of young lady men notice."

He gave the porter a brief description.

"She does sound a beauty, sir, no mistake. Wish I could say the same of most of the ladies I see passing through to Gretna. That Derbyshire heiress, now…"

The porter made a face and shuddered. "No doubt she had a pretty purse to make up for her face and figure."

The jest hit Thorn with the force of a physical blow as he thought of such things being said about he and Felicity.

"I've a word of advice for ye, sir," continued the porter, "and no extra charge for it, neither. Once ye've got young missy back, ye'd best marry her off to some good steady fellow, so ye won't be back here in six months' time doing this all over again."

"Sound advice, indeed," agreed Thorn. "I'll just go fetch that money before the traffic gets busy."

The man had a point, he decided as he fought his way up the stairs to Felicity's room against a tide of departing guests. A serious-minded young man like Oliver Armitage might seem an odd choice for his headstrong, vivacious little sister, but she could do far worse.

Better Armitage than the kind of charming wastrel Thorn had often feared Ivy might take up with.

"Any sign of Oliver and your sister?" Felicity held her dressing gown closed with one hand as she unbolted the door to admit Thorn.

"Not yet. If they spent the night in Penrith, it could be a while before we see them." He shifted from foot to foot, fumbling with his hat. "I'm sorry to wake you."

"I was stirring before you arrived," she lied. "Thinking of getting dressed and ringing for some breakfast, as a matter of fact."

"You should have a nice, late lie-in." Thorn glanced toward the bed. "Try to catch up on your sleep while you have the opportunity."

And go back to that awful dream she'd been having? One in which she was a fox with a luxurious red tail being driven by a pack of hounds into a narrow gorge from which there could be no escape? No, indeed!

"I've had all the sleep I care to." She drew closer to Thorn. His presence, his very scent, gave her an illusion of safety she needed just then. How much safer would she feel wrapped in the sanctuary of his arms?

"I might be persuaded to return to bed, though." She trailed one end of her dressing gown sash along the sleeve of his coat. "If I had some congenial company…"

He glanced toward the bed again with a thinly veiled expression of horror, as if it was the trap she'd barely escaped in her dreams. "A…tempting invitation, but I can't just now. Someone needs to keep an eye out for Ivy and your nephew."

Though she endeavored to hide her disappointment, Thorn must have perceived it.

Lifting one hand to her face, he stroked her cheek with the backs of his fingers. "Soon enough I'll be making a nuisance of myself so often you'll grow tired of my company. You should enjoy this last opportunity to have the bed all to yourself."

Though he spoke in a tone of gentle jest, it seemed to Felicity that he was in greater earnest than he might realize.

"I shall never grow tired of you, my dearest." She raised her own hand, pressing his more firmly against her face. "The more I come to know you, the better I love you. If it keeps up, I shall be quite besotted presently."

"That will make two of us." Thorn chuckled. "So treacly sweet, we'll make all our acquaintances quite bilious."

Felicity felt her grip tighten on Thorn's hand. If only she could keep him close by until they had made their vows before some Scottish clergyman, blotting out all her misgivings with hot passion or fond repartee.

"Once we return to Bath as man and wife, we must pay a call on Weston St. Just and amuse ourselves watching him strive to hold his gorge!"

As they laughed together, imagining it, Thorn bent toward Felicity and she raised her face to him. Their lips met in a kiss of infinite restraint that still managed to send ripples of urgent desire romping through her flesh.

After a long, sweet moment, Thorn stirred and pulled away with obvious reluctance.

"I should return." He sounded winded, as though from a fast run. "To keep watch for Ivy and Oliver. Before there is a line of carriages backed up all the way to Penrith."

Felicity touched her forefinger to her lips. "Pay me one more small penalty, and I'll release you."

"Penalty?" Thorn shook his head. "Say rather a prize. One I'm always more than eager to claim."

Claim it he did, this time with less restraint, as though the banked fire of his passion for her was consuming his self-control.

Again he pulled away from her, this time with greater force, as if it required more energy to resist.

His words confirmed Felicity's impression. "I must go. While I still can."

When the door had closed hard behind him, she

wilted against the wall and let out a long tremulous breath.

It would be all right. Enough delicious moments like this would be worth whatever price she must pay for them.

The door thrust open again, setting Felicity's heart in a dizzy dance. Thorn must have changed his mind about a warm, rumpled morning tryst with her.

It seemed as though a different man reentered the room from the one who had just left. His facade of fond assurance had crumbled away, leaving behind a manner so ill-at-ease it was almost painful to watch.

"You have a lamentable effect upon me, my lady." His gaze made a restless circuit of the room, looking at anything but her. "You made me forget the very reason I came here.

"I...that is..." Thorn hesitated as though he couldn't force the words out.

Would a sound clout on the back help? Felicity wondered.

At last, like a cork loosed from a bottle of champagne, the words burst free in a rush. "I need to ask you for some money."

More came tumbling out after them. Some convoluted explanation about the inn's porter...? Stopping carriages...?

Money? Was that all?

"Why, of course, my dear." Felicity rummaged through her bags until she found her reticule. "Take whatever you need, by all means."

She tossed it to Thorn, who appeared more flustered than ever as he tried to juggle her reticule and his hat, only to end up dropping both to the floor.

As Felicity looked on, caught between amusement

and exasperation, he mastered himself enough to pick them up again and extract a handful of large coins from her reticule.

"Thank you." He passed the purse back to her with a look of shame that could not have been much greater if he'd stolen the money. "This should be more than sufficient. I trust the investment will prove worthwhile. Once I have Ivy and your nephew in my custody, I'll bring them here so we can talk about what's to be done."

Jamming the hat onto his head and the money into his pocket, Thorn withdrew again.

Felicity considered going back to bed, but decided against it. Without the diversion of Thorn's company, she would have nothing to keep unsettling dreams at bay.

Besides, she did not want to be caught in her dressing gown for their confrontation with Ivy and Oliver. Her suitably dignified appearance might help impress upon the young pair the imprudence of their actions.

To that end, the interview called for the one dark gown she'd brought with her from Trentwell, Felicity decided. And perhaps the stylish turban shot with gold threads. Pleased with her choice, she set her reticule on the bed and began to remove the necessary garments from her luggage.

She smiled to herself remembering how Thorn had fumbled the bag, as if it was a hot potato. A further thought, chasing fast on the heels of the first, wiped the smile from her lips.

This time tomorrow morning, Thorn would not need to ask her for money. Every particle of her property would be his, by law. If she wanted or needed funds, she would have to apply to her husband.

For the first time since her spell of sickness in Gloucester, a powerful wave of nausea gripped Felicity's stomach.

She barely reached the basin in time.

Chapter Seventeen

The porter raised his hand to flag down another carriage and give away more of Felicity's money.

Thorn strove to keep his hopes from rising. Or falling.

Who would have guessed that this early an hour on a spring morning would have seen so much traffic through the heart of this northern town? A surprising fraction obviously were *not* lovers heading across the Scottish border for a speedy wedding against the wishes of their families.

Thorn had lost count of the number of vehicles he'd peered into, praying to catch a glimpse of red-gold curls, blue-green eyes and a pair of disarming dimples. Aside from all the other considerations, it had been several days since he'd laid eyes on his little sister. He wanted to satisfy himself that she was safe and well.

As the coach slowed, Thorn ventured a glance toward the passengers. One that he hoped might be mistaken for casual curiosity.

No doubt it would be some respectable Scottish matron, returning home from a visit to her daughter in the Lake Country. Or a man of business bound for one of the prosperous border ports.

Instead, Thorn found himself gaping at the back of a young woman perched upon the knee of a young man. The pair were wrapped in a particularly ardent embrace. Natural discretion set Thorn's face blazing and made him avert his eye.

As he had a great many times that morning, the porter tossed a coin to the coachman and prepared to nod him on his way.

Just then, a memory stirred to life in Thorn's mind, of Ivy showing off a new bonnet she'd purchased with some money their wealthy brother-in-law had given her. Though Thorn seldom took particular notice of women's apparel, he thought Ivy's matched that of the girl in the carriage.

It was enough to make him put modesty aside and look again.

This time the young man's hand had lowered from the young woman's nape. A cluster of golden-copper curls peeped from beneath the back of her bonnet. Dismay at how close he'd come to missing them made Thorn wrench the carriage door open with more force than he'd intended.

It also turned his greeting to his lost sister into a gruff demand.

"I suggest you take your hands off my sister, Mr. Armitage!"

The way they started and the bewildered countenances they turned upon him nearly compensated Thorn for everything he had been through since the night he'd discovered Ivy missing from Bath.

"Thorn!" The little minx had the impertinence to

round on him as though *he* was the one in the wrong. "What are you doing here?"

Fortunately for Ivy, her brother was not a man disposed to violence. Otherwise, he might have tossed her over his knee then and there and given her young backside a thumping she'd have cause to remember.

"Spoken as if you had no idea." He settled for seizing her by the arm and pulling her out of the carriage.

Every qualm of anxiety he had felt on her behalf over the past few days struck him afresh. "Have you made it your sworn aim in life to turn me gray-headed before I'm forty?"

His righteous wrath seemed to awaken some proper sense of shame in his sister at last. Ivy's pert little chin began to tremble and her luminous blue-green eyes looked ready to gush forth a torrent of repentant tears.

"Pray don't be angry with your sister, Mr. Greenwood," a manly young voice bade Thorn.

Oliver Armitage unfolded his lanky frame from the coach and brought his hands to rest on Ivy's shoulders in a heartening, protective gesture. "The responsibility is mine."

The lad could hardly have uttered any words more apt to win Thorn's approval, yet he did not soften the severity of his tone. These two needed to understand just how much distress their little escapade had caused him and Felicity.

"I have plenty of outrage to go around, Armitage." He shot the young man a stern glance, but was secretly pleased when Oliver did not quail before it. "You'll come in for your share, never fear."

Thorn looked from Ivy to Oliver and back again, unable to guess whether the young lovers had consummated their marriage in advance. "I'm hardly surprised to discover my sister up to such high jinks, but I had credited you with better sense."

Throwing off her manner of proper remorse, Ivy twisted out of her brother's grip and scowled at him with the kind of bold defiance he would never have expected from her...until today.

"I will not permit you to speak to my fiancé in that tone, Thorn. Kindly apologize at once."

Of all the impudence! The little baggage had led him a chase the length of the country. And now that she'd been fairly caught she made it sound as though he had no right to be vexed with her.

"That young man is not your fiancé," Thorn growled, "and I will speak to him in any tone—"

He suddenly noticed how many curious stares their confrontation had drawn. Not wanting to make himself more of a spectacle than he had already, Thorn struggled to curb his outrage.

Of all the things he expected Ivy to say next, he did not anticipate the question she posed. "Is Lady Lyte with you?"

What difference did that make? Still, Thorn seized the opportunity to continue their discussion away from prying eyes.

"She is." He nodded toward the inn. "Let's go inside and see what she has to say to the pair of you."

He bowed to the porter to acknowledge his assistance, then strode through the door of the inn and headed up the stairs to Felicity's room. Now and then he glanced back to make certain Ivy and Oliver were following him.

They were—clinging to each others' hands and looking for all the world as if they were being led away to summary execution. As often happened when he was called upon to discipline his little sister, Thorn's ire began to soften.

After all, if these two hadn't run off together, he would not be on the brink of marrying the woman who had captured his heart. That favor deserved a little forbearance, did it not?

The sound of footsteps coming up the stairs put Felicity in mind of the night Thorn had barged into her town house. Could it have been less than a week ago? With all that had happened, it felt as though every day of a month had passed.

The footsteps halted outside her door and a firm but quiet knock sounded. She was not the least surprised to hear Thorn's voice. "Lady Lyte, I have my sister and your nephew with me. May we come in?"

She sniffed the air, hoping her liberal application of rosewater masked the sour smell of morning sickness. Soon it would no longer matter if her condition became known. But she wanted to share the good news with Thorn before anyone else, and at the time and manner of her own choosing.

"You may enter," she called, rising from her chair by the fire.

Thorn pushed open the door and stood back to let Ivy and Oliver in.

They clasped hands tightly as they stepped into her presence. Oliver looked chastened, yet determined, and Ivy...

The young woman regarded Felicity with an eager curiosity that seemed to divine far more about her situation and feelings than she wished to reveal. In an effort to steady herself, Felicity fastened her gaze upon Thorn.

He closed the door behind him, then moved to stand with her so they might confront the younger couple together. Felicity caught his eye and a look of fond reassurance passed between them.

"It worked!" cried Ivy, hurling herself upon them. "I knew it would. I just knew it!"

Had Thorn's sister gone mad? Felicity wondered as the girl kissed her on the cheek then threw her arms around Thorn. What had Ivy known? What had worked?

The explanation came in a breathless, giggly tumble. "I told Oliver if the pair of you were cooped up together in a carriage all the way to Scotland, you'd soon realize how much you cared for one another."

Ivy looked from Thorn to Felicity, her young face the very picture of gloating triumph. "And you did, didn't you?"

As the truth crashed down on Felicity, it felt as though a rough hand had thrust itself inside her and clenched around her stomach. She wrested herself out of Ivy's impulsive embrace, in part because she feared she might be violently ill all over the young woman's gown.

And also because she could not bear Ivy's touch or Thorn's nearness. They seemed to swarm around her, forcing their will upon her. Like a pack of hounds, driving the desperate fox to her doom.

"Do you mean to say you *planned* all this?" The words retched out of her, sour as bile.

Did she even need to ask? It should have been obvious to her from the first. This was the only explanation that answered all the questions and inconsistencies that had been nagging at her since the night she'd left Bath.

How could she have been so blind? How could she have let herself be manipulated this way...again?

"Did you not have any intention of marrying my nephew?" she demanded.

"Not at first," Ivy admitted in a cheerful chirp that made Felicity want to cuff some sense into the girl. "It all started as a ruse to bring the pair of you together, but one thing led to another...and..."

A ruse to bring the pair of you together. The words rang like a taunt in Felicity's head. A trap had been laid for her, and she'd bolted straight into it. Had the past taught her nothing about being wary? Or was she too stupid to learn?

Her horrified gaze met Thorn's. A scatterbrained creature like Ivy Greenwood could never have contrived a scheme like this on her own. "You were in on this, as well, weren't you? Did you put them up to it?"

Something hard and cold reared in Thorn's gaze, confirming her worst suspicions.

She backed away from him, only to find herself trapped against the hearth. "I can't believe I was gullible enough to let you twist me 'round your finger this way."

Thorn pushed past his sister. "I knew no more of this than you did, I swear." He tried to take her in his arms. "Surely you can't believe I'd stoop to such a thing?"

How desperately she longed to believe him and to feel safe in his arms again. To plan a future together. But the safety and the future Thorn Greenwood offered were both lies of the worst kind.

"Keep your distance." She shrank back from his touch, more afraid of her own traitorous yearning to believe him, than of the man himself. "Don't touch me!"

With all her considerable will, Felicity struggled not to betray her weakness. But as she looked from Ivy Greenwood to Thorn, she saw instead the faces of the disagreeable governesses of her youth and her grandfather. Looking from Thorn back to his sister, she saw her philandering late husband and his top-lofty mother.

Only when her gaze fell on the dear, trusted face of Oliver Armitage did her mounting panic lessen.

"I don't hold you to blame for any of this, my dear boy. We have been abominably used, both of us."

She extended her hand to him and with it a plea. "Just take me home...please."

The lean planes of her nephew's face canted at sharp angles, the way she had often seen when he puzzled some scientific enigma. Felicity saw something more, too. A pained perplexity that sometimes took hold of him when he could not reconcile two facts that both appeared correct, yet flatly contradicted one another.

"Don't be angry with Ivy," he begged his aunt. "She only wanted to make the pair of you happy."

Oliver glanced toward Thorn. "And her brother knew nothing about it, of that I can assure you."

Felicity shook her head. For such a learned young man, her nephew had much to discover about the world and its deceit.

Before she could cajole any sense into him, Oliver spoke again, in a more determined tone than she had ever heard him use before.

"In any case, I cannot take you home just now. Ivy

and I mean to wed.'' Oliver glanced toward Thorn. ''Before nightfall, if I can persuade her brother to give us his blessing.''

Bad enough that the Greenwoods had tricked her in this way, but to use her dear Oliver as the means to advance their plan outraged Felicity even more.

Her nephew flashed her an encouraging smile. ''I know this has all fallen out like a comedy of errors, but that will not signify if we can give it a happy ending. Won't you and Thorn come with us to Gretna and make it a double wedding?''

To think how recently she herself had entertained such a possibility. Now, the notion made Felicity sick with disgust.

''You stupid boy!'' she cried. ''Can't you see Ivy Greenwood is just like all the others—after you for *my* money?''

If she had descended upon him and soundly boxed his ears, Oliver could not have looked more dismayed. Though she reproached herself for being so harsh with him, Felicity would not take back what she'd said. For his own good, the boy must be made to understand.

A swift glance at Ivy restored Oliver's composure. ''All evidence to the contrary, I believe Ivy loves me, Aunt Felicity. And I know I love her.''

All evidence to the contrary? Felicity could scarcely believe she'd heard him utter such words. What scientist worth his salt ignored a mountain of contrary evidence?

Oliver turned to Thorn. ''Will you please permit your sister to marry me, sir? I promise to do everything in my power to make her happy.''

Was she in the midst of another nightmare? Felicity asked herself. If only it could be. But life seemed bent on teaching her that disappointment, frustration and betrayal were the true way of the world. Trust, security and happiness were no more than ridiculous dreams.

Ivy Greenwood grasped Thorn's hand and beseeched him with her winsome eyes. "Oh, please, Thorn, please say yes! Don't do to me what Father did to Rosemary by forbidding her to wed Merritt."

"Well..." Thorn wavered, just as Felicity had known he would. "...if the two of you have made it all this way without killing one another..."

Felicity could not keep silent a moment longer. "I don't believe this! Don't tell me you mean to indulge this silly whim of theirs, after everything we went through to stop them?"

Unless her worst suspicions were correct and this whole journey to Gretna had been nothing but a conspiracy to lure her into marriage?

Staring Thorn down, she offered him one final chance to refute her doubts. "If you ever had the least genuine feeling for me, Hawthorn Greenwood, you'll forbid this match and fetch your sister back to Barnhill, where she belongs."

For an instant some flicker in his eyes made her hope he might yield.

Then that flicker went out, and Thorn regarded her with a look of wistful regret, as if *she* had wronged *him.* "If you have the least feeling for me, Felicity, you wouldn't ask me to sacrifice my sister's happiness."

He put his arm around Ivy's shoulder, glancing from her to Oliver. "If the pair of you are set on getting married, I will give the bride away."

Felicity flinched. "You are all in league against me, I see."

Her eyes prickled with the sting of a thousand nettles. Whether they were tears of anger or hurt, she would not give anyone in this room the satisfaction of seeing them fall.

"Very well, then." She prayed her voice would not break. "If you persist in this folly, Oliver, I shall have no choice but to cut you off without a penny."

It was more than a threat calculated to deter him. If she must fall back on her original plan, to sever ties with Thorn and retire to the country to raise her child, Felicity knew she could not afford to maintain contact with her nephew if he threw his lot in with the Greenwoods. "See if *that* does not change Miss Greenwood's inclination to marry you."

Though Oliver tried to appear confident, he could not hide a passing qualm of doubt from the woman who had been like a mother to him for so many years. Ivy looked positively stricken by the news that Oliver would lose his grand expectations if he married her. Thus confirming every ugly suspicion Felicity had ever entertained about her.

"May we have a few moments' privacy to talk this over?" Ivy asked.

The young woman's subdued manner and plaintive tone touched Felicity's heart in spite of her determination to resist. She could not afford to be duped by whatever show of sentiment the Greenwoods might now stage for her benefit.

"Take as long as you like." Felicity gathered up her wrap, gloves and reticule as she made her way to the door. "I shall wait in the carriage for ten minutes. If Oliver does not join me by then, I will return to Bath without him and instruct my solicitor to write him out of my will."

While she issued her ultimatum, Felicity kept her gaze averted from Thorn, fearful of the power he wielded over her heart, power he might not scruple to use.

As Lady Lyte shut the door behind her with firm finality, Thorn struggled to rally his wits. He felt almost as if he'd been thrown, once again, from a fast-moving horse into a cold, dark river.

He had been galloping toward a happy future with everything coming neatly into place. Felicity had agreed to marry him. They had succeeded in recovering Ivy and Oliver. Then, without any kind of warning, it had all shattered around him.

With cold loathing in her eyes, Felicity had accused him of conspiring with his sister to trick her into marriage. That the woman he loved could believe him capable of such infamous conduct stung Thorn Greenwood to the depths of his dutiful heart.

Looking from his sister to Oliver Armitage, he struggled to find words that might make sense of what had just happened, for they appeared as bewildered as he. Part of him wanted to thank Ivy for what she had tried to do for him, while another part could not help wishing she had minded her own sweet, meddlesome business.

He was too stunned by this sudden reversal to say anything coherent, Thorn decided. He'd already wasted one minute of the ten Lady Lyte had granted her nephew. Once Oliver made his decision, there would be time for Thorn and his sister to talk, if either of them could bear it.

With a sigh and a rueful shake of his head, Thorn

left the room and wandered downstairs, muffled in a thick daze of regret.

As he paused on the landing just out of sight of the posting room, he overheard Lady Lyte settling her bill with the innkeeper.

"Have my servants summoned at once," she ordered, "and have my luggage brought down. Instruct the hostlers to ready my carriage for the road. I must leave without delay."

A tidy sum must have changed hands, above the usual reckoning, for Thorn heard the innkeeper bellow Lady Lyte's instructions, followed by the sound of scurrying feet.

He told himself to stay put or to steal out the front door and go wander the market square until Felicity had departed Carlisle. He told himself pleading with her would do no good, only further erode his self-respect.

Unfortunately, his feet were not well under control. Before Thorn knew what was happening, they bore him down the final dozen steps and face to face with the woman he had hoped to wed in a few hours' time.

One stern glance from Thorn sent the innkeeper bustling off, issuing orders left and right.

"Please, Felicity." As he spoke, Thorn felt his knees stiffen. He'd gone down on them to this woman once before. He would never do it again. "Won't you take a few minutes to reconsider? You stand to lose as much by this as any of us. More, perhaps."

He tried to convince himself that he would not lose anything that had ever truly been his. Nor anything he truly wanted.

But when he looked in her eyes and saw beauty unmarred by the anger and anguish that haunted them,

Thorn remembered every ray of sunshine Felicity had brought into his life. Every glitter of starlight, every blush of candle glow.

Suddenly, it was all he could do not to bow his head and weep for that loss.

Felicity shrank from him, as if she feared he might strike her. In doing so, she struck him a far more grievous blow.

"Leave me be, Mr. Greenwood." She spoke through clenched teeth. Indeed, every part of her seemed clenched tight against him.

Her heart tightest of all.

"Have you and your sister not done me enough harm, today?"

"I would *never* harm you!" Prudence and propriety cautioned Thorn to keep his voice down, but he refused to heed them. "And my sister is guilty of nothing worse than a generous impulse taken to ill-considered lengths. I told you she fancies herself a matchmaker."

"Ah yes, Lady Cupid." A subtle venom tipped Felicity's words. "If I recall my schoolbooks correctly, Cupid made all sorts of mischief among gods and mortals. I wish your sister had saved her arrows for some other quarry."

"No one *made* us fall in love, Felicity." Why could he not make her see? "Or perhaps I should amend that. You made me love you. And until a short time ago, I believed I had made you love me. All Ivy and Oliver did was throw us together when we would rather have run away from one another."

At that moment Felicity's driver and footman burst into the entry hall. Ned had misbuttoned his livery, and he was rubbing sleep out of his eyes.

Mr. Hixon looked from Thorn to his mistress in some alarm. "Is it true, ma'am? That we're to leave at once? Is something wrong?"

"A great deal is wrong," replied Felicity, "though none of it that you need fret about. We will return south as soon as the horses can be harnessed."

Without a further word to Thorn, she swept out of the room, a pair of baffled servants following in her wake.

Ned paused at the door. "Are you not coming with us, Mr. Greenwood?"

Thorn shook his head. Though he hadn't meant to speak, he heard himself say, "Take care of her for me."

"I'll try, sir," replied the lad. "Lady Lyte doesn't make it easy."

The ghost of a smile tugged at Thorn's lips as he gave a knowing nod.

From off in the distance came the sound of Mr. Hixon calling the young footman.

Still Ned hesitated. "Whatever happened, I'm sorry, sir. For you…and for her."

With that, he hurried away, rebuttoning his coat as he went.

Though Thorn had no intention of doing so, he found himself following. Perhaps at the last instant Felicity would realize precisely what she stood to lose. Particularly if Oliver Armitage held his ground.

If the sight of Thorn served to drive that vital knowledge home, he would do it. Pride be damned.

He strode from the inn, around to the narrow alley that led back to the stables. In that courtyard, beside the watering trough, stood Lady Lyte's fine carriage. The hostlers had just finished harnessing the horses, in record time, no doubt. Another servant came down a flight of outside stairs bearing Lady Lyte's luggage, which he hoisted up to Ned in the boot.

Thorn trained his gaze on Felicity, who sat stiff and still as a wax statue inside the box. Staring straight ahead of her, she gave not the slightest sign that she was aware of Thorn's presence.

Silently he willed her not to let her troubled past destroy her future…and his.

Behind him the bells of Carlisle Cathedral chimed the half hour. Lady Lyte's coachman bid the horses to get moving, and the carriage began to roll.

As it came toward him, Thorn stepped out of the way. Yet he still stood close enough to mark a pair of tears that rolled slowly down Felicity's ivory-sculpted cheeks.

She knew what she was giving up, those tears assured Thorn. But to hold on to it would have cost his lady of fortune more than even she could afford to pay.

Chapter Eighteen

Felicity cursed the two mutinous tears that betrayed her weakness. Not for anything in the world would she expose further vulnerability by letting Thorn see her wipe them away. So she stared straight ahead, refusing to acknowledge either his nearness or the distressing effect he had on her.

But when her carriage passed beyond the old walled town that lay at the heart of Carlisle, and she was certain Thorn could no longer catch a glimpse of her, Felicity's brittle composure crumpled tear by tear.

She tried to convince herself she was weeping for Oliver.

That her nephew would abandon her after all the years of their acquaintance and all she had done for him grieved her sorely. And to have turned his back on her for the sake of a young woman he'd known such a short time spoke ill of Felicity's ability to inspire and hold the loyalty of those she cared for.

Percy. Thorn. Oliver. Would everyone she loved end up hurting her?

"Not my baby!" Felicity vowed, wrapping her arms around her body in a fierce, protective embrace.

Not unless she'd been foolish enough to tell Thorn the truth while he'd held her in his thrall. Then her poor child would have become the rope in a tug of war between its mother and father. Thank heaven she'd had the sense to hold her tongue!

The day wore on as Lady Lyte's carriage rolled south, through a narrow valley nestled between the Rivers Eden and Petteril, both of which cut a swath through the old Forest of Inglewood.

On either side of the road, lines of gray drystone walls separated absurdly small plots of farmland. At intervals, a group of tidy white houses, a small church and sometimes a posting inn would cluster together in a village. Off to the east stretched the crooked gray hump of England's backbone, the Pennines.

It had been too dark to see any of this on the previous night when she and Thorn had driven the final stretch into Carlisle. Now, the peaceful, remote charm of the place settled over Felicity, soothing the turbulent outrage that battered her spirit.

The interior of her carriage suddenly felt so large and still and empty without Thorn's presence.

Not that he had a *presence,* as such. At least not in the vivid, high-flown, effusive style of his friend Weston St. Just. Thorn Greenwood had a character not unlike the Cumberland countryside. Quiet, steady and unassuming, yet rich in true worth, gentle strength and durable virtue. Or so Felicity had come to believe.

How could she have misjudged him so?

Had she misjudged him?

In her solitude, Felicity could not hide from the truth. Perhaps she had not been mistaken in Thorn's character during the long, sweet days and nights they had shared on the journey north. More likely she had judged wrong in those brief anguished moments when old fears had overwhelmed her and a lifetime of bitterly cultivated suspicion had blighted the vulnerable bud of her trust in him.

Though there was no one to see her, Felicity hid her face in her hands. Her shoulders shook with mute, dry sobs that the gentle moisture of tears might have eased. Except she had squandered all her tears in an unworthy cause.

She had believed there could be no worse heartache than to suffer domination or betrayal by those closest to her. But in that, too, she'd been wrong.

It was a far more cruel blow to see her few admirable qualities governed by her faults. And to live with the bitter certainty that she had betrayed her own happiness out of blind, selfish pride.

A sharp pain gripped Felicity deep in the belly, making her cry out. Mr. Hixon must have heard it, for the carriage slowed to a halt almost at once.

Barely a moment later, the carriage door flew open and the young footman peered inside. "What's the matter, Lady Lyte?"

The pain had loosened its clutches on her, leaving her weak and shaken.

"Nothing of consequence, Ned." Felicity tried to sound a good deal better than she felt.

She couldn't be taken ill now. Not so far from home, with no one to care for her but a couple of servants—menservants at that. "Once we reach Trentwell, I shall be right as rain, again. Now be a good fellow and tell Mr. Hixon to drive on."

The boy did not obey her order with the alacrity Lady Lyte expected from her servants. "Begging your pardon, ma'am, but you don't look well."

"Of course I don't look well," Felicity snapped. She could feel another wave of pain beginning to build, and she did not want the young footman to witness it. "Neither do you, to be frank. Who would expect us to after such a long journey in such haste? I order you to leave off pestering me and instruct Mr. Hixon to make haste for Trentwell."

When he continued to hesitate, staring at her with an anxious countenance, she cried, "Now!"

Before Ned could obey, the pain swept her up again like a rat in the powerful jaws of a terrier. Determined not to cry out this time, Felicity bit into her lower lip until she tasted blood, warm and salty.

To her surprise and vast relief, Ned slammed the carriage door shut, and the carriage soon began to move again.

But not for long.

The pain had tamed to a constant, almost bearable pitch when her carriage drew up in front of a red brick coaching inn.

"What is the meaning of this?" she demanded through clenched teeth when her driver and footman edged open the carriage door.

Ned stared at his boots, as if expecting to find the answer to his mistress's question written on the toes. "You're not well, ma'am. You need rest, or a physician, or...something. Mr. Greenwood asked me to look after you, and I don't mean to let him down."

Perhaps the knowledge that Thorn had cared enough for her to bid her servants so should have eased Felicity, but it did not. After the things she had said to him and to his sister, she did not merit such consideration.

Her coachman appeared even more troubled than

the young footman at the prospect of disobeying orders. Yet Mr. Hixon supported young Ned in his well-meant mutiny.

"What you don't need, ma'am, is another long drive. You may dismiss the pair of us without character when you're well again, but until then, we won't budge another mile."

"Very well." She was too sore and spent to argue with them just then. The prospect of resting on a bed, even a hired one far from home, appealed to her.

Felicity managed to pull herself out of the carriage box, but then her strength deserted her and she collapsed into Mr. Hixon's muscular arms.

She must be losing her baby. There could be no other explanation for the location and intensity of the pain.

Yet even as her heart quailed with grief at this final loss, she had to concede it might not be unjust. After the way she had so recently bullied the young man she claimed to love like a son, how she had questioned his choices, threatened his happiness and tried to control his actions, Lady Lyte was forced to acknowledge that she might be too selfish a creature ever to make a satisfactory mother.

"I wish Mother could have seen you today, my dear." Thorn pressed his lips to his sister's brow as they prepared to enter the small parish church in Gretna Green. "I believe she would have been as proud of you as I am."

Ivy's delicate chin trembled, and her usual bright smile crumpled until she looked half her present age. Like a mischievous little girl whose latest prank had gone dangerously awry.

"Dear brother, you mustn't make me blubber right before my wedding, though I'm sure I deserve it."

Thorn fished out a handkerchief and passed it to her, just in case.

Ivy dabbed her nose. "To think I fancied myself a matchmaker! Match-wrecker, more like. After the way I spoilt everything between you and Lady Lyte, you'd have been well within your rights to bundle me home to Barnhill and lock me in the attic until I grew some sense."

"Now, now." With the crook of his finger, Thorn tilted her pert little chin up to its customary cheerful angle. "Locked in the attic at Barnhill? That sounds rather harsh to me. Why not just transport you to Botany Bay and be done with it?"

Ivy rewarded his clumsy jest with a crooked smile. "You really mustn't pretend to take it so well. You'll make me feel far worse than if you lit into me."

"I'll own I'm not pleased over how things fell out between Felicity and me," Thorn admitted, "but that's hardly your fault. I know you had the best intentions for our happiness. If she could believe that you and I plotted this whole scheme as a means to entrap her and her nephew, then perhaps I am well rid of Lady Lyte."

And perhaps if he repeated those words to himself often enough, he might come to believe them.

The spring breeze ruffled Ivy's curls and the Scottish sunshine anointed them with a deep golden lustre. Her blue-green eyes seemed to see past Thorn's proud protest and into his turbulent heart.

"I don't believe that now any more than I did when Oliver and I left Bath. And I feel certain that in her heart of hearts Lady Lyte doesn't believe any of those dreadful things she said about all of us.''

Shaking his head, Thorn treated his sister to an indulgent half smile. ''I wish I could share your boundless optimism, my dear.''

''This is more than just me hoping for the best, Thorn.'' Ivy clasped his hand and looked deep into his eyes, as if willing him to partake of her own ardent conviction. ''Remember how Merritt accused Rosemary of entrapping him when he found out we'd lost our fortune?''

''I'm not likely to forget, am I?'' It had all but torn him in two, watching his beloved sister and his dear friend make each other so unhappy.

''They'd probably never have reconciled if it hadn't been for you,'' Ivy said, ''though I know you'll never own to playing matchmaker.''

Thorn affected his most stern brotherly tone. ''If you have any notions of interceding for me with Lady Lyte, you may put them out of your mind, young lady. I will not have it. Do you hear?''

''I hadn't any thought of the kind!'' Ivy protested. ''You and Lady Lyte must serve as your own matchmakers, Thorn. I know you can if you will only try.''

She nodded toward the sanctuary where her bridegroom awaited her. ''I've done a good deal of growing up this past week, you know. After some of the things Oliver told me about he and his aunt, I feel quite sorry for anyone with a large fortune. How are they to trust that anyone cares for them?''

Felicity had once believed he had no designs on her fortune. Thorn remembered how her admission had touched him.

Ivy gripped his hand harder. Thorn had never seen

his blithe, flighty little sister so passionately earnest. "When Lady Lyte said those things, what she meant was that she doesn't believe she deserves to be loved for herself alone. It's not you she mistrusts—but herself."

He opened his mouth to tell Ivy that she'd let the romantic fancies of her wedding day get the better of her. But before he could get the words out, a swarm of memories unfolded in his mind. The most vivid was less than a day old, as they'd been driving into Carlisle. Thorn could hear Felicity's wistful murmur as clearly as if he'd been holding her in his arms.

"I'm not half good enough for you."

Could what Ivy said be true? Or was he only clinging to a hopeful falsehood because he wasn't man enough to face the truth?

"You must go after her, Thorn." Ivy grasped his hand with such force it almost made him cry out. "I know once she's had a chance to think things through, Lady Lyte will realize she was wrong. And what else is there to do on a long carriage drive *but* think?"

If only his innocent little sister knew! A searing blush crept upward from Thorn's collar.

Just then, Oliver Armitage appeared at the church door with an anxious expression on his lean, clever face.

Ivy glanced toward him, her eyes dancing with devilish glee. "Unless one has congenial company, that is!"

Perhaps the little minx knew almost as much as he did, Thorn decided, remembering the passionate embrace in which he'd caught Ivy and Oliver that morning.

Oliver Armitage cocked an eyebrow at his bride as

if to ask what she found so confoundedly amusing while he was a perfect bundle of nerves. "I feared you'd got a case of cold feet and persuaded your brother to fetch you back home again."

"Never!" The sparkle in Ivy's eyes deepened into a fond glow as she gazed at her husband-to-be. "I was only giving Thorn the benefit of more matchmaking advice...after I swore to myself I'd never play Cupid again."

"Come along then, Lady Cupid." Thorn tucked his sister's hand in the crook of his elbow. "Let's not keep your bridegroom waiting any longer."

Oliver ducked back inside the sanctuary again, while Thorn and Ivy followed at a more decorous pace.

As they reached the church door, Ivy hesitated on the threshold. For a moment Thorn wondered if she was having second thoughts.

His sister glanced up at him. "Will you do something for me, Thorn—as a wedding present?"

How had she known that he regretted having no gift for her on this special day?

"Very well, my dear. Name your favor."

"Go after Lady Lyte, if only to make certain she gets back to Trentwell safely. I know Oliver is worried about her and feels badly for going against her wishes after how good she's been to him."

The little minx! "Hadn't you ought to be thinking about your own romantic connection, now, rather than meddling in mine?"

She turned her sweet imploring gaze upon him, the one Thorn had never succeeded in resisting. "You wouldn't disappoint your little sister on her wedding day, would you?"

Young Armitage would have his work cut out for him managing this one. Thorn rolled his eyes and muttered a grudging, "Very well, then, but only because I'm afraid you'll keep me here arguing at the church door until your poor bridegroom does something desperate."

Ivy squeezed his arm and treated him to the warm doting smile she always wore when she had gotten her way. "You won't be sorry, I promise you. Love has great power, you know, if only we have the courage to use it."

A shiver went through Thorn. Where had he heard those words before?

"Come on, then," whispered Ivy, tugging him forward. "I don't want to keep poor Oliver waiting."

As he made his way to the foot of the altar, with Ivy on his arm, Thorn cast an approving glance around the simple Scottish church. Oliver and Ivy might have eloped to Gretna, but Thorn had insisted on a proper Christian ceremony to bless their union. No hasty, furtive rite performed over an anvil by a "blacksmith priest" for *his* sister!

The vicar cleared his throat and scarcely glanced down at his prayer book as he began to speak the familiar words, "Dearly beloved, we are gathered here in the sight of God and these witnesses to join this man and this woman in holy matrimony."

A short time later, when he asked who gave this woman to be joined in wedlock, Thorn answered, "I do" in a firm, confident voice. Yet he placed Ivy's hand in her bridegroom's with a sense of wistful reluctance.

Why, it seemed just the other day he'd gathered the downy little creature from her cradle and borne her off to say one last goodbye to their dead mother, even though he knew the baby would never remember it.

Here she stood before him, after those swiftly passing years, speaking her vows in a clear melodious voice. A beautiful young woman, sometimes impulsive and frivolous but always kind-hearted and hopeful. He'd done his best for her, ill-equipped though he'd been for the task.

Now he must entrust responsibility for her to a young man who looked anxious and adoring, in equal measure. A young man who, unless Thorn missed his guess, had little experience with the fair sex. Oh well, Ivy had managed to thrive in spite of an unseasoned surrogate father. A green husband would not likely put her off her stride.

A mellow warmth settled deep in Thorn Greenwood's heart, unkindled by any doing of his. As if his mother were trying to tell him, in the only way she could, that she approved the loving, muddled job he'd made of bringing up her baby.

Suddenly, he knew where he had first heard Ivy's naively wise advice about the power of love and the courage to use it. Long ago, when his mother had told him fairy stories of enchanted princesses rescued from the spells that held them captive by the kiss of true love.

Certainly Felicity was everything he had ever imagined in a fairy-tale princess. Had her past woven an evil spell around her heart?

He was no fairy-tale prince, more like the frog in another of his mother's stories. Was it possible he might have the power to break Felicity's curse? After the loathing he'd seen in her eyes and heard in her voice this morning, did he have the courage to try?

Perhaps, but first he had one final brotherly duty to discharge.

Once they'd finished signing the marriage register, while Ivy inquired of the vicar and his wife if they could recommend a good inn, Thorn drew his new brother-in-law aside for a private word. "Be patient with her tonight, my boy, and treat her gently."

It could have been worse, he supposed. At least he hadn't had to repeat the agonizing embarrassment of informing his sister what sharing a bed with her husband would entail. He'd needed a very deep snifter of brandy after his brotherly wedding eve chat with Rosemary.

"I love Ivy very much, Mr. Greenwood," said Oliver…as if he needed to when his face glowed with an ardor almost too bright for Thorn to bear. "You have my word, I'll never do anything to harm or frighten her."

Staring at the church floor as he scuffed it with the toe of his boot, the bridegroom confessed, "Just between us, your sister seems to have more information about the whole process than I do."

Thorn tried to stifle a smile. Apparently Rosemary had done a better job than he at preparing their younger sister for what awaited on her wedding night.

"It sounds as though you're both in good hands, then. Once you get back to England, the two of you are welcome to make your home at Barnhill for as long as you need or wish."

Oliver's eyes shone with gratitude, as though Thorn had just given him the most precious wedding gift in the world. "I promise you, I will do everything in my power to make certain Ivy never regrets her decision to wed me."

"Do that, and I will be proud to call you my brother." Thorn extended his hand, which Oliver clasped in a firm, warm grip.

"Now I must go." Thorn's gaze strayed south, toward Solway Firth and England as he wondered where Oliver's aunt might be by now. "Ivy insists I pursue Felicity and see that she doesn't come to any harm on the journey south…even if I'm obliged to watch over her from a distance."

He still had Weston St. Just's horse and the porter in Carlisle had refunded him enough to finance frugal meals and beds on his journey. Though Thorn chafed a bit at the idea of using Felicity's money, he excused himself on the grounds that he would be doing her a service, whether she wanted it or not.

Ivy appeared at Oliver's side. "You had better get on your way if you're to have any hope of overtaking Lady Lyte."

Catching her brother in a fierce embrace, she kissed him soundly on the cheek. "Take care of yourself, Thorn, and don't worry your head about me." She cast a fond glance at her new husband. "I'm in capable hands."

"So you are." He had better not linger, Thorn warned himself or he might begin to wax maudlin. "Behave yourself and heed your husband. He has a good sensible head on his shoulders, and I can bear witness that you made a vow to obey him."

"Men!" protested Ivy with an impish grin that announced she'd obey her husband only so far as *she* was inclined. "How you all club together! I'm going to make Oliver the most devoted wife you can imagine."

"I believe you shall, dear heart." Thorn quashed a

tiny spark of envy for the happy years he pictured stretching before Ivy and Oliver. ''Now, I mustn't trespass on your honeymoon a moment longer.''

A short while later he was riding toward Carlisle, wondering how he'd let Ivy wind him around her finger yet again.

It had been one thing to follow Felicity from Bath, against her express wishes. At least then he could honestly claim to be acting in the interests of his sister. Even if part of his aim had been to keep watch over Felicity. In his secret heart of hearts, perhaps he'd nursed a faint hope that they might reconcile...for a little while, at least.

This time, for all he might protest otherwise, it would appear as though he was trailing after his former mistress, hoping he could persuade her to give him one last chance. When, in fact, he wasn't certain he dared take another chance on her.

A prudent man knew when to cut his losses.

Thorn's father had not been a prudent man, throwing good money after bad in a vain and increasingly desperate effort to recoup his fortunes. More than anything, Thorn did not want to follow in his father's unfortunate footsteps.

His sister had been right about a long journey providing time for reflection, Thorn decided as he traveled south, through the austere, rugged beauty of the borderlands. Too much time, perhaps, for regrets and worries, which seemed to wait around each bend in the road to ambush him.

Would he be able to find Felicity, even? Unless he stopped to inquire after her at every inn he passed, he ran the risk of outstripping her without knowing it. Yet, if she had resolved to press southward with all haste, each stop he made would put him farther and farther behind her.

Perhaps that would provide a convenient excuse for failing to do what he had promised his sister, Thorn told himself as he happened upon a northbound carriage halted by the side of the road.

A liveried footman flagged him down.

Thorn reined his mount to a stop. ''Is something the matter? Can I help?''

''Aye, sir, if you'd be so kind.'' The young man nodded toward his employer's carriage. ''Our back wheel got damaged when it dipped into the ditch. We came through a village two miles back that had a smithy.''

A stocky middle-aged man who might have been the driver appeared just then from behind the carriage, his shirtsleeves rolled up to the elbows and his hands well blackened. ''I offered to unhitch one of our team for the lad to ride back and bring help, but he's frighted about managing a carriage horse bareback.''

The man's thick gray brows bristled as he glared at the lad. ''Time was I could ride anything four-legged that was big enough to bear my weight with naught but a hank of rope for a bridle. But my riding days are over, I fear.''

''I'm bound that way in any case.'' Thorn leaned forward, extending his hand to the boy. ''I doubt my horse will notice your weight.''

He swung the slight young footman up behind him and urged his horse forward.

''I'm much obliged for your kindness sir.'' The way the lad clung to Thorn's coat told him the footman was far from comfortable on horseback under any circumstances.

"Have you come a long way today?" Thorn called over his shoulder, hoping to distract the young fellow, and perhaps gain some news of Felicity into the bargain.

"Not a very great way, sir," replied the lad. "Only from Brough."

Little chance they'd meet Felicity on the road, then, since the town of Brough lay a few hours south of Penrith on the coach route to London.

"I don't imagine you met a fine traveling coach on the road between here and Penrith?" Thorn heard himself describing Felicity's carriage down to the Lyte coat-of-arms painted on the doors, though he knew perfectly well it was useless to ask.

Useless it might be, but the footman still needed something to divert his attention from the speed of the horse and their distance from the ground. And Thorn had made a promise to his sister. However distasteful he might find it, he would keep that promise to the best of his ability.

"No, sir…"

Ah well, he hadn't expected so, but worth a try.

"…not on the road, sir."

What? Thorn started, provoking the horse to toss its mane and gallop faster.

The young footman abandoned all dignity, throwing his arms clear around Thorn's waist and clinging for dear life. "A-at an inn h-halfway between here and Penrith, sir, when we stopped for a bite of supper. I saw that rig in the courtyard and thought how fine it looked."

Despite all his misgivings, a strange eagerness kindled itself deep inside of him at the thought of Felicity so near at hand.

"Godspeed, sir." The young footman waved Thorn on his way a short while later. "I hope you find the lady better than she was when we left."

"What's that you say?" Thorn bridled his horse sharply.

"That lady, sir. The one with the fine carriage. I heard tell she'd stopped at the inn because she'd been taken ill on the road."

"Dammit, lad, why did you not say so before?" A blaze of concern for Felicity consumed all the other conflicting emotions in Thorn's heart.

The young footman at least had the decency to look ashamed of himself. "I thought if you knew...you might make the horse go faster, sir."

What the lad said was true enough, and understandable, but that did not make it a whit more palatable to Thorn. Cursing under his breath, he pointed his mount south and gave it a taste of leather.

Though the beast galloped like the wind, it could not outrun the dark fear that stalked its rider.

Chapter Nineteen

"Will I lose my baby?"

Though her pain had vastly diminished after a mild purging, Felicity still braced herself for bad news. She had been disappointed too often by life to summon much hope.

The innkeeper's wife, a big raw-boned North Country woman, tucked the bedclothes around Felicity with a surprisingly gentle touch, but she gave her answer in a vigorous, bracing voice.

"Miscarry, ye mean? Nay, lass, I think not."

She straightened from her crouch over the bed and planted her hands on her broad hips. "Ye may trust my judgment in the matter, too, for I've brought scores of babes into this world these past twenty years. I get called into Penrith for a lying-in often enough. Lasses from these parts who've wed town lads. Naught will do for 'em but to have Mother Merryvale attend their lying-in."

The weight pressing down on Felicity's heart eased a little. "How fortunate I should land in your care, Mrs. Merryvale. You've been most skilled and most kind."

She could not remember ever having been *taken charge of* in such a forceful, yet agreeable manner, except on one or two occasions when she had let her guard down with Thorn.

"Better fortune than ye deserve, I daresay." Mrs. Merryvale scolded gently as she bustled around the room, lifting a small kettle off the hob and pouring steaming water into a mug. "And yer husband. What can he have been thinking to let ye make such a long journey when ye're breeding?"

"I have no husband, Mrs. Merryvale." Might as well get used to telling the story she would be obliged to tell for many years to come. "I'm a widow."

It was no lie, she protested to her conscience. Mrs. Merryvale didn't need to know how long her husband had been dead or that Percy had not been the father of her unborn child. In a curious way, her parting from Thorn felt like widowing in a way Percy's death had not.

"Poor lass!" The innkeeper's wife clucked in sympathy. "Then I reckon it's not much wonder ye haven't taken proper care of yerself. But ye must, ye know, for the sake of that little one yer carrying."

Felicity gave an obedient nod.

"Ye don't mean to give that pleasant-spoken Master Ned the sack do ye?" asked Mrs. Merryvale. "For making ye stop here when ye would have driven on?"

The prospect must be weighing heavily on her servants, if they had communicated their worries to the innkeeper's wife.

Felicity shook her head. The fright she had taken, on top of the emotional reverses of the day, must have sapped her strength...or perhaps broken her stubbornness.

"No, I shan't sack him or my driver. Rather they deserve a reward for looking after me better than I was prepared to look after myself."

Her servants had stood to gain nothing—and risked losing much—by challenging her authority.

It was not an easy notion for her to digest, that someone might oppose her will, yet have *her* well-being at heart, not their own. From her earliest years she'd been conditioned to look out for her own interests, certain that no one else would. Her marriage had bolstered that belief.

Or perhaps fallen victim to it?

Now her relations with the two people she loved best in the world had been soured by it, as well.

"Has the pain got worse again, my dear?" asked Mrs. Merryvale. She strode toward the bed bearing the mug she'd just filled.

"No." Felicity tried to smile. "It eased a good deal after that physic you gave me."

The ache in her belly, perhaps. But the one in her heart had grown more severe. Even an experienced midwife like Mrs. Merryvale could have no remedy for that.

The innkeeper's wife appeared to think otherwise. "Sip away at this." She wrapped Felicity's hands around the warm mug. "It's a brew of this and that from my garden. Naught that'll harm ye or the babe, but it may ease ye. It's rest ye need as much as anything, and I don't just say so to keep ye lodging here the longer."

To her surprise, Felicity believed the woman. She took a wary sip from the cup and found it a strange taste, though not unpleasant.

Mrs. Merryvale nodded her approval. "If ye're like

most folk, ye'll mend faster under ye're own roof, my dear. Rest easy tonight, and I'll give yer men leave to take ye on yer way in the morning.''

She wagged her forefinger. "As long as ye promise not to make too great a haste, mind. Stop often to stretch your legs and take the air, then put in for a good supper before it grows dark."

"I promise." Felicity took another drink of the strange tea. Now that she knew what to expect, she quite liked its queer taste. "I will take better care of myself from now on."

The innkeeper's wife beamed. "Of course you will, my dear. Now I'll leave ye to finish yer tea and get some sleep. That's the best remedy for most ailments, I expect. Ring if ye need aught, whatever the hour."

"Thank you, Mrs. Merryvale. I hope I shan't need to disturb you during the night, but there is one small task you could do for me now, if you would."

"And what might that be?"

"Kindly assure Ned and Mr. Hixon that I'm in no danger and that their places in my household are secure for as long as they wish."

Their obvious loyalty to Thorn would make it impossible for her to take them with her when she retired to the country to raise her baby, which Felicity regretted. She would see them well-situated before then, however.

Mrs. Merryvale beamed. "I shall be as pleased to pass that message on to them, lass, as I believe they will be to hear it. So don't trouble yerself more on that or any other account."

"I'll try," whispered Felicity, as the innkeeper's wife marched out of the room, knowing she could not promise more.

Whether it was some power of Mrs. Merryvale's brew or simply Felicity's own weariness, a peculiar sense of peace stole over her. Though she did not understand it, nor entirely trust it, she gave herself up to it with a grateful sigh.

A while later—Felicity could not tell whether it had been an hour or only a moment—the soft sounds of the door easing open roused her from a light doze.

She coaxed her eyelids open just a little and glanced toward the door, expecting to find that Mrs. Merryvale had come back to check on her. Instead she beheld a familiar figure she had feared never to lay eyes on again.

Thorn? Could this be but a sweet dream brought on by Mrs. Merryvale's wholesome herbal draught? If it was, Felicity did not want to do anything that might dispel it.

The man in her dream made no move to wake her, only stood silent, watching. Not daring to open her eyes farther, yet resolved not to close them as long as his dear image hovered in her view, Felicity gazed at Thorn, seeing him with a new clarity of heart.

She had chosen him as her lover for all the wrong reasons, mistaking his obliging manner for weakness, his quiet constancy for dullness. She had turned a blind eye to his fine qualities, and when that had become impossible she'd fought a desperate, sometimes vicious, fight against her growing love for him.

What had he seen in her that had made him tolerate her worst excesses? Felicity wished she could catch even a fleeting glimpse of herself through his eyes. How she yearned to be the kind of woman he had mistaken her for!

After some considerable time, yet not nearly long

enough to suit Felicity, Thorn backed toward the door with soundless steps. Since he seemed determined to go, she need not worry about some sound or movement of hers driving him away.

"Please don't go!" She struggled to rise from her pillows.

Thorn started at the sound of her voice, then stopped as she had bidden him.

He must be real. He must be here.

Now what could she possibly say that would not drive him away again?

"Y-you found me?"

Even as the words left her mouth, she knew she was failing. Thorn's features took on a tense, guarded cast.

"What else could I do?" he asked. "These roads are no safer than they were when we came north, and I could not be certain you'd have the prudence to stop at a decent inn before dark."

She should have known. A vulnerable bud of hope in Felicity's heart began to wither. Just because Thorn had come after her did not mean he still cared.

He'd escorted her to Carlisle, so of course he would consider it his duty to escort her south again. No matter how he might abhor the task.

"I was told you had taken ill." Thorn could not mask the genuine concern in his voice.

"I'm much better now," said Felicity, anxious to make light of it. "Wrought up nerves on top of the long journey."

If she blurted out the truth, that she was carrying his child, Thorn would do his duty by her, even if he could not forgive the way she had treated him.

She would not entrap him that way. Nor would she subject her child to life in a home full of veiled hostility and resentment on the one side, bitter regret and hopeless yearning on the other.

But what if…?

Was there a chance she could win Thorn's forgiveness? Reawaken the love he had felt for her?

"Oliver and Ivy?" she asked, determined to distract him from the subject of her indisposition.

How ironic that the match she had worked so hard to prevent might now provide a bridge between her and Thorn.

"Man and wife some hours now."

The severe set of his features lightened as he spoke of it, setting hope aflutter in Felicity's heart on tiny, fragile wings of heartbreaking beauty.

"I insisted they make their vows in front of a proper clergyman, at least."

"Thank you for that." Felicity could not coax her voice above a whisper. Oliver married, and she had not been there, by her own selfish choice.

Thorn took a step nearer the bed, but with an air of reluctance, as if drawn against his will. "Hard as this may be to credit, Oliver does love my sister, you know. And she him. No doubt they'll have a squall or two over the next year as they come to know each other better…."

His voice trailed off, but he soon rallied it. "With the support of their families to sustain them, I believe they'll weather those early storms and come to see that their impetuous decision was a wise one after all."

Did she hear a pleading note in his voice when he spoke of the need for Ivy and Oliver to have the support of their families? Or was that only an echo of the pleading from her own heart?

"I will not disown my nephew." She sat up slowly

so as not to ward Thorn off. Neither did she want to risk rousing the pain with him present. "It was wicked of me to threaten such a thing."

Thorn did not contradict her.

"I remember how I hated being controlled by those who had power over me," Felicity continued. "Today I used my power over Oliver—his inheritance and whatever feeling he may once have had for me—to control him."

Thank heaven she had wept herself dry of tears in the privacy of her carriage box. If she wept now in front of Thorn, she knew she might touch and turn his tender heart. But she did not want to win him back with pity any more than with duty.

"I am so vastly ashamed of how I behaved this morning, I may never be able to bear the sight of myself in a looking glass again." She hung her head.

The soft sound of a footstep made her glance up through her lashes. Thorn had drawn nearer the bed. If she stretched out her arm, she might brush her forefinger against the breast of his coat.

As he eased himself into a crouch, Felicity held her breath. In her heart, she prayed as she had never prayed before to a deity she'd previously never given more than lip service. One who had been invoked against her frequently during her childhood—powerful, controlling, exacting.

Shadows had begun to lengthen in the late spring dusk. From off in the distance came the murmur of horses being stabled, luggage fetched and the muted hubbub of the taproom. Within the snug walls of Felicity's room an expectant, fearful hush hovered, begging her to fill it with the anxious thunder of her heart.

Now, if she extended her arm, she might brush the

backs of her fingers against the warm, springy softness of Thorn's side whiskers. Her whole arm tingled with the sweet threat to rise of its own accord.

But while she struggled to keep it in check, her tongue turned traitor. "I don't know which of you I maligned the worst today—you, Oliver or Ivy. You must all hate me now. I suppose I don't blame you if you do. I am not very fond of myself, just now."

A question rose to her lips, unbidden. Not for Thorn to answer, but for herself. "I wonder if I have ever been?"

Thorn gathered his composure around him like a wall, for he could feel a great wave of excitement building from deep in his toes that might crash down upon him, sweeping away everything in its path.

"None of us hate you, Lady Lyte." His tongue stumbled on the unaccustomed formality, but at the moment he did not trust himself to call her by a more intimate name. "Put that out of your mind once and for all."

He tried to ease the unspoken intensity between them. "It was Ivy who bid me come after you, though she swears today's events have cured her of chronic matchmaking. I think that remains to be seen."

His attempt at a chuckle failed miserably.

"Your sister is generous beyond her years," whispered Felicity, "to take pity on me after I falsely accused her of fortune-hunting."

Then why did his sister's gesture of forgiveness make Felicity look so stricken?

She expelled a rueful sigh. "The fact that she wed my nephew in spite of my threat to disinherit him proves her feelings for Oliver are genuine. It grieves me to think I almost prevented him from knowing that happiness.''

"But you didn't.'' Thorn ached to take her in his arms, if only he could be certain she would welcome it. "In a roundabout way, you may have done them a favor. Now your nephew will never once doubt Ivy's love is for him alone. And she will treasure the assurance that he was willing to give up his very considerable expectations for her sake.''

Felicity shook her head. "How I wish that was all it were—a ruse like the one you played on Rosemary to convince her and Mr. Temple of the sincerity of her affection for him.''

An idea took Thorn by storm, kindling a smile that warmed his face from the inside out.

"Who is to know that's not all it was, if we support each other in that story?'' His words gathered speed and conviction as he spoke. "We can claim we were only trying to prove to ourselves and to Oliver and Ivy that their feelings for one another were strong and true.''

A chuckle bubbled out of him, a real one, this time. "By heaven, I wish I *had* been clever enough to come up with such an idea.''

Felicity raised her eyes to his. The depth of pain Thorn saw in them choked off his laughter.

She lifted her hand to shield her lips or perhaps to still a tremor. "You would do that? For me?''

He nodded. "For Oliver and Ivy, too. I would rather they believe you a brilliant actress carrying out a convincing deception for their benefit, than…''

Thorn could not make himself say the rest.

To his surprise Felicity did not flinch from the harsh truth. "…than to have our future relations poisoned by the knowledge that I truly thought my darling nephew a fool and his dear wife a fortune huntress.''

''Better for all, wouldn't you say?''

She had seldom looked more beautiful to him, though grief and weariness haunted her face. Her rich dark hair spilled over the shoulders of her white nightgown. The fine fringe of her lashes once again stood delicate guard over the secrets in her eyes. Her wistful-looking lips beseeched him to kiss them into a smile.

How often in the past months had he come to her bed? For all the delight he had found there, Thorn had never quite trusted that he deserved his place in her arms. To know she had believed him capable of conspiring with his sister to dupe her and her nephew into marriage made him feel sorely in need of a bath.

And yet...

Felicity glanced up at him again. ''I have done nothing to deserve such generous treatment from you, sir.''

Venturing another look into her eyes, he saw such gratitude, as if she'd owed an unpayable debt that had suddenly been cancelled.

Who, then, was the richer of them?

Felicity, with her full purse, but so much else in her life empty? Or him, with a wealth of love from his family on deposit in his heart, yielding bountiful interest?

Surely he could afford to extend her a little generosity?

''On the contrary, Lady Lyte.'' Thorn held his hand out to her, willing it to stay steady. ''You have given me the happiest weeks of my life.''

Her hand inched over the coverlet toward his, but hesitated before completing the journey. ''They cost me nothing to bestow. In truth, I believe you gave me more than you received.''

He beckoned her hand with his fingers. ''Perhaps when a man and a woman both give freely to one another, without counting the cost, they both reap ample reward.''

Slowly she bridged the physical gap between them, bringing the cool delicacy of her hand to rest against the firm warmth of his. ''Can *you* ever forgive me, Thorn?''

''Are you asking me to?''

''Begging.''

He closed his fingers over hers before she could withdraw them. ''No need to beg. I believe I know why you said what you did, this morning. It was because of the way you were treated as a child, wasn't it? And later, by your husband and his mother?''

''Yes, but I make no excuse on that account.'' Felicity raised her chin in a flash of defiant spirit. She might crave his forgiveness, but clearly she wanted none of his pity.

''You have never treated me with anything less than kindness and sincerity. To compare you with those others was an undeserved insult of the worst kind. All the more so because I know how much your integrity means to you. *Asking* your forgiveness does not seem sufficient, somehow.''

Before Thorn could answer, she hurried on, as if fearful of hearing his answer. ''I can hardly say which I regret more—maligning you so cruelly or ignoring your excellent advice to reconsider my actions. Once reason caught up with my runaway suspicion I realized what a fool I'd been.''

And that bitter knowledge had sickened her.

Thorn could not find it in his heart to compound the punishment she'd already suffered at the hands of her own conscience.

"I cannot pretend your accusations left me un-moved." He raised his free hand to encase hers. "I should be grieved if you truly believed me capable of conspiring to entrap you—"

"I didn't!" Twitching her legs around until they dangled over the edge of the bed, Felicity brought her other hand to close over his. "I only thought the cir-cumstances made sense, like the plot of a bad play."

She shook her head. "But when I tried to cast you in the villain's role, you didn't fit at all."

"I know," said Thorn. "*I* know your fortune means nothing to me but a nuisance. I know I want you in my life, not your property. That's what matters, in the end. That's why I can and do forgive you."

He wasn't certain what sort of reaction he'd ex-pected from her. A tear or two, perhaps? An embrace would have been welcome. But Felicity held her place on the bed, gazing at him with a peculiar look he could not fathom.

"Y-you want me in your life?" She spoke in a tone of hushed wonder that kindled a strange giddy joy in Thorn's chest. "Still?"

A slow teasing smile spread across his lips.

"Well, of course," he replied in the same tone he would use to answer whether the sky was blue or whether there were twenty shillings in a pound.

For the rest of his life Thorn would remember her squeal of delighted astonishment as she wrenched her hands from his and threw her arms around his neck, sending them both sprawling onto the floor.

It was not enough to hear his words. Felicity needed

to feel his arms, strong and dependable around her. She needed the familiar reassurance of his kiss to be certain Thorn's feelings toward her had not altered.

All her senses quivered to a feverish pitch, attuned to any subtle sign that might contradict Thorn's declaration.

His arms closed around her as he lay on the floor, with her draped over him. His lips found hers with unerring aim.

The kiss did feel different, somehow, than any they had shared before. But Felicity approved the difference—a new masterful confidence that set her flesh aquiver even as it soothed her afflicted spirit.

She had been forgiven.

Like a warm rain over parched fields, the enriching power of that unfamiliar sensation soaked into her heart.

Her family had never forgiven her for not being a son. The Lyte family had never forgiven her for not bearing a son. And she, in turn, had never been able to forgive her husband's infidelities. Not that he'd ever asked.

Time and again on their trip north, Thorn had seen the worst side of her character—imperious, distrustful, insecure. Yet he had persisted in caring for her, even when she'd been bent on driving him away.

Did Thorn also feel a difference in the way she responded to him? Until this moment she had always held part of herself back, fearful of giving away what she could not afford to lose. Now she offered herself to him completely, confident that he would accept the sum total of who she was, even those parts of herself she did not much care for.

Oh, the warmth of his hands as they stroked her

body through the thin barrier of her nightgown! The delicious potency of his kisses! Both the sweeter because she had expected never to feel them again.

"If I were a fanciful fellow," Thorn murmured between kisses, "I would say that even a wooden floor feels like a feather bed as long as I have you in my arms."

He made a droll face of exaggerated pain. "I hope you will not think it an insult if I say that bed of yours looks deucedly appealing after a long day in the saddle."

"Certainly not." Her laughter came out a trifle thin and shaky as she rolled off Thorn. "If you spouted any such nonsense, I would fear you'd taken a fall from your horse straight onto your head."

"Come on, then." She grasped his hands to help him off the floor. "Let this be the first night of a new beginning for us."

"I like the sound of that." Thorn perched on the edge of the bed to pry off his riding boots.

He shrugged off his coat, then went to work on the buttons of his waistcoat.

Caught up in her anticipation of the night to come, Felicity did not hear the approaching footsteps.

The door eased open, then burst the rest of the way as the innkeeper's wife barrelled in.

"Lord-a-mercy, what's all this?"

Felicity screamed.

Mrs. Merryvale bore down on Thorn like the brawny arm of some vengeful goddess, yanking him to his feet by the ear. "I'll have yer hide, scoundrel, accosting defenseless ladies in my house!"

"Ouch!" Thorn struggled to free himself from the

woman's remorseless grip. "You're mistaken, madam. I'm not accosting anyone. This is my...wife."

"It's the truth, Mrs. Merryvale," cried Felicity, anxious to spare Thorn any worse punishment at the landlady's hands. "My...husband heard I'd taken ill on the road, so he came to me at once."

"Ye gave me the fright of my life," the innkeeper's wife scolded. But she did let go of Thorn's ear. "I heard a noise and came to see if there were aught amiss."

"Thank you for your concern." Felicity tugged Thorn back toward the bed. "But I'm feeling much better now that my husband is with me."

"Husband?" the innkeeper's wife muttered. "I thought ye told me ye were a widow."

Felicity scrambled to remember what she had said. "Perhaps you misunderstood me."

Mrs. Merryvale shook her head. "A queer thing if I did. Don't ye recollect? I asked what yer husband was thinking, letting you trundle about the country in yer condition—"

Felicity sprang from the bed, pushing the other woman none too gently toward the door. "I hardly knew *what* I was saying, then."

"What condition?" asked Thorn.

Pretending she hadn't heard, Felicity rattled on. "I'm feeling ever so much better now. I swear to you, this man *is* my husband, and we are both very tired, so if you don't mind—"

"*What* condition?"

"Men!" The innkeeper's wife heaved an exasperated sigh as Felicity urged her out the door. "What condition do ye think, ye great simpleton? With child, of course. Now if ye have any sense, ye'll put yer foot down about her gadding all over the country. Or next time she's taken poorly away from home, ye might not be so lucky!''

Felicity slammed the door behind the woman, not caring if it hit her broad backside.

If only she could have similarly evicted Mrs. Merryvale's damning revelation, which hung in the air like a cloud of noxious gas.

Chapter Twenty

"Please, Thorn, I can explain."

Felicity's voice seemed to reach him from a great distance while a vast swarm of his own thoughts crowded between them, all clamoring at once.

He gave voice to the most insistent one. "With child?"

"Yes."

"My child?"

"Of course!"

Thorn's knees gave way. Luckily, he was near enough the bed to sit down hard upon it.

His child. How could that be?

The cruel truth kicked him deep in the belly, mocking him for a fool that he'd let himself be so easily duped.

You wondered why she'd taken a man like you into her bed! it roared, heaving him headfirst into the mud. *Well, there's your answer, you daft ass!*

He groped on the floor for his boots.

Felicity snatched them away, just as she'd snatched the candle from his hand that night in Bath when he'd come to tell her about Ivy and Oliver.

"I won't let you leave here until you've given me a chance to explain, Thorn."

"Explain?" The word retched out of him on a gust of harsh laughter. "I prefer not to tax your powers of invention, my dear. I marvel that after a week like this, you have not strained them beyond recovery."

Everything that had puzzled him about Felicity's behavior this week suddenly made sense. Brutal, revolting sense.

"I was going to tell you." In the fading light, she looked the very picture of guileless sincerity.

Thorn hardened his gullible heart.

"Indeed? When? On the child's fifth birthday? His tenth? On my deathbed?" He held out his hand. "Stop lying to me, damn you, and give me my boots!"

She stepped in front of the door, hiding his boots behind her back. "At first I didn't ever mean to tell you."

"Now, *that* sounds like the truth." Denied his boots, Thorn grabbed his coat from the bed, jamming his arms into the sleeves. "After such a steady diet of falsehood, I wonder that I can recognize such a rare delicacy when I hear it."

He loathed the scathing mockery he heard in his voice. But Thorn could do nothing to prevent it. If he did not spew out the poison brewing inside of him, he feared it would eat away his heart.

"Perhaps you think I should be flattered that you chose me for a stud to sire your little foal."

Felicity's mouth fell open.

Thorn took some perverse pleasure in shocking her with his show of crudity.

"Is *that* what you believe I did?" she asked.

"What else am I to believe, pray?" The faintest hint

of a doubt flickered within him, but Thorn trod it under his heel. "You assured me you were barren, which is clearly not the case. By your own admission, you meant to keep your condition a secret from me, and I have only your word that you ever intended to tell me."

To think he'd flattered himself that a woman like her could care for him. When all the time he'd been no more to her than a convenient object of use. Once they'd set out from Bath, he had become an inconvenient burden, to be placated with hollow flattery and false promises until he could be safely discarded.

Though Felicity shrank from his reproaches, she did not budge from in front of the door.

"I know I've given you no reason to trust my word, Thorn, but I beg you to listen just the same. I see now that what I meant to do was wrong, but at the time I felt I had no other choice. Bad as that was, it is not half so bad as it may look to you now. If you hear me out, I feel certain you will believe me."

"Of course I'll believe you, dammit!" Thorn ploughed his fingers through his hair. "Haven't I swallowed every other honey-dipped lie you've ever fed me? I am a fool, Lady Lyte—a daft, besotted fool, ready to let you lead me 'round by the nose...or some other portion of my anatomy."

This was probably how his father had brought their family to the brink of ruin, by giving ear to lies he wanted so desperately to believe.

The realization that he had let his soft, partial heart overrule his sound judgment shook him to the core. It made him feel as if he no longer recognized himself. He despised what he had become—what Felicity Lyte had made of him.

"I will not stay and be persuaded of what I wish to believe." He strode toward the door. "I can do without my boots if you insist on keeping them from me. The night is not cold enough to prevent me riding barefoot."

But how would he shift her out of the way without touching her? And how would he stop touching her once he'd begun?

The anger that surged through his veins like fire had not seared away the bedeviling itch of his desire for this woman. Rather, each fueled the other—two sides of the dangerous coin that was passion. He had been right to keep it out of his cash box until now.

Yet, torn as he was, Thorn Greenwood had never felt so fully alive.

Felicity did not cower as he approached her. Neither did she move. "No matter how much you hate me at this moment, I know you will not harm me."

How well she knew his every weakness, and how skillfully she played upon them.

"Get out of my way, woman, or I will not be answerable for my actions!"

Felicity held her ground. "When I told you I was barren, I believed it to be the truth."

Why would she have permitted that insufferable Norbury cub in her house if she had reason to know the young man was *not* her husband's natural son?

The wheedling little voice in his mind only stoked Thorn's fury, for it proved what an easy mark he was for this woman's well-aimed lies.

Taking firm but restrained hold of her upper arms, he lifted her off her feet and moved her clear of the door. If he could only keep his renegade desire in check for a few moments more, he'd put himself beyond her seductive power…forever.

And count himself lucky to have escaped her clutches with a few shreds of his self-respect intact.

She was losing him!

If she let him get away now, the Thorn Greenwood she had come to know in the past week would disappear—stifled by propriety, stabbed through the heart by her deception, buried under a mountain of suspicion and resentment.

Is this not what you wanted? whispered the loathsome little voice of her selfishness. *Thorn Greenwood conveniently out of your life and your child's?*

"No!" Dropping Thorn's boots, she grabbed hold of his coat cuffs the instant he released her arms.

For her own sake she could not have humbled her pride to cling and plead with him like this. But she could not permit her child to be deprived of such a father. Better if…

Suddenly, Felicity knew what she must do.

For her, that brief timeless interval between one heartbeat and the next ached with loss and remorse enough to fill a lifetime.

"Would you abandon your child to a woman like me?" The question stung her throat.

"Eh?" Thorn froze.

Felicity willed her voice to keep steady. If she became overwrought, she would drive Thorn away. Perhaps, forever.

"I have greater confidence in your judgment than you appear to, my dear. I am asking you, for the sake of our child, to hear what I have to say with an open heart and mind. If you will do that, I promise I will give you the baby to rear once it is born.''

"If this is another trick of yours…" Thorn jerked his coat free of her hands, but he made no move toward the unblocked door.

Felicity shook her head. "I would *never* say such a thing if I did not mean it with all my heart."

For a moment that stretched almost too long and tight to bear, Thorn did not move or speak.

At last he found his voice. "Why?"

"Why would I give you my baby?" The prospect made Felicity tremble. "Because today I proved I cannot be a good aunt, let alone a decent mother, while you have proven you can be mother and father both."

If she stood another minute, she would swoon. And Thorn would probably catch her, as he had on the night this whole fateful journey to Gretna had begun. Then some compound of pity and desire might overpower his reason, and he might accept what she told him without truly believing it.

Much as she wanted to hold on to him, she could not do it at that price.

Her legs had just enough strength to carry her back to the bed. "If you still wish to go, I will do nothing more to prevent you."

She drew the bedclothes up to her chin, knowing that neither their warmth nor the glowing coals in the hearth could protect her from the chill of Thorn's leaving.

Darkness had fallen in earnest, now, but the embers of the small fire gave off enough rosy light that Felicity could see Thorn bend and pick up his boots.

When he straightened again and walked toward the

door, Felicity had to bite her lip to keep from crying out his name.

Perhaps something in him heard and responded to her mute plea, for he turned, leaned back against the door and slowly slid to the floor.

"Go ahead and speak then." The words wafted out of him on a weary sigh. "I will hold you to your promise about the child, mind. Whatever it takes."

Now that he had given her the chance to explain herself, Felicity could scarcely rally her voice to begin.

"Whatever else you doubt, trust this. I did not take you as my lover to sire a child. I believed what I told you on the night St. Just introduced us, that I was barren and therefore as free as any man to take my pleasure."

"I remember."

So did Felicity. If she could go back to that night at the Upper Assembly Rooms, knowing what she knew now, would she take Thorn Greenwood as her lover again? Or would she settle for requesting a dance and spare herself all that had happened since?

The answer that welled up from the depths of her heart surprised and frightened her. Had she changed so much during this mad dash to Gretna?

"When I realized I must be with child, I was as dumbfounded as you were, just now. I must have asked myself a hundred times how it was possible until finally I guessed the truth—that the women with whom my late husband had been unfaithful might not have been faithful to him."

A soft, sharp grunt from the direction of the door told Felicity the idea had never occurred to Thorn, either.

"I cannot think why I never saw it before, espe-

cially since none of Percy's *natural children* resem-
bled him except in his own fancy.''

"Tsk, tsk, tsk. Poor Lady Lyte," muttered Thorn.
"All those years a childless wife, then your gay widowhood spoiled by an inconvenient infant.''

An angry retort rose to Felicity's lips, but she reminded herself that the bitterness of his tone was only
a measure of his hurt.

"I thought no such thing. I was beside myself with
joy and more grateful than you can imagine. I believe
it was from that moment I began to fall in love with
you.''

"Ha!" Thorn mocked her...as she deserved. "You
have a most singular means of showing gratitude and
affection, I must say. That charming note, for instance,
in which you told me to make myself scarce. The way
you threatened to have me tossed out of your house
when I came in search of my sister.''

"I know I treated you abonimably, and I have never
been sorrier for anything in my life. But what was I
to do, Thorn? If I'd told you about the baby straightaway, what would you have done?''

"Offered to marry you, of course.''

"Of course.'' It was small comfort to know she'd
been right about that, at least. "All the while wondering if I had lied about my barrenness to entrap
you?''

"Never!''

"Never?'' she challenged him in a whisper.

After a thoughtful pause, Thorn admitted, "Perhaps
it would have crossed my mind.''

"I told you how reluctant I was ever to wed again
and all the reasons why.''

"You did.''

"And you seemed to understand, better than I did myself. Can you not find a cold crumb of that understanding left in your heart, now?"

"I might." Thorn's shoulder's bowed as if they had been asked to bear one burden too many. "But why should I? Did you spare a thought for me when you decided to cut me out of your life and rear our child without my knowledge?"

"No," Felicity admitted. "At least, not enough. I have told you time and again that I am a selfish person, Thorn. Always you made light of it or claimed to understand. What did you call it once—self protective? I did what I believed I had to do to protect myself and my child."

"From me?"

"From a man I hardly knew except as a pleasant companion and a considerate lover."

"Do you know me so much better, now?" From across the room his dark gaze bored into her. "Well enough to give your child away to me in return for an hour of listening and no promises?"

"I know that if our child needs to be protected from one of its parents, that one is me."

Was she reaching him at all? Or had exhaustion sapped the energy from Thorn's anger, making him sound more forbearing than he felt? At least it seemed she'd put to rest the ugly suspicion that she had deliberately used him to sire her child.

A minor consolation, to be sure. But Felicity took it and was grateful.

If only Thorn would lower the shield protecting his heart. Then he might employ the special wisdom that had nothing to do with reason, and he might judge her less by past failings than by future promise.

But if he held her to any measure other than his bountiful compassion, Felicity knew she would fall woefully short.

Just as he had predicted, Thorn found himself wanting to believe every winsome word that passed Felicity's lips. Which was precisely why he must not.

A pretty riddle that! And Thorn too tired to puzzle it out.

He had to grant her one point—she probably did know him a good deal better after this one turbulent week than she had after their pleasant tranquil interlude in Bath. He certainly knew her a good deal better than when they'd set out for Gretna.

Or so he'd thought until an hour ago.

"Suppose I'm willing to believe what you've told me so far." He paused to indulge in a deep yawn. "Were you only leading me on, since we left Bath, with all this talk of marriage? How am I to know you didn't seize on Ivy's innocent matchmaking scheme as a convenient way to get rid of me at last?"

"All that talk of marriage was true!" Her words pealed with a desperate conviction.

"Except the great hue and cry about not being able to bear children. When I think how I struggled to accept that, all the while you were carrying my child." If he hadn't been so confoundedly tired, Thorn might have walked away then.

"I had to know you cared for me as more than a source of children. If you recall anything I told you about my marriage to Percy, perhaps you'll be able to understand."

Perhaps if he had a good night's sleep, a hot breakfast and several cups of coffee, he could go back over all that had passed between himself and Felicity to sift out the true from the false. Yet Thorn doubted he would sleep soundly until he had resolved it to his satisfaction.

From out of the darkness Felicity challenged him. "Was what I did really so much worse than when your friend Mr. Temple told Rosemary he'd lost his money when he hadn't?"

Her question roused Thorn from his lethargy. "Of course it was different! Rosemary didn't give a fig about Merritt's fortune."

"Whereas you cared a great deal about having a family." The plaintive note in Felicity's voice told him she was near tears. "Yet you were still willing to marry me, even though you thought I could not give you children. You cannot imagine what that meant to me, who have never been loved on my own account."

Amid the shifting quagmire of truth and falsehood where he now wallowed, Thorn could feel something solid beneath him for the first time. But was it large enough to build on?

"You were the one who said we must weigh each thing that stands between us against the prospect of a future apart. I know this all must weigh very heavily against me, Thorn. Too heavily."

She seemed to shrink before his tired eyes, and her voice sounded bereft, yet curiously resigned. "Somehow you found a way to forgive me for the way I behaved this morning. I know you well enough to be certain you cannot forgive me this. I only wanted you to hear my side. You have been more than patient in that. I will not detain you any longer."

Just then a very old memory roused in Thorn's mind while all the others were falling asleep. A quote from back in his school days. Pythagoras, was it? Or Archimedes? *Give me a solid place to stand and I can move the world.*

Other words came to him, as well. Words he had first heard long ago, and which his sister had echoed today. *Love is a powerful force, if only we can find the courage to use it.*

It took courage for a man of reason to say, "I was wrong."

"What?"

Thorn wanted to ask himself the same question.

From some strange newborn place inside him came an answer that surprised him at least as much as it seemed to surprise Felicity.

"I was wrong to talk of weighing love like so many cabbages in the market. It's not like a bank balance, either, with deposits, withdrawals and interest charged for an overdraft."

He didn't remember getting to his feet, but all of a sudden Thorn found himself standing. Which way his feet would carry him, he hardly knew.

"What is it then?" asked Felicity in a murmur that sounded hopeful, yet frightened.

"Love is an all-or-nothing wager," Thorn heard himself say as he took a step toward the bed.

"For more than you can afford to lose." He took another step. "Against very long odds."

If his father had risked telling Thorn the true state of their affairs, they might have worked together to recover his losses. Instead Royce Greenwood had taken his secret shame to his grave. Had he been too proud to reveal his folly to his children? Or had he feared they would never forgive him?

Thorn heard a rustle of bedclothes.

"That doesn't sound like something a sensible man would do," whispered Felicity from only a few inches away.

Thorn shrugged. "It isn't."

"After everything that's happened, are you reckless enough to gamble your happiness on a risky proposition like me?"

Felicity sounded so forlorn and vulnerable, nothing like the clever, confident lady of fortune who'd recruited him to become her lover. Now Thorn understood her show of assurance had been a brittle facade. In the rich soil of his love, true confidence would take root and flourish, proof against the insecurity that had led her to test him again and again.

He held his arms open to her. "I believe the winnings will be worth the risk...for us both and for our child."

"You are a hundred times too good for me." Felicity drifted into his embrace. "But I will strive with all my heart to make you happy."

Thorn inclined his head by gentle degrees until his brow rested against hers. "Allow yourself to be happy, my love, and you cannot fail to bring me happiness."

She lifted her lips to his like a parched flower to the warm, gentle rain, and deep in his heart Thorn knew it would be so.

Epilogue

Lathbury, England
February 1816

"I vow, I never saw a sweeter-tempered baby." Ivy Armitage nuzzled the downy cheek of her infant niece and namesake, Ivy Olivia Greenwood. "Not a peep out of her at the christening. Not even when the vicar dribbled that cold baptismal water on her dear little pate."

As a soft, gentle fall of snow blanketed the Buckinghamshire countryside, a merry blaze crackled in the sitting room hearth at Barnhill, where all the Greenwood family had gathered for Miss Olivia's christening breakfast.

"Do you hear that, Master Hawthorn?" Rosemary Temple demanded of her sturdy little son as she bounced him in her arms. "Your Aunt Ivy means to remind everyone that you wailed loud enough at your christening to make all our ears ring for hours afterward."

The child blinked his enormous blue eyes and chortled at the droll face his mama had made.

Merritt Temple paused in the story he was reading to his elder son. "Don't laugh, you young rascal. The vicar's nerves haven't been the same since."

From his post at the sideboard, where he was ladling hot punch into cups, Thorn Greenwood called, "The prospect of a tribe of lusty young Armitages at the baptismal font will likely drive the poor man into retirement."

"Indeed," said Merritt, casting a searching look from Oliver to Ivy and back again. "Is there some chance of that happening in the near future?"

Oliver made no reply, except to stare at the floor and blush.

"Aha!" Thorn and Merritt cried in perfect chorus.

"Congratulations!" Rosemary stooped to kiss her sister's cheek. "When may we expect the new arrival?"

"Thorn!" wailed Ivy, "I was saving the news for a surprise announcement at breakfast."

"Did somebody mention breakfast?" Felicity Greenwood breezed into the sitting room. "You must all be famished for it."

Though Ivy had seen her sister-in-law often during the summer and autumn, she continued to be surprised by the alteration that marriage to Thorn had wrought in Felicity. Everything about her seemed to have softened and ripened. The special radiance of motherhood had further enriched her dark, delicate beauty.

"I've come to tell you everything's ready, at last." Felicity beckoned them all. "Let's eat while it's piping hot. And what's this I hear about an announcement? You haven't told them already, have you Thorn?"

"No, my dear." Thorn handed his wife a cup of punch and passed another to Oliver. "I just happened to divine that the Armitages have a happy event in the offing. Now Ivy's vexed at me for guessing. Will you be vexed at her and your nephew for making a woman of your tender years a great-aunt?"

"Indeed not." Felicity caught Oliver's hand and gave it a squeeze. "Especially if they are kind enough to furnish Olivia with a little girl cousin for a play-mate. I'd hate to see her too badly outnumbered by the boys."

"Don't try to divert us, you two." Merritt Temple hoisted three-year-old Harry onto his shoulders. "What's this news you haven't told us, Thorn? People are letting cats out of bags left and right this morning."

Master Harry wiggled around, peering all over the room. "I don't see any cats, Papa!"

Thorn laughed as Merritt tried to explain the queer figure of speech to his son. "Never fear. You shall hear my news soon enough. Let's go tuck into that breakfast before it gets cold."

As if on cue, a trio of maidservants appeared to bear the younger guests off to Barnhill's newly refurbished nursery. Meanwhile their parents, aunts and uncles re-paired to the dining room for a feast of good things, all seasoned with laughter and congenial talk.

"Kippers, Oliver?" asked Merritt as he helped him-self to a generous portion. "They say fish is good for the brain. How's your research progressing, by the by? Made any great discoveries?"

Oliver held out his plate. "No great ones, but a number of small ones that each build on the others, which is very gratifying. I'm working out some specialized factory applications for the steam engine, which will save many hours of human labor and pay me quite handsomely to boot.''

Beneath the table Ivy nudged her husband's foot. When he glanced across at her, she darted a sly smile his way. "Oliver has been intrigued by the workings of steam engines ever since we ran off to Gretna.''

It was still one of their favorite private jokes from their wedding night—how Oliver had likened the act of lovemaking to a piston and cylinder!

Her husband cleared his throat and adjusted his spectacles. Though he managed to keep a sober face and continue his conversation with Merritt, Ivy sensed that he was struggling to hold back a sheepish grin. He shot her a look that told her she would pay for her impudence in some very pleasant manner, as soon as they were alone.

Glancing to her left, Ivy saw Felicity and Rosemary with their heads together like two lovely mirror images, one dark and one golden. From what little she could pick up of their whispered discussion, it appeared to be all about babies.

Ivy had never had much patience for the subject before, but lately her feelings had begun to change. She suspected they would undergo a complete reversal the first time she held her own little one in her arms.

At last, Ivy's gaze wandered to the head of the table, where she found her brother watching his family with quiet pride and satisfaction. An echo of those emotions stirred in her own heart. Three of the happiest married couples in the whole kingdom sat around this very table, and she'd had a hand in bringing each of them together.

When the serving platters were almost empty and

conversation had begun to ebb, Rosemary spoke up, "Don't keep us in suspense any longer, Thorn. What's this news you planned to tell us?"

Thorn rose from his chair. "Nothing as momentous as Oliver and Ivy's, but I'm keen to share it with my family just the same. I thought you might like to know that I have finally succeeded in clearing all of Father's debts and have begun to accumulate capital in my own right."

The Temples and the Armitages cheered this news. Though her brother had made light of their situation to her and Rosemary, Ivy knew it had weighed on him.

"Thank you, thank you." Thorn acknowledged their applause and congratulations. "Everyone else of my acquaintance probably believes I owe this renewed prosperity to my wife's fortune."

Felicity shook her head. No one seeing the gaze of transparent admiration she directed at her husband could doubt that Thorn had succeeded entirely by his own efforts.

"In truth," said Thorn, "I owe far more to my wife's confidence in my abilities than to her property. As long as we here know the rights of it, the rest of the world may think what it pleases."

As Thorn took his seat again, Merritt Temple stood up. "I believe this calls for a toast. To my dear friend and brother, who has persevered and triumphed in his business affairs. That achievement is eclipsed only by his brilliant success in raising two dear, delightful sisters."

"To Thorn!" They all drank to his accomplishments with a warm will.

"I hope you have not drained your cups," said Felicity, rising from her place opposite her husband, "for

I have a toast to make, as well. Let us drink to Ivy and Oliver's wonderful news. May they be as happy in their new family as Thorn and I have been, thanks to their efforts.''

Everyone drank to the Armitages' happiness as eagerly as they had saluted Thorn's newfound prosperity.

Ivy blinked back tears of joyous fulfillment even as she quipped, ''With three happy marriages to my credit, you will all be relieved to hear that I plan to retire from matchmaking so as not to risk tarnishing my perfect record.''

As her family chuckled and drained their punch cups a final thought occurred to Ivy.

''At least until the next generation of Greenwoods are grown and need a little help from Auntie Cupid!''

* * * * *

From Regency Ballrooms to Medieval Castles, fall in love with these stirring tales from Harlequin Historicals

On sale March 2003

THE SILVER LORD by Miranda Jarrett

Don't miss the first of **The Lordly Claremonts** trilogy!
Despite being on the opposite side of the law,
a spinster with a secret smuggling habit can't resist
a handsome navy captain!

BRIDE OF THE TOWER by Sharon Schulze
(England, 1217)

Will a fallen knight become bewitched with the
mysterious noblewoman who nurses him back to health?

On sale April 2003

LADY ALLERTON'S WAGER by Nicola Cornick

A woman masquerading as a cyprian challenges a
dashing earl to a wager—with the stake being an island
he owns against her favors!

HIGHLAND SWORD by Ruth Langan

Be sure to read this first installment in the
Mystical Highlands series about three sisters
and the handsome Highlanders they bewitch!

  Harlequin Historicals®
Historical Romantic Adventure!

SAVOR THE BREATHTAKING ROMANCES
AND THRILLING ADVENTURES
OF THE OLD WEST
WITH HARLEQUIN HISTORICALS

On sale March 2003

TEMPTING A TEXAN by Carolyn Davidson

A wealthy Texas businessman is ambitious, demanding
and in no rush to get to the altar. But when a beautiful
woman arrives with a child she claims is his niece,
he must decide between wealth and love....

THE ANGEL OF DEVIL'S CAMP by Lynna Banning

When a Southern belle goes to Oregon to start a new
life, the last thing she expects is to have her heart
captured by a stubborn Yankee!

On sale April 2003

McKINNON'S BRIDE by Sharon Harlow

While traveling with her children, a young widow falls
in love with the kind rancher who opens his home and
his heart to her family....

ADAM'S PROMISE by Julianne MacLean

A ruggedly handsome Canadian finds unexpected love
when his fiancée arrives and he discovers she's not the
woman he thought he was marrying!

Harlequin Historicals®
Historical Romantic Adventure!

HHWEST24

COMING NEXT MONTH FROM
HARLEQUIN
HISTORICALS®

- **THE SCOT**
  by **Lyn Stone**, author of MARRYING MISCHIEF
  After overhearing two men plotting to kill an earl and his daughter, James Garrow, Baron of Galioch, goes to warn the earl. Instead, he meets the earl's daughter, freethinking, unruly Susanna Eastonby. Despite the sparks flying between them, James and Susanna enter into a marriage of convenience. Will this hardheaded couple realize they're perfect for each other—before it's too late?
  HH #643 ISBN# 29243-0 $5.25 U.S./$6.25 CAN.

- **THE MIDWIFE'S SECRET**
  by **Kate Bridges**, author of LUKE'S RUNAWAY BRIDE
  Amanda Ryan is escaping her painful past and trying to start a new life as a midwife when she meets Tom Murdock. As Tom teaches Amanda to overcome the past, they start a budding relationship. But will Amanda's secrets stand in the path of true love?
  HH #644 ISBN# 29244-9 $5.25 U.S./$6.25 CAN.

- **FALCON'S DESIRE**
  by **Denise Lynn**, Harlequin Historical debut
  Wrongly accused of murder, Count Rhys Faucon is given one month to prove his innocence. In order to stop him, the victim's vengeance-seeking fiancée, Lady Lyonesse, holds him captive in her keep and unwittingly discovers a love beyond her wildest dreams!
  HH #645 ISBN# 29245-7 $5.25 U.S./$6.25 CAN.

- **THE LAW AND KATE MALONE**
  by **Charlene Sands**, author of CHASE WHEELER'S WOMAN
  Determined to grant her mother's last wish, Kate Malone returns to her hometown to rebuild the Silver Saddle Saloon and reclaim her family legacy. But the only man she's ever loved, Sheriff Cole Bradshaw, is determined to stop the saloon from being built and determined to steal Kate's heart....
  HH #646 ISBN# 29246-5 $5.25 U.S./$6.25 CAN.

KEEP AN EYE OUT FOR ALL FOUR
OF THESE TERRIFIC NEW TITLES

HHCNM0103